DEADSIDE
REVOLUTION

I0685615

TERRY GRIMWOOD

Terry Grimwood

First published in 2016 by
Horrific Tales Publishing
http://www.horrifictales.co.uk
Copyright © 2016 Terry Grimwood

The moral right of Terry Grimwood to be identified as the
author of this work has been asserted in accordance with
the Copyright, Designs and Patents Act, 1988.
All rights reserved. No part of this publication may be
reproduced or transmitted in any form or by any means,
electronic or mechanical, including photocopy, recording or
any information storage and retrieval system, without
permission in writing from the publisher.

A CIP catalogue record for this book is available from the
British Library

ISBN: 978-1-910283-15-8

This book is a work of fiction. Names, characters, busi-
nesses, organisations, places and events are either the
product of the author's imagination or are used fictitiously.
Any resemblance to actual persons, living or dead, events
or locales is entirely coincidental.

ACKNOWLEDGEMENTS

A heartfelt thanks to Graeme Reynolds, for believing in this story and to Kerri Patterson and Steve Lockley for their invaluable editing work.

To Steve Byrne, a fine writer and friend

PROLOGUE

She told him afterwards and he was angry.

"Why didn't you ask?" Robert Lewis tried to keep his voice level.

"Because you would have said no." Caitlin lay on her side, elbow on the pillow, head resting in her hand. "I'm sorry, I..." She sounded close to tears and Lewis knew he shouldn't be angry with her.

But she had lied to him. Christ she was a doctor; they both were. How could she have stooped to such a pathetic deception?

Caitlin sat up. "For God's sake, it was a mad impulse. A stupid mistake, okay?"

"Have you done this before?"

"What?" She swung round to sit on the edge of the bed, her back to Lewis. Caitlin was naked, her pale skin smooth and flawless, her red-dark hair reaching between her shoulder-blades. And she was beautiful. But Lewis was too angry and exasperated to make any move towards her.

"You heard me, Caitlin. Is this the first time you've neglected to take your pill?"

"No it isn't." She looked at him over her shoulder. Her eyes were red. "A child, Robert, would that be such a terrible thing? A new life?"

"Ah, now we have it; Dr Caitlin Lewis and her bloody new life crusade."

"Yes, new fucking life. It's a damn sight more natural

and healthy than the resurrections."

"We agreed..." Lewis tried. "You know how I feel about our careers, children...I don't want children, Caitlin. I like the life we have. Why spoil it?"

No response, until she grabbed her clothes, walked out and slammed the bedroom door in her wake.

Despite his anger, Lewis knew why this was so important to her. The new life crusade might have been a sarcastic jibe, but it was true. Caitlin was a neurologist, highly respected and, before the resurrections began, tipped for a consultancy post at the Central Middlesex. But who needed doctors now? Death really had lost its sting. When illness became too painful or debilitating to bear, why not simply make the Great Transition and join the ranks of the resurrected?

It had started eighteen months before, the dear departed returning first from mortuary slabs and undertakers' parlours, then literally from their graves as shock gave way to panic-stricken mass exhumations. A year deceased seemed to be the limit, any corpse older than that remained a corpse. Their ranks, however, swelled daily. No one remained dead for more than a few minutes anymore.

For some of the Living, it was a time of unbridled joy. Loved ones, thought gone forever, were returned to the bosom of their families, death was no longer the end, life-bought wisdom and experience would never again be lost to the grave. It became politic to re-name the formerly dead, the Returned, to ignore their special odour and avoid disparaging comments or jokes about their pallor.

Others, Caitlin among them, regarded the resurrection with suspicion, loathing, and in some, more extreme quarters, hatred. While most governments and societies celebrated, some persecuted and burned. Fire, they had discovered, was the only way to rid the world of the Devil's great deception.

A weeks ago, the resurrection had even threatened to bring down the UK government when, in an unguarded moment, unaware that the microphones were switched on, the Prime Minister had used the inappropriate term *stenchers* to describe the Dead. There was outcry, a call for his resignation and an opportunistic leadership challenge led by the Home Secretary, Jonathon Baker. The Prime Minister, ever the survivor, quickly appeased the offended then went on to subdue the mutineers. Rebellious foot soldiers were exiled to the back benches, the ring leaders, including Baker, were sent home to spend more time with their families.

Robert Lewis had little time for unease, politics or philosophy. The wealthier Dead were even vainer than their Living counterparts. Especially since post-mortem animation did not prevent post-mortem degeneration. As a result, the cosmetics industry which included Lewis' own Harley Street practice, was flourishing.

Snow smudged itself on the window. This should have been one of those comfortable, warm times, the two of them basking in afterglow, cocooned and happy. Instead the iciness outside had penetrated the world in here.

Hating the silence, Lewis reached out to switch on the bedside radio. It was time for the Sunday afternoon play, a Lewis post-coital tradition. And also a practice run, Caitlin would joke, for middle-age. Radio Four had adapted The Shining. Damien Lewis played Jack Torrance. But not this Sunday.

"...confused, but it seems that fighting has broken out in towns and cities across the entire country. We are also getting reports of similar battles in other parts of the world. The picture, however, is far from clear."

Fighting?

Lewis turned up the volume.

"We can now go to Abhik Dhawan, who is in Central

London. Abhik, are you there?"

"Yes, Jim. I'm in Trafalgar Square, which is, as you can hear, overflowing with people. Everyone is confused and panicked. The police..." The correspondent's already hoarse, breathless voice was interrupted by the din of the crowd. "The police are out in force but there seems little they can do. It's the same all over the city. The streets are choked with traffic. No one knows whether to stay at home or run, although, quite frankly, where do you run to?"

There was a heavy *crump* sound.

"Was that an explosion, Abhik? Abhik? Can you hear me?"

"Yes, yes. I'm still here. There have been a few explosions in the last half hour or so. They seem to be coming from south of here, although people are telling me that there are fires and running battles everywhere. A few minutes ago a convoy of armoured cars and troop lorries managed to push its way down towards Westminster, their presence indicating that the violence in the capital has escalated to unprecedented levels."

"There is talk of some kind of civil war between the Living and the Dead, do you think there is any truth in the claim, Abhik?"

"The trouble certainly seems to result from clashes between the two factions. We know there have been increasing tensions in certain quarters, fire bomb attacks on Dead homes by religious and other extremists. As for the spark that ignited this? Nobody can say for - oh my God..."

"Abhik what's happening? Abhik? We seemed to have lost...Abhik, can you hear me?"

"...Dead," the correspondent shouted, his voice breaking with fear. "There are Dead charging into the Square, from Westminster, no, from all sides. They're armed...my God, they're armed. I can see khaki...there are soldiers among them...and police...people are..." He was running, panting, the sound barely audible above a wall of screams.

A gunshot. Another. A volley. Silence.

"Uh...we'll try to get Abhik Dhawan back on air as soon as possible." The newsreader sounded badly shaken. "But in the meantime we can go over to Manchester."

Lewis clambered out of bed.

"Caitlin!" he shouted as he ran downstairs. "Turn the television on. Caitlin where are you? It's important. It's..."

She was in the lounge, still naked apart from a long cardigan she had draped over her shoulders. She stood in front of the television which flickered with chaotic, almost incomprehensible images of riot and panic.

"Now do you believe me?" she said. Her voice was tightly calm.

"We don't know." Lewis went to her and put tentative hands on her arms. She stiffened and shrugged him off.

"We have to get away," she said. "Pack some suitcases."

"In this weather? We won't get as far as the A1."

Good old weather, reassuringly bad, a debilitating security blanket and eternal excuse for inaction.

"And where do we go, Caitlin? You heard what they're saying, it's everywhere. We're probably safer here."

Everyone is safe here in dear old Arkley. Money is our barbed wire and battlements in this little haven of civilisation that clings to the northern coat tails of London, but is far enough out to avoid getting too much of the city's dirt on its soft, well-manicured hands...

"They'll come for us," Caitlin whispered.

"Listen, the army is out, the police. Things will be calm by the morning."

Would they? Didn't that reporter scream that there were soldiers and police among the ranks of the Dead? Casualties didn't fall in this war, they changed sides.

The lights went out.

Caitlin jerked back as if stung. "Jesus…"

"It's just a power cut. The snow –"

"Don't bloody patronise me Robert. This is a war."

"Okay, okay. We'd better check the doors and windows. Lock everything, just in case. Come on Caitlin. Now!"

Action, purpose, a way for him to quell his own panic.

"Leave the front door until last. I need to go out to the garage."

"Why, Robert? For God's sake –"

"There's a can of petrol."

"Why do we need petrol? For God's sake, Robert."

"Fire…Doesn't fire kill…" Kill what? Those who were already dead?

"Be quick, please."

Was that a hint of thaw? Ridiculously, Lewis felt a moment of relief, and was immediately astounded at his own superficiality. The world was descending into apocalyptic chaos and here he was euphoric because his hurt wife had shown a flicker of concern for his well-being

Lewis hurried into the hall, where he fumbled for keys, shoes and a coat in the burgeoning, non-electric dark. A moment later he was out on the gravel drive that fronted the property. The road, hidden behind a high hedge, was no longer illuminated by street lights. The neighbouring houses, each half-concealed by their own hedges and trees, were lightless silhouettes in the late afternoon dusk.

Snow stung Lewis' face as he trudged to the double garage. The wind was violent and bitter. A frozen-fingered struggle with the lock and he had a door open.

He had forgotten to bring a torch so had to pick his way carefully between his Jaguar and the bare block wall, blundering first into the lawnmower and then the edge of the workbench. He crouched down and gingerly felt around until his hand brushed over the plastic handle of the petrol can. He hauled it out, reassured by its shifting, liquid weight.

Outside again, he turned to pull down the garage door.

Something...movement...

He spun around. Snow drove across the garden. Wind stirred the white-encrusted bushes and creaked the leafless branches of his neighbour's oak tree.

Movement, again.

Then figures, on the drive, moving fast.

Four...five... The closest, a man wearing a roll-neck sweater but no coat. He was thick-set, but light on his feet despite his bulk. A woman moved round to the man's left. She wore a dress and, like the man, no coat. Lewis felt a momentary relief. It was Brian and Nicola Thurrow, his neighbours, the owners of the oak tree. Bloody hell they must be cold.

"Brian, are you okay? The power..."

"Don't 'Brian' me, you warm flesh bastard," Thurrow shouted back.

The words slammed into Lewis, confusing, hurtful even. Then Thurrow surged into a run, his gaunt-to-skeletal wife on his heels. The others arced round, pincer-like, all carried weapons; lengths of pipe, spades and garden forks, a kitchen knife.

Lewis stumbled back as two of the attackers rushed the

house and burst in through the unlocked front door. Then his heel caught on some snow-buried obstacle and he was on his back, wallowing and winded. Thurrow and Nicola slid into his field of vision. It was Thurrow who carried the iron bar and Nicola the kitchen knife.

There was screaming from inside the house that went on and on.

Caitlin.

Oh Christ...Caitlin.

CHAPTER ONE

THE LIVING AND THE DEAD

Dead flesh was far from dead. Dead flesh was hungry, its will to survive relentless. Even when detached from muscle and bone it curled about the scalpel blade, twisting and writhing as it was transferred quickly from patient to electric incinerator by Lewis' theatre technician. Only then, as it convulsed in heat agony, did it finally dissolve and cease to be.

Organs were worse. Intestines imbued with the speed and strength of steaming, blue-grey snakes; stomachs that were lethal, acid-filled slugs; hearts, thrashing cephalopods with blood-vessel tentacles. Operating on Dead, required speed, dexterity and a full set of personal protective equipment.

It did not require the tremors that shook Lewis' hand with increasing frequency, or the sweats and cravings that snatched away his concentration at the most critical moments.

Like now.

He stopped, struggled to slow his breathing and waited for the tremors to pass. He had to regain control or he would end up in one of the charnel houses that passed for restaurants among the Dead, The Savoy for instance, famous for the quality and freshness of its live meat.

"Melissa," he said to the nurse, who was also gowned and armoured. "I'm sweating here."

Lewis's Perspex face-shield was pulled up and the sweat dabbed from his forehead and eyes. The nurse had long ceased to be Sister Foster. Such formalities were irrelevant among the small cadre of medical staff, the Vitally Skilled as the Dead called them, who now lived out their lives imprisoned in the Harley Street Compound.

Hands steady again, Lewis resumed his work. The patient's face had been stripped down to bare muscle, and bulging eyes stared up at Lewis, unblinking windows to a soul that was far from human. This Dead was muscled and athletic. His hair was blond, his ever-open eyes, blue. His name was Brad, appropriate somehow.

Hair-like filaments waved from Brad's raw meat face, sensing Lewis's living skin and blindly groping for it with minute, barbed tips. Lewis elbow length surgical gloves were the strongest available. Living flesh was never exposed to the Dead.

"Why so slow?" Brad asked and gave a carnivorous, yellow-toothed grin. There was no need for anaesthetic because the Dead felt no pain. "Lost your nerve?"

"Please don't speak." Lewis forced professional neutrality into his voice. "You need to remain absolutely still."

"But I'm hungry," Brad said and snapped his teeth.

Lewis instinctively snatched his hand back. Brad laughed.

"Andy," Lewis said, voice a little shaky. "I'm ready."

Andy Campbell, the technician opened the chiller box and drew out a sheet of Living human skin. He brought it over to Lewis, laid on a tray and protected by two layers of foil. Skin was kept frozen in a large unit in the far corner of the theatre. Sheets of it were placed in the chiller box to defrost at the start of the each day. The amount had to be calculated from measurements taken during initial consultations. Living skin was precious and every square centimetre had to be accounted for.

Lewis laid the skin over Brad's forehead. As he smoothed it gently into place he felt the ripples and undulations caused by the filaments as they hooked into, and drew the flesh tight over the Dead muscle beneath.

More Dead tissue crept in from the sides of the Brad's head, and down from the scalp, moulding into the edges of the new layer. The join was delicate and would take several days to strengthen. Until then the new skin needed to be stitched in place.

Another spasm tightened Lewis's hand, more from revulsion than delirium tremens this time. He swallowed bile, closed his eyes for a moment then picked up the first of the sutures from the bowl Melissa had brought to him. There was no need for sterilisation. No bacteria could survive the Dead's hungers.

Lewis worked quickly, deftly. He had always been fast, his touch light and sure. More sutures, then the next sheet of skin, the process repetitive, mechanical and nauseating. Lewis never allowed himself to wonder where the Living skin actually came from. He knew that the Dead owned what they quaintly called Farms. Rumour in the Harley Street Compound was that the cattle on these farms were not of the four-legged kind. Lewis had stopped listening, or thinking, long ago, because therein lay madness.

Skin and organs were delivered once a week and that was the end of it.

Except there never would be an end of it, would there?

Every day the slavery of the operating theatre and the claustrophobic confines of the Compound, surrounded by an uncrossable sea of affluent Dead. And, eventually, inevitably, Death itself; either the waking hell of a Dead restaurant or the everlasting nightmare of Dead-state. Not yet though, not this hot June evening. Another day survived, another day breathing.

Exhausted, Lewis pulled the last suture tight, tied it off

then straightened. He blinked sweat from his eyes. The room was summer bright, despite the blinds, and chilled to discomfort by the air conditioning. The Dead insisted on it. Summer was not their time.

Lewis turned away from the patient and walked across to the window.

"Thanks, Doc," Brad said. "Didn't feel a thing." He laughed, a throaty, gritty sound that stopped abruptly. "You'd better sort that tremor out, Lewis. One botched operation is all it'll take. And if you go down, your pretty little nurse and handsome techie will go down with you."

"Fucking stencher," Campbell muttered after Brad had left. He was a gangling, raw-boned Scot, his head shaved, eyes hard and glinting with malice for the Dead. "Thank Christ that was the last one for today." He set to work cleaning up, using an industrial vacuum cleaner to clear the floor of even the minutest scrap of Dead tissue.

The drone of the cleaner jarred through Lewis' skull, but he couldn't bring himself to leave the theatre. Instead he opened the blinds and pushed up the big sash window, desperate for air.

Harley Street was silent and deserted but for a few big luxury saloons and gleaming sport coupés, parked by the pavement. None of these belonged to medical staff at any of the clinics in the Compound. All were owned by their Dead patients. As Lewis watched, Brad emerged from the main door downstairs, climbed into a Ferrari and roared off towards the barbed-wire fence and gate that secured the Marylebone Road end of the street.

Campbell finished cleaning and was emptying the bag into the incinerator when Melissa returned. She had removed her scrubs and was now wearing her civvies; a tee shirt and jeans. She was gaunt, middle-aged, earthily attractive, and Andy the technician's lover.

"Everybody okay?" she said, as she said at the end of

every working day.

"Okay as okay goes," Campbell answered.

"You're such a misery," Melissa chided him. "I really don't know what I see in you."

"It can't be charm," Lewis said.

The banter ran like clockwork, a litany that had become ritual.

"There's a letter for you, Robert," Melissa said.

Now that wasn't part of the script.

"A letter?" Campbell said. "I'd almost forgotten what one of those is."

"It was on the doormat. No stamp or anything. Mind you, does anyone use stamps now?"

"Melissa it may have escaped your notice but there isn't a Post Office anymore. No postmen or red vans or sorting offices or -"

"Andy."

"Yes, my love?"

"Shut up." Melissa turned to Lewis. "I put it on your desk, Robert."

"Yes, yes thanks." Lewis used feigned disinterest to hide his panic. Campbell was right. No one wrote letters, in fact no Living compound had any contact whatsoever with any other Compound or with the outside world (whatever that was, these days), other than through their patients. They were prisoners, held in a somewhat gilded cage, but prisoners nonetheless, and slave labourers, alive because they had something the Dead wanted. So a letter could only mean trouble.

"Goodnight, Robert," Melissa said. She and Campbell were at the door, on their way out and up to their private apartment on the top floor of the clinic.

Loosening his tie Lewis descended to the ground floor consulting room, which was adjacent to his own apartment. The room was traditional enough; heavy oak table with leather inlay, big comfortable chairs for himself and his patients, a screen, a couch and the usual medical paraphernalia in glass-fronted cabinets on the walls. Most of it was window dressing. The Dead only came to him for one thing.

Despite its professional prettiness, the room was grimy, dusty, and smelled of damp. There were dark, cloud-shaped patches of mould in the corners of the ceiling. Like all the houses in Harley Street, this one was old and, since the Uprising, neglected. Age was rapidly peeling away its mask.

The letter lay on the desk, sealed in a white envelope, his name printed on the front. Innocuous but deadly. Dry-mouthed, Lewis tore it open. It could, of course be from one of the other clinics in the Compound, but messages were usually delivered in person. The medical slaves took any opportunity they could for human contact, for prowling, even briefly, around the confines of their cage.

The fact that his name was printed, along with the quality of the envelope and of the paper inside, were ominous signs. Only the Dead had access to word processors, printers and good paper. As Lewis unfolded the letter, an object dropped out onto the table. It was the size and shape of a credit card, but plain, except for the faint light that pulsed from somewhere deep inside its thin interior.

A Pass.

A patient then, in need of a home visit. It wouldn't be the first time.

Lewis turned his attention to the letter and saw more printed text.

"To Jack, don't let it creep. Please come tonight."

Jack? What the hell...

It was from 'Wendy' Under that, another phrase: "Shreds Remain." There was also an address. Onslow Crescent, South Kensington. Home visits required discretion, the Dead were sensitive about their treatment. But if this was some sort of code, then it was taking discretion to ridiculous new heights.

Shreds Remain...

Shreds, of what? Sanity?

He stared at the letter. Jack and Wendy. If this was some sort of code, did it refer to Peter Pan? No, he didn't think there was a Jack in that story.

Don't let it creep.

What the hell did that mean?

Perhaps he should just take the Pass and get the visit over with. He was tired, he didn't want to do anything tonight except sit, listen to music, read something from the new pile of scrappy paperbacks acquired from last intra-Compound literature exchange, and drink.

Oh yes, he would drink and he would drink. It was the only way. Even the Dead understood that and kept him well stocked. Hands shaking, Lewis lit a cigarette and read the brief correspondence over and over again.

Jack. Jack and Wendy. Jack Spratt, Jack the Ripper, Jack the Lad, Jack O'Lantern. He scraped about his memory for all the Jacks who had hidden themselves there over the years. Jolly Jack Tar, Jack Bruce, Jack and the beanstalk, Spring Heel Jack, Jack Frost, Jack Torrance, Jack Kennedy, Blackjack, Jackknife –

Wait.

Jack Torrance, playwright and live-in winter caretaker of

the Overlook Hotel. And husband of Wendy. That was her name wasn't it? Wendy. Jack Torrance who did let it, the hotel's lethal old boiler, creep. And it was his undoing...Jack Torrance, main character from *The Shining*, the last Radio Four Sunday adaptation ever aired...

Who would know about that?

Except.

Oh Christ, oh Christ...

Caitlin.

But she was gone. He had left her in the house on that final day and never seen or heard of her since. Her screams still rattled through his skull every night, tearing at the veneer of self-control, exposing the raw, bloody vitals of his guilt. Unless he could drink himself into peaceful oblivion, of course, before honest sleep took him.

Caitlin had written to him. She wanted him to come to her. She was outside the Compound. She had sent a Pass. So she must be a Dead. And he didn't want to see her if she was. He couldn't...

But a Pass was a Pass. A Pass was not to be refused. Somewhere in the labyrinthine bowels of Dead bureaucracy there was a record that he, Mr Robert Lewis, had been summoned to the house of a Dead. A refusal would lead to arrest, which, in turn, would lead not to a cosy interview at the local nick, but to the kitchens at the Savoy.

***

At seven pm Lewis, stifling in his threadbare suit and carrying his medical bag, exited the Compound at the Marylebone Road end. It was still daylight. A breeze troubled the trees at the edge of the park, tepid and devoid of relief.

There was always a momentary sense of release when you were allowed out of the Compound, a sense of space and freedom. But it was just an illusion, Lewis knew from bitter experience. He had been called on by the more affluent, high level Dead to carry out home visits a handful of times before. Each visit was enabled by a Pass, which shrivelled to dust once the visit was complete and Lewis was safely back behind the Harley Street fence.

There was another reason for the falseness of this particular form of parole. Evening and night were the Dead's time and the first of them were already out and heading city-wards for the night's entertainment. There would be food, countless ravenous orgies held behind the respectable frontages of the capital's restaurants. Whited sepulchres every one, wherein lay blood and torn flesh and the screams of the farm-raised Living. Then there would be all manner of sensual pleasure. The Dead craved touch, taste and physical delight.

Walking the city streets meant walking among the Dead and although the Pass would protect him, Lewis would still be in their midst and the object of their carnivorous lust. A journey into night time London was a journey into Hell.

Hands in pockets, head down, Lewis hurried towards Regents Park Underground Station. Dead streamed in from both sides, chattering noisily, pretending to be oblivious to his presence. Another illusion. They knew, they smelled him. But they also felt the presence of the Pass. It was Lewis's crucifix to their vampire. The only thing that stood between his warm, living flesh and their desperate hungers.

Into the station then, where it was hot, crowded and stinking. Lewis gagged, his stomach spasmed, but he pressed on, hurrying from any bumped contact. He waved his Pass over the reader at the turnstile. The reader's eye glistened wetly, pupil momentarily dilating. The gate unlocked and he was through. Freedom turned to claustrophobia and panic. He was immersed in the Dead, trapped in a river of them, wrapped in their perfume and necrotic stench.

The escalator bore him down to the platform, which was cooled by chillers that roared deafeningly in the enclosed space. For all their auditory bluster, they were only partially successful at cleaning the stink and heat from the air. The Dead crowded the platform, smartly dressed, heavily made-up. They laughed and sported, embraced and kissed, deeply and hungrily, public carnal performances ignored by the rest.

The Pass would keep him safe. Hungry as they were, the Dead would never dare attack a Pass carrier.

Would they?

Hot air puffed from the tunnel, there was a rumble, then the train hurtled into the station. Its driver was a glimpsed Living slave chained to his post, his heartbeat saved by his engine-driving skills. Doors hissed open. No one got off but scores, Lewis among them, swarmed into the already crowded carriages.

Lewis clung to the overhead rail. There was no room to move, bodies pressed in against him, scent-soaked and expensively clothed. Lewis felt hard muscle and soft dissolution. He felt broken bones move awkwardly beneath flesh, shirt and jacket. He felt spilled vitals, spongy and writhing through silk and cotton. And always, there was the odour.

Dead stared at him. He tried not to blink. It was an automatic response, to keep his eyes wide until they burned for moisture. There was a young woman in a tight black dress, a tall, balding, distinguished-looking man in a pinstripe suit, his almost hairless scalp mottled with necrosis, a stocky younger man in tee-shirt and jeans, whose jaw looked to be broken. Crushed against him, was a large woman whose stench was all but intolerable, whose hair was falling out and whose face was turning black.

All stared at him.

The Pass, the Pass, my safety is the Pass...

South Kensington's near-empty side streets were a relief after the crushed hell of the tube.

Caitlin will be there, waiting for him...

Dead Caitlin who was no longer Caitlin. Shreds remain, that's what she had written wasn't it? Did that mean shreds of herself, of her soul? She needed him. He didn't know why, but it was important. Perhaps she just needed him.

Onslow Crescent was a terrace of large, white dwellings, Victorian perhaps, or maybe Edwardian. Lewis was no expert in architecture. Each front door was guarded by a pair of fluted pillars and accessed via a wide flight of steps. They had been mostly converted to apartments before the uprising. Now they were houses again, the homes of High Levels, those with authority and privilege in whatever hierarchy that structured the Dead society.

Lewis checked the address he'd been. Number 14. He strolled past the frontages until he found the one he wanted.

Its large, deep blue door, stood ajar. She was waiting for him then, no mistake, no last minute change of heart. Lewis laughed at that, albeit humourlessly. If one organ was useless to the Dead it was that one. A moment to compose himself then he mounted the stairs and rang the bell. The door was open, but the courtesy was habitual.

No reply.

He pushed at the door then entered the main hallway. It was wide, plushly carpeted and furnished in an antique style his wife loved; Queen Anne and Regency, eras that retained some lightness of style in the years before the sledgehammer solidity of Victorianism. There were oils, plundered, Lewis suspected, from London's galleries. With the Dead it seemed, beauty was not to be shared but hoarded and lusted over.

Another open door.

23

"Caitlin? Caitlin it's me, Robert."

No answer, just a heavy, tight silence. Another hesitation, another bracing intake of breath then a push at the door. Which opened into what was a sitting room.

And devastation.

Furniture lay upended and smashed, books spilled from their shelves, paintings torn down and destroyed, and worse, huge gouges, like claw marks, raked into the wall. Lewis tried to breathe and, instead, choked on rotten air.

One of the books...

Now he shouted her name, overwhelmed by the same desolation he had felt on the night of the uprising. She had been taken again. Even though she was no longer his Caitlin, something had happened to her and the grief of it ripped into him and reduced him to a shivering wreck, oblivious to any lingering threat that might still lurk in the house.

The book, it's wrong somehow...

He should get out. The Pass linked him to Caitlin and suddenly it seemed more liability than privilege.

Odd. That book, isn't it?

Who or what the hell had done this? A Living raid perhaps? Rumour had it that the Resistance had grown bolder in the last few months, striking out from their ghettos, deep into the capital to steal food and other supplies and to take revenge. But the Resistance usually burned what they left behind.

The book. Wrong.

And those claw marks in the wall...

The book, look at the bloody book...

It lay, upturned on a coffee table that had somehow

remained intact among the ruin. It was a paperback, *The Shining*.

Caitlin still read King?

Shreds remain, that's what she had told him.

Lewis picked the book up, and a folded sheet of paper fell out. He opened it to find it covered in handwritten numbers. "9-2-12, 10-39-1, 16-18-9, 15-42-6, 9-2-12, 190-1-2, 171-35-2."

Another code?

The numbers were in patterns of three; page, paragraph, line? No, page, line, word. He would try that. He fumbled the pages. The code was laborious, awkward. His fear and panic stiffened his hands, forced re-counts.

First word, "The..."

Second, page ten. "First".

The first...

He dropped the book, stopped, tried to calm down and take his time. Whatever had visited this house had been and gone. It was okay. He owed this to Caitlin, to get it right.

Third word. "house".

The first house...

Christ no.

"now"

The first house now...

"ask the"

The book was tatty, pages fell out.

The first house now ask the mad...

Last word. "am".

No, he had made a mistake; mad am. It made no sense. He re-checked. It was correct according to the code. Caitlin must have made the mistake then.

mad am

No, wait.

mad-am, madam.

The First House...Christ Almighty. "The First House now and ask for the Madam"

CHAPTER TWO

FIRST HOUSE BLUES

Westminster was a seething mass of Dead. There was noise, relentless movement and blatant sensuality manifested as animalistic coupling. What passed for sex among the Dead was shared, social and violent.

To Lewis, huddled by the lamp-lit railings of Westminster Bridge, it seemed to be more about need rather than pleasure. Thankfully, it utterly absorbed its practitioners and Lewis was ignored.

The activity ebbed and flowed about the First House itself, like a carnal ocean lapping against the honey-coloured, Clipsham Stone walls of the once venerable old building. Few of the Dead gathered about its skirts could ever enter. But it was as if the scent of the pleasures it offered to the high level Dead and their privileged guests, was enough. Perhaps it permeated the very air of the surrounding streets and that was what drew the Dead moth-like, to its hormone-rich flame.

Lewis fingered the pass in his jacket pocket and supposed that he was Caitlin's honoured guest in that house of mirth. Shouldn't he go in?

On the far side of the bridge, the London Eye was a dark, skeletal framework and what was once St Thomas's hospital, was now a blackened ruin. Below was water, cold, deep and riddled with treacherous currents. A moment's shock and pain then –

- he would crawl out onto its muddy bank, dripping and hungry, to take his place among the foul mass of necrotic flesh who ruled the city.

Even suicide was no longer a choice.

So he turned back to stare at the First House. Built as a temple to democracy the building had become an altar to unimaginable lusts and pleasures.

Lewis withdrew the hip flask from his inside jacket pocket. Caitlin had bought it for him many years ago, to help take the chill off those winter weekend golf mornings. He swigged scotch then picked up his medical bag and set off towards The First House.

What a vast, grim joke it had been to turn the Houses of Parliament into the biggest brothel in London, if not England - if there was an England, Britain or United Kingdom anymore. What happened outside the city environs was a mystery to Lewis, and the others who clung to life within the capital. Be it Heaven or Hell, Lewis knew he would never go there. He would live out the rest of his days in the Harley Street Compound.

If his days didn't end here tonight.

He pushed a shaking hand through his sweat-damp hair and tried not to think about what he was about to do or what had happened - or was happening to - Caitlin, or the fact that he had no reason to trust her because she was, it seemed, a High Level Dead and this could simply be some lethal game.

Buffeted and cursed at by lust-crazed Dead, Lewis wrestled his way into Parliament Square. Cars raced by, no thought given for any speed limit or pedestrian safety. Horns blared, and there were metal-on-flesh thuds and cries and shouted curses as the cars forced their way through.

What was death anyway? What was mutilation but the spawning of yet more grotesque life forms?

The chimes of Big Ben rang out eleven pm. Around Lewis, Dead shouted and fought and touched. Someone grabbed at his arm and he spun round to stare into the face of a blonde, gaunt youth, one eye whole, the other a festering lava flow of pus that spilled from the socket and down his cheek. The Dead backed away, snarling, spitting obscenity.

Lewis pressed on, trusting the pass to keep any others at bay.

Parliament Square.

Lewis grabbed at the spiked iron fence that guarded the First House and clung on like a drowning man. He glimpsed Churchill's statue. What the hell would the old man think of this? Too long dead to think of anything. Thank God.

Entrance to the First House was through a gate in the fence, guarded by a pair of large males, both in a pseudo-military uniform of bulging tee shirt and khaki trousers. They carried guns, although, what good would bullets do if the crowd tried a mass forced entry? Exploding bullets perhaps? Incendiary shells?

Lewis took a step towards the guards, who looked perfect, not marred by necrosis or any other sign of post-mortem deterioration. Then one of them blinked.

Living?

"Who the fuck are you?" The speaker was the taller of the two, an intimidating, shaven-headed bull of a man.

Lewis held up the pass and the guard nodded towards the reader which stood just inside the gates. Lewis stepped through and swiped the card.

The other, a shorter, stockier version of his fellow, took a menacing step forward. "Yeah, we're Living," he said quietly. "So don't stand there like a fucking judge. You do whatever whoring you do to keep your heart beating, we do ours. You wear a suit, we carry guns, but we've all sold our stinking little souls to the stenchers, so that makes us exactly the same."

It made sense, Lewis decided, as he hurried towards the main doors. Living would retain their muscle tone and strength. It was hard for the Dead to remain in that sort of shape. Their strength lay in sheer numbers and that overwhelming, relentless energy that drove their bodies and made them invincible.

***

And so, into the First House stepped Mr Robert Lewis, Consultant Cosmetic Surgeon.

There was no necrosis here, no leaking eyes or ruptured guts. These Dead were immaculate, their much-repaired flesh as pristine and beautiful as it was possible for dead flesh to be. But they were no better behaved.

The chambers and hallways were packed with a seething tangle of dancing, whirling, shouting, laughing and rutting bodies. Music was the engine, played at jet-engine volume, a repetitive, electro-pound that hammered at Lewis's skull and drove brutal fists into his abdomen. The light was disorientating and hypnotic, a relentless colour-shift that paled, then greened then bloodied the revellers. There was no alcohol as far as Lewis could see. The orgy was driven by lust.

Lewis moved cautiously, keeping to the edge, quickly disorientated by the noise, the light, the labyrinthine chaos of corridors and vaulted ceilings. He was moving deeper into the House's rotten heart and had no idea who to speak to or how to find the Madam. The Living who served the Dead looked drug-dazed, of no help to anyone but their customers. Then he saw the woman.

She stood, a little to one side of the throng, aloof, haughty. Her dark was hair hanging almost to the floor and she wore a skin-tight dress of some shiny material, which could have been satin or equally could have been plastic. It was bright yellow.

She stared, unblinking, but there was a keenness to her

dead stare. She had some authority here, probably over the Living servants. Lewis swam towards her, finally daring to push into the mass. Head down he elbowed and barged, was bounced and buffeted but held his course. The woman caught his eye and glared at him. As he closed on her he drew the pass from his pocket. She grabbed his arm and wrenched him round then slammed him against the wall, hiding them both behind a balustrade.

"What are you here for?" the woman demanded. Her teeth were close to his ear. He smelled the stink beneath her perfume.

"The Madam..." Lewis couldn't shout, His strength had gone. "I want to see the Madam."

The women shook her head. Lewis noticed that her thick make-up was melting in the heat and revealing the truth beneath. "You can't."

"I must."

"Go away, or I'll call for security."

"Caitlin sent me." Lewis tensed, waiting for shock, anger or violence.

The woman backed away a little.

Lewis pressed on. "She told me to ask for the Madam -"

"Shut up, cretin. Dance with me. And listen carefully."

Lewis held her close despite the unutterable coldness of her flesh and the realisation that this would be how Caitlin would feel in his arms.

"We have to slip away unnoticed."

Lewis nodded.

"Hold my hand, make it look as if I've chosen you." She smiled, as if enjoying a private and very dark joke. "Kiss me."

Lewis shook his head, no...

"Kiss me or I'll throw you to the House, pass or no pass."

No choice then. Lewis put down his bag, took her icy face in his hands and pushed his lips against hers. She became urgent and trapped him in her arms. He tasted foulness, he tasted rot and decay and almost vomited into her. Things reached into his mouth; those hair-like tendrils feeling for live flesh. The woman broke away and laughed scornfully.

She led him through plushly carpeted corridors, and past countless doors, beyond which were rooms that he assumed were once offices, but now, perhaps, places for private pleasures. The turns and junctions became a repetitive blur. Lewis knew he would never find his way back. Too late to worry about that now. Another door, this one opening onto a set of stone stairs that descended into a red-tinted gloom.

The woman released his hand. "She's down there. You'll find her."

Then she turned on her considerable heel and strode away. Lewis stared into the shifting crimson glow and told himself that no one could descend into a place like that and stay sane, could they?.

So what was he going to do, wander these corridors looking for escape?

He took the first step, one hand on the stone-block wall. The steps ended at the entrance to a narrow, cramped, tunnel. There was a damp stink down here. The walls sweated stale moisture. There were roots too, fibrous, growing over, and into, the stone. He felt them under his fingertips recognising their pulsing life.

The light was organic, emanating from the swollen abdomens of the rat-sized centipedes that covered the wall and low, low ceiling. Their needle-thin proboscis plunged in and out of the fibrous roots. Feeding? Lewis shuddered, repulsed by the swarms of invertebrates and their sudden, unprovoked bursts of movement. He walked carefully, not wanting to brush against any of them.

There was a wooden door, low and insect-free. Lewis leaned against it. He breathed hard, muscles aching from tension.

"I want the Madam," he called out.

The door opened at his touch and Lewis did not hesitate in stepping through and into a chamber, where he discovered the source of the roots. It took a few moments for Lewis to comprehend what was sprawled on the floor in the centre of the room, to understand the structures and complexities of it.

Vaguely human, the thing was perhaps fifteen feet from hairless head to bloated, useless feet. It was naked, a mass of slick, mottled flesh, its head featureless but for a mouth, no eyes, no ears, no nose. The mouth was covered by a thin curtain of membrane, which meant that it could not be used for feeding. The roots emanated from its carcase. The thing lay on its side, its body covered with rows of teats, at which human-looking creatures suckled. One of them turned to glare at Lewis and revealing a vast fang-lined mouth, empty, soulless eyes and waist-length, rough black hair.

The bloated creature at the centre of the chamber spoke and its voice was soft and shockingly feminine. "I'm the Madam, one of the Seven who were sent by Hell to administer the new order imposed on your sorry little world." She sighed, "But no longer. The Seven are now Six, because I started feeling sorry for you all. And besides, I received a better offer from another quarter."

Other figures stepped out of the shadows; men and women, wearing dinner jackets and cocktail dresses, unblinking, silent, Dead.

The creature groaned, the sound apparently calming, because the suckling returned to its meal. Lewis saw that the creature held something, crooked tenderly in one huge, fat-smothered arm.

"Caitlin sent me." Lewis held out the pass, his hand shaking.

The creature moved its head and Lewis sensed her regard.

"Caitlin? Oh, so you're Mister Lewis."

She had known that already of course, but games had to be played, he supposed."Where is Caitlin?" the Madam asked.

"I don't know. I went to her house, but she's gone. I think there had been a struggle."

Had he said too much? Impossible to know.

"Gone?" The Madam shook the part of her that constituted a head. "Poor, poor Caitlin."

"Do you have any idea where she might be?"

"I don't know, Mister Lewis. Let us hope she escaped, because, if Reeder has her, it will be dark for her."

Something whimpered. The sound was child-like, yet not real. In his head, while at the same time, emanating from the bundle in the Madam's arms.

"Come closer, don't be shy," said the Madam. "I won't hurt you, nor will my sucklings. Unless you try to harm me of course."

Lewis steeled himself and moved towards the monstrous thing. He sensed tension from the feral, many-fanged sucklings, despite the Madam's reassurances. The Madam rolled herself further onto her side and slowly uncurled her arms to uncover the thing she held. It was an ovoid of some gelatinous, fleshy substance. Something dark but indistinct stirred beneath its translucent surface.

"You have to look after her," The Madam said.

Her?

"What are you talking about? What the hell is that thing?"

"Caitlin must trust you a great deal." The Madam's voice was oddly soothing, its honey curled about a kernel of great authority. "There's a reason she left it here with us. She knew she was in danger. She wants you to take the child who is both an ending and a beginning. They're always one and the same."

"No riddles. Just tell me what it is."

"She's your daughter, Mister Lewis."

"That...That thing? No. This is bullshit, this is some sort of fucking trick. It's not even human."

"Not yet. She has no soul. Her mother is Dead, therefore the child is an open page, unfinished. She cannot grow and remain in this state forever, unless she is quickened by another soul and what better soul then that of her own father? She is also a rarity, precious and much sought after. Most of those born to women who were with child when they became Dead, are nothingness, howling fragments of darkness. Shape-changers who suck-in and make their own, whatever, or whoever, is to hand. Your task is to nurture and form this child. And to get her to safety."

So, was this object, the creature in the Madam's arms, really his daughter? Was it the child Caitlin had deceived him for? Had it been conceived on the afternoon of the uprising, in the moments before their final argument? Whatever it was, it...she...was the child of a Dead. A half-formed thing. The idea repulsed him.

"No...I can't. I'm confined to a Compound, I work for the Dead..."

"If she stays here, Reeder will take her." It was one of the Dead, who had spoken, a young man with thin, fair hair. His voice a gravel-choked whisper. "He's coming for us. We're finished."

Reeder? Lewis glanced nervously towards the entrance to this chamber, the action instinctive. Everyone, Living or Dead was terrified of this near mythic Lord of Law and his army of enforcers. It was claimed that he was answerable only to the Seven themselves.

Lewis shook his head. "I can't get involved with this"

"You're involved already. Your pass brought you here, so there will be a record of your visit to the First House," another of the Dead, a stout, pearl-wearing woman said. "The child is the only way to save yourself and everyone else."

"Save myself? By taking this...child...back to the clinic?" Lewis shook his head. "No, no this is a mistake. I have to go -"

"Do you want her to stay here?" said the young man. "In this place? We're all Half-Deads. We're all fugitives from Reeder and The Seven."

It sounded like the name of a rock band. Lewis almost chuckled, despite his fear.

"Her name is Anna," said the Madam.

Yes, that sounded like the sort of name Caitlin would have given to a child, simple, sweet, intensely feminine.

"What...What am I supposed to do with her?" What any father was supposed to do with his child, surely, look after her, nurture and protect her.

But it wasn't a child.

"Get her to the Resistance," the woman said.

"How the hell am I going to do that? They'd kill me. I'm

a collaborator."

"You will help her," the Madam said. "Willingly or not."

Lewis swallowed hard. He couldn't do this. It would mean his death. He had survived by doing as he was told, by keeping his head down and remaining as invisible as it was possible to be. He wouldn't be able to cope with this pressure. He would crack.

And what did he owe the Dead Caitlin anyway? Or this child, who must have formed and grown in the womb of a walking corpse? But Anna wasn't Dead, she was Living. Not his responsibility though; compassion and selflessness were long gone from this world.

"I'm sorry..."

"We're disappointed, Doctor."

He backed away, trying not to look at the child, unable to find any words that were not self-justification or excuses.

One of the suckling, almost forgotten by Lewis, growled softly and the others were suddenly alert, sniffing the air, emitting hisses and low growls. For a moment Lewis doubted that he was going to get out of this room alive. The sucklings clambered down onto the floor and crouched, fangs bared. Lewis froze, wondering if his bladder and bowels would hold up long enough for him to die with any sort of dignity.

They came at him and he screamed as the first of the creatures slammed into him and knocked him to the ground. Winded, he clawed for air. He saw only its open jaws, the rows of needle fangs, its forked, serpent tongue. Saliva dripped onto his face, hot and stinging. He thrashed in panic, but the creature was strong. It thrust its cavernous mouth into his face and hissed. He whimpered, unable to shrink away. Rough hands wrenched at his tie, his shirt, ripping the material, popping buttons. Another suckling came closer, holding the child. She looked to be soft in its hands, hanging over the edges of its palm. The suckling brought the quivering mass down onto Lewis' chest.

Lewis cried out again as he felt the soft, dank, warmth of it against his skin. Then there was pain. It stung him like some sort of grotesque jellyfish. He writhed and his heels drummed the floor as things pierced his chest. He tried to breathe then scream, but his mouth was locked open, his breath trapped in his lungs. The child-thing spread and settled itself and he felt its hooks and roots press into his flesh.

Then it stopped. Images poured into his mind. He saw Caitlin smiling down at him. He felt her close to him, heard her whisper, but could make out no words. He closed his eyes but a moment later was hauled roughly to his feet. Two of the sucklings supported him. He tried, feebly, to claw at the mass clinging to his chest, now spread-out over him like a second skin. He became aware of tension. The sucklings drew back into a defensive circle about the Madam.

"Go, Mister Lewis, get out, away. Reeder has come."

CHAPTER THREE

SHREDS REMAIN

The Half-Dead shrank back into the shadows.

"Follow Eve and you'll be safe." The Madam said, urgent now.

Presumably Eve was the suckling who had broken out of the defensive circle and was opening the door.

"In return you must look after the child, *your* child."

Screams drifted from the House above, followed by an animal roar. Lewis swallowed hard, half-paralysed by his terror. He had to get out of there, now.

He could not face Reeder.

The man with the Stanley knife. Such casual butchery, so much blood.

And who's next, eh?

"Yes," Lewis said, the word almost sobbed out. "Yes, yes I'll take care of her."

Anything, please get me out of here...

Another roar rolled down the passageway.

The Madam emitted a long, mournful groan and, without hesitation Eve rushed out of the chamber and into the passage. The suddenness of her departure caught Lewis unawares. Most of the Half-Dead had galvanised themselves into following her before he was able to move. He clutched his shirt and jacket tight to him and blundered through the narrow, insect-ridden tunnel. He realised that the Madam was staying behind, along with her faithful sucklings. The realisation brought him a moment of shame As grotesque and monstrous as she was, she did not deserve whatever Reeder would inflict upon her.

They reached the steps out of the tunnel without incident. At their head, Eve paused, sniffed, dog-like, then ran up to the door. She opened it cautiously. A moment, then she beckoned for Lewis and the others to follow.

Doors opened as they passed by, Dead stumbled out, many of them naked, their ever-open eyes bright with something that looked like genuine fear. Eve snarled and snapped at them as she passed, and they flinched away.

Corridors, more corridors. And Dead, milling, pushing and shoving as they crowded through doorways and onto the stairs. Lewis found himself cut-off from Eve, trapped in a tangled press of stinking, smartly-dressed bodies. He glimpsed the suckling, darting right through a set of double doors. Lewis forced his way through the melee and followed her.

Into Hell.

At first he could not comprehend the horror of the place. Then, slowly, it dawned on him that he was in the kitchen. There were steel tables, blood-drenched and piled with raw meat. Offal slicked the floor, and hanging by their chained ankles from huge metal hooks were the Dead's screaming, struggling, delicacies. People, Living, farmed for freshness most of them, although there were, no doubt, Vitally Skilled among them, those who had transgressed or outlived their usefulness. And there might even be choice cuts of captured Resistance fighters. Stories of their legendary exploits, and acts of brutal vengeance on Living collaborators regularly filtered into the Compound as scraps of news and rumour. The Resistance were both heroes and bogeymen, admired and feared in equal measure. Whoever they were , most of them were already mutilated; limbs hacked, slabs of flesh peeled and torn, and still bellowing out their horror at what was being done to them.

Eve darted between the hanging bodies with Lewis hard on her heels. Bloodied, desperate hands clutched at him as he passed by, upside-down faces howled their miseries into his own. A door swung open to admit more panic-stricken Dead, followed by a deafening, bestial roar. Lewis glimpsed green leather, pew-like seats, and realised what the dining hall had once been.

He forced himself to focus only on Eve, on her glistening, vein-webbed back and her long, matted, black hair. Eve lashing out with her clawed feet and hands as she ploughed a furrow through the knots of fleeing Dead. Lewis staggered on in her wake, out of breath and in pain from unaccustomed exertion.

Then she crashed through another door and they were out onto a small park, Lewis saw the river to his left and recognised the place as Victoria Tower Gardens. He stumbled to a halt, hands on his knees. He smelled smoke, saw it on the air. There was fire somewhere in the First House. All around him Dead boiled out, and surged into the already panic-maddened crowds on Westminster's streets.

Lewis straightened, scanned the chaos and saw Eve, sprinting towards the road. He forced himself to follow. A white Mercedes skidded to a halt. Eve headed directly for it. Confused and alarmed, Lewis did the same. Eve opened the front passenger door then looked back.

Looking for me, Lewis guessed.

He reached the car unhindered. An order was snapped from inside.

"Get in!"

Lewis slid into the front seat and found himself next to the smaller of the two security guards he had encountered on his way into the First House. If this was some sort for trap, then he was caught. There was nothing he could do about it now. As the car jerked into motion, Lewis clutched at the child, the action instinctive but awkward. There were other cars racing along Millbank and away from the First House..

"I shouldn't be surprised," the driver growled. "I thought there was something wrong about you."

"Where are we going?" Lewis asked.

"Your place," the driver answered. "Wherever that is."

"Harley Street?"

"Harley Street it is then."

"We'll never get back in, not with...with this -" child "-thing. Look, who are you working for?"

"The Madam, who do you fucking think? Everyone who works in the First House works for her." The driver swung the Mercedes right onto Vauxhall Bridge Road, narrowly missing a sports car. Horns blared.

"Who is she?"

"If you don't know I'm not going to be the one to tell you – fuck!"

Enforcers, four or five of them, ran across the road ahead, clumsy and anonymous in their fireproof suits. They clutched flame-throwers in their gloved hands, connected by hoses to small tanks strapped to their backs. The driver wrenched the steering wheel to the left and the Mercedes swung violently into a narrow, ill-lit side street. The nearside wheels shuddered over the pavement. Dead pedestrians, buildings, all flickered through Lewis's view.

Had the Enforcers seen his face through the windscreen, or the registration number? Did they know who was in the car?

A junction, the traffic lights rusting and long disused. The driver turned right and Lewis soon saw the cavernous, burnt-out ruins of Victoria Station. There had been fierce fighting here during the Uprising. There were Dead everywhere, running and driving for their homes. He glimpsed more Enforcers moving through the crowds, taking up positions at junctions and roundabouts. What if they set up roadblocks to stop and search vehicles?

"This was always going to happen," the driver said. "Reeder has just been biding his time." He slammed the heel of his hand against the steering wheel. "Why the fuck doesn't *He* help us?"

"Who? Reeder?"

"Of course not bloody Reeder -"

"Tell me for God's sake. I'm involved anyway."

The driver glanced at him sharply then sighed, as if defeated. "Azazel, fuck him. I'm looking after myself from now on. To hell with the revolution." The driver chuckled mirthlessly. "You still don't know what I'm talking about do you? The Dead are not all stencher bastards, some of them are fighting back, the Half Dead, the ones who've managed to keep hold of a little spark of their souls."

"Shreds remain."

"What?"

"Nothing."

"Nothing? That's the fucking battle cry and you don't say it unless you deserve to. And you don't."

They were on Park Lane now, one of a stream of wildly racing vehicles. Hyde Park itself was to the left, trees and fences flashed by.

Shreds remain...

Caitlin, then, was one of the rebels. One of those who had managed to keep hold of a little spark of their souls. The thought brought more anguish than joy.

***

They made it to Regent's Park without encountering any more Enforcers, but Lewis still had to get back into Harley Street. The driver stopped the car just out of sight of the Compound gate. Lewis still had his pass which meant that there was nothing to stop him simply getting out of the car and walking back in. Except the state of his clothes, his torn shirt, his smoke-smudged face, his hair wild and awry. Did it matter? There was no guard, only a pass-reader. But there might be a camera. His hand went to the door handle but he hesitated.

"Out," the driver said.

"Wait...I can't..."

"Yes, you can. Me, I'm going try to make contact with the Resistance. I don't want to be trapped in the Deadside when the shit hits the fan."

"The Deadside? What are you talking about?"

"This is the Deadside, you moron. This fucking sewer full of stenchers."

"So, there is an outside?

"If course there's an outside. Where do you think the Resistance operates from?" He seemed to relax for a moment. "They say there are communities, way out in the sticks, people who got away and are not involved in any of this shite. That's where I'm heading once I get out. Fuck the revolution, I've done my bit."

"Take me with you. This thing...this child is supposed to be delivered to the Resistance -"

"Fuck off. I probably won't get anywhere near them before the Enforcers catch me and I'm not hobbling myself with you. Stay here, in your cosy little surgery, and wait. If the resistance want you that badly they'll come and get you. I'm on my own."

"I can't..."

The driver turned away then back round, the movement, sudden, fast and fluid. He was holding something and bringing it up close to Lewis's' face. A gun, a pistol of some kind. Lewis could see few details but he knew that the tiny black eye of the weapon was level with his own.

"I said, I'm travelling alone. What part of that don't you understand? Out, now."

There had been guns held at his head before, used to prod him into motion and club him into submission. Rifles, handguns, shotguns. They had killed the weak and disobedient, noisily, messily, painfully and briefly…

"Please," Lewis said, his mouth dry.

"I'm fucking warning you." The man thrust the weapon against Lewis's forehead and the familiar bite of metal against flesh made him want to drop to his knees and sob for mercy. "Out."

"Okay, okay…" The child clenched herself more tightly across his chest. "Put the gun away. If you shoot me I'll become one of the Dead and you know what that means don't you? The moment you pull that trigger every Dead in London will know where you are and what you've done."

Because the Dead knew, they had a web, a network that, if not exactly telepathic, enabled them to *know*. Many in the Compound believed that whatever animated the dead was actually one being, one ID, and that it was aware, at any one moment, of what its component parts were doing, thinking or feeling. Which meant that he was finished anyway, because there had been Half Dead in the Madam's chamber, who had seen it all.

The gun wavered, then disappeared into the driver's jacket. Lewis clambered out of the car. He was shaking but he felt that he had won some tiny victory. He pulled his shirt over the child-thing as best he could, re-buttoned his jacket and ran his hand through his hair before setting off towards the gate. He glanced up but saw nothing that looked like a camera. He swallowed dryly and, swiped the pass over the reader. The gate opened.

Behind him, the tyres of the Mercedes squealing, then it raced away.

As he walked quickly towards house number 131, Lewis felt the pass disintegrate in his hand. Dust streamed between his fingers and then it was gone. Its absence disturbed him. He was trapped again, imprisoned. And this time with the mark of death clinging to his flesh. Everything had changed. Now there could be no rest, his guard must be up, at all times. Reeder would take all of them if the child was discovered, Lewis, Melissa and Campbell.

Lewis stepped into the clinic's darkened hallway. As he struggled to remove the key from his pocket and fumbled it into the lock, he remembered his medical bag. He had left it in the First House, in the Madam's underground chamber. His medical bag, his identity. Something gave way inside him and he was suddenly too weak to move. It was already over. He had to get the others out of there before it was too late -

The lights came on. Startled, Lewis spun round to see Campbell at the top of the stairs.

"What the hell happened to you?"

"I was called out on a visit."

"A pub brawl more like."

"There was a...a riot...I..." Lewis shrugged. He wanted to escape into his room.

"Why didn't you tell us?"

Lewis shrugged. It was difficult to think. He was suddenly exhausted. His head felt light. The child-thing was moving, clawing into him again. He leaned against the wall.

"Are you all right?" Campbell asked. Lewis sensed him

coming down the stairs towards him. "Your clothes...Come on. I'll fix you a drink, man."

"Yeah...Yeah...I..." The world drifted away from him. The walls raced outwards. And Caitlin was there again. The way she had been that last afternoon, her back to him, naked and weeping. He reached towards her. Said her name. She turned and smiled through her tears and said "It's going to be all right -"

Lewis felt the strength leave his body.

"Robert!"

Caitlin. It really was Caitlin, calling to him.

He fell, the floor slammed into his back and he opened his eyes to see Campbell crouching over him, concern on his face. Campbell fumbled at Lewis' torn shirt, mumbling about air. Lewis tried to push him away but his arms were too heavy.

Campbell recoiled. "Christ! Jesus Christ!"

Lewis fumbled weakly at his shirt as Melissa's face swam into view.

"Robert? Robert, what happened to you? And what the fuck is that?"

"Child...My child..."

The darkness closed in, grey and singing.

***

"Did you say child?" Melissa said.

Lewis was on his bed though he had no idea how he got there. The blinds were down, the light on. The bed was dishevelled, the room small, dank and untidy. He rested his arm over his eyes for a moment, then sighed and tried to explain.

"It...She was forced on me. It was a set-up."

"Are you out of your fucking head?" Campbell was in the room as well, his eyes alive with panic.

"I had no choice."

"We don't interfere," Campbell said, without waiting for any explanation. "You said it yourself. The Dead are dangerous. They play games and we don't play with them. Never, ever."

"Andy," Melissa snapped. "For God's sake shut up and calm down. We need to understand what's going on here."

"What's going on is that we're fucking dead."

"Robert, who forced this on you?" Melissa asked.

"Something called the Madam, I was sent to the First House."

"What the hell is the Madam?" Another loud oath from Campbell.

"I don't fucking know, but she seems to be on our side."

"Our side? There are sides now?" Campbell moved in close. his eyes were ablaze, his breathing hard. "We're not on anyone's side, Lewis. Only our own. It's us against the whole fucking lot of them. We're all that matters, do you understand that?"

"There's nothing I can do. I'm supposed to get the child to the Resistance."

"Can this get any worse?"

"Shut up, Andy," Melissa snapped. "Robert, you need to tell us what happened?" "That letter, it was from Caitlin. She was taken and made Dead when the uprising happened. She's disappeared, but I was given instructions." Lewis told them about the First House the Madam, the guards, the driver.

"So they are some sort of rebels. And you say Reeder

raided the place?" Campbell sounded calmer.

"Yes."

"So this thing, this fucking abomination, is to do with the rebels."

"It's obviously important," Melissa said.

"Our death warrant, more like. They would have known that Robert was in the First House because he had a pass."

Lewis remembered his medical bag and forced himself to ride out a moment of panic. The bag would make little difference to the outcome of this. He closed his eyes. There was a decent thing to do here. He grit his teeth and managed to utter the words.

"I should leave."

"Yes, you fucking should," Campbell said.

Melissa made to speak, but Campbell got there first. "But you can't. Listen, it's too dangerous for a start. How long would you last out there? The second reason?" He sighed. "It would be the end for Mel and me. We're only breathing because of you. Without you we're of no use to the Dead. And, like you said, this isn't your fault."

"Andy's right. We need help from Resistance."

"The Resistance will kill us," Lewis said. And the old despair was back. There was no easy way out of this. Other than trying to hide and keep themselves alive here for as long as they could.

"Perhaps not," Melissa said. "Whatever that child is, it...she...is important. And if the Madam and those others really are rebels, well, my enemy's enemy is my friend." Melissa moved away, arms folded, head bowed. "And there's one other thing. You've been back for three hours, Robert. If the Enforcers were coming for you, surely they would have been here by now. That might mean that Reeder doesn't know anything about the child."

Or Reeder could be playing with us, Lewis added silently.

"We need to sleep," Melissa said. "There's nothing we can do right at this moment." She moved back to the bed and took Lewis's hand. "Does it hurt?"

Lewis shook his head "Just leaves me feeling weak. It's as if she's feeding off me."

He closed his eyes.

And

Suddenly he was alone, lying in the snow. His attackers had gone. There was only the icy wind and the darkness. Lewis struggled to his feet, shivering. The trees hissed and groaned. Snow was whipped into an abrasive mist that ground at Lewis's face. He stumbled towards the house. The front door was wide open.

"Caitlin! Caitlin!"

She called back to him. A windborne snatch of voice. Which meant she was safe. Thank God, oh thank God. Lewis broke into a shambolic run. He grabbed at the door frame while he recovered his breath. The house was a well of blackness, but she was in there, somewhere. He could hear her calling, her voice distant, and melded with the wind that was sucked in through the open doorway to spiral through the house. Lewis groped his way to the stairs. He tripped and bumped into familiar objects; a chair, the kitchen door.

"I'm here. I'm here, Robert..."

He began a careful ascent. There were other voices now, coming from the radio in the bedroom.

How could that be? There was no power. This was wrong...

"Come to me, Robert, please hurry."

He struggled on up the stairs, shivering and exhausted by both the cold and fear. He dropped to his hands and knees and crawled.

The light snapped on. The electricity was back. Things were returning to normal -

He started, looked up and saw that the stairs stretched upwards forever. She *was* up there. She was calling to him, increasingly desperate and frightened. He climbed and climbed. A baby cried, the sound ghostly, chilling his soul. And he became aware that he was not alone on the stairs. There were things were behind him, growling, chuckling, their breath liquid and asthmatic. More of them, behind the walls, pushing at the plaster to form bulges that stretched and split the paint. Things that dripped and boiled and stank of corruption.

He woke suddenly, panting, a handful of grubby, sweat-dank sheet in each clenched hand. The darkness was full of shapes and sounds. The child moved on his chest. He lay for a moment, knowing that Caitlin was alive. The child had shown him that she was out there, somewhere, waiting for him.

CHAPTER FOUR

THE HALF-DEAD

"Help her."

The Dead stood in the centre of the operating theatre, supporting a woman who looked to be almost unconscious. The man wore a dinner jacket and black tie, the woman a black cocktail dress. Both they and their clothes were smoke-smudged and dirty. They smelled of fire and scorched cloth, hair and flesh.

"I can't," Lewis said. "You're not on my list"

List? How pathetically British that sounded.

"To hell with your fucking list, you warm flesh bastard. Help my wife or I'll have the Enforcers in here. Non-cooperation with a High Level will do for a start."

The Dead was close, teeth bared, eyes wide and alive with the fury and malevolence that Lewis tried never to see when dealing with the non-living. It boiled behind the pupils, the flames of a soul that was far from human. The stench of the man was overpowering. His make-up had run to a clown-mask, exposing cheeks webbed with necrosis.

"Well?"

Lewis glanced at Campbell who stood apart from them, gloves and mask off, his face sweat-shiny and etched with tiredness. Melissa was by the door. She looked flustered.

"I'm sorry," she said. "They barged in, I couldn't stop them."

Lewis nodded to her. It was all right, not her fault.

"Let's get the lady onto the table." Lewis's own

exhaustion seemed to overwhelm him at that moment. His limbs were heavy and the pounding in his skull immune to the handful of painkillers he'd washed down with his breakfast black coffee. The headache was no hangover. He had barely slept. And there was the child. The thing called Anna.

The Dead seemed reluctant to let go of his wife which resulted in an awkward tangle of arms and struggling bodies. The woman snarled and rolled onto her front. The back of her dress was burned away, as was most of the flesh beneath.

"Heal her," the man commanded. "Quickly. She's in pain."

The Dead didn't feel pain did they?

"I'll do what I can," Lewis answered. "But you'll have to wait outside, or at least get out of our way."

The man glared at him then nodded and backed into a far corner of the theatre, arms folded, eyes fixed on the operating table.

"How the hell did this happen?" Campbell's question was a harsh whisper.

"I don't know," Lewis answered.

Yes he did, because he had been there. These two must have been at the First House.

Fire, the scourge of the Dead.

Brushing his unease aside, Lewis worked as fast as his exhaustion and headache would allow. He cut away the burned skin which bore no sign of the life that Dead skin normally displayed when removed from the body. Each charred layer simply fell to the floor and crumbled to ash. The injuries extended from scapula to hips, and by the time he had finished clearing it away, Lewis had essentially flayed the woman's back down to the scorched and blackened bone. What had not been fire-damaged, was blue with decay. Beneath them, her organs squirmed, restless with Dead life. A deep growl issued from her throat, Lewis saw her hands crushed into fists.

Efficient as always, Campbell had sheets of Live flesh ready for Lewis, who moulded them carefully in place. Fusion between her uninjured Dead flesh and the replacement skin was slow, as if the Dead tissue was afraid to encroach onto the fire ravaged territories of her body. Every join had to be sutured.

An hour passed, and another. There would be other patients by now, filling the waiting area, impatient, angry. The Dead's hold on their tempers was fragile. At any moment one of them might burst in, raging and looking for warm flesh to tear. Once it began, it wouldn't stop.

Fingers stiff, wanting to close his eyes and sleep forever, Lewis struggled on. Melissa and Campbell were at his side. Without them he would have been lost. The patient's husband paced, irritable, snapping out orders for Lewis to hurry. More flesh, more stitching.

Then it was done.

The husband strode over and examined Lewis' work. When he spoke it was to the woman. His voice was soft, almost tender. "Are you okay, Laura?"

"Weak," she answered and her voice was small and hurt, not the low growl of the Dead. "I can't travel anymore. Not today."

The man turned his stare on Lewis.

"She stays here until the morning." It wasn't a request. "You must have beds."

"This isn't a hospital…"

Christ, they can't stay here.

"It's all right, I'll handle it," Melissa said. "We'll use one of the empty consulting rooms upstairs on the second floor. There're some old examination couches up there. Andy, help me get her onto a trolley."

Lewis could only stand aside, gowned, gloved and bloody while his two assistants lifted the Dead woman onto a trolley then quickly pushed it towards the doors. The man stayed behind in the operating theatre. He positioned himself between Lewis and the door, arms folded.

"You were there last night, Doctor Lewis," he said. "In the First House. I saw you."

Lewis shook his head, an instinctive denial he knew to be futile because a pass, such as the one Caitlin had sent him, left a trail.

"Why you? Why a warm flesh?"

"I have no idea what you're talking about."

The Dead took a step towards him, arms by his sides now, fists clenched. The smell of burnt skin and decay was overwhelming. "You have it, don't you, the key, the thing that's going to save us." The man was suddenly weary. "The Seven are hunting us down, they've unleashed Reeder. We have to get out of the Deadside."

"I can't help you -"

"I think you're helping us already."

"What do you mean?"

The child, of course.

"With some of us, shreds remain."

Christ, there it was again. What had the driver called it last night? The battle cry of the Resistance.

"Shreds of what we were, buried alive in these stinking rotten carcasses." Lewis stood his ground, fought to hold the Dead's stare, and the thing that glared back through the man's eyes. "Can you imagine what that's like? No, of course not, but you will if you're one of the strong ones, like us, like Laura and me. We're fighting it you see, fighting the filth inside us."

He took a step back.

"Something's been found, a key. We're been organising around it, the strong ones, the Half-Dead, I suppose you'd call us."

So was Caitlin one of the strong ones?

"The Seven want it too. That's why they sent Reeder to burn the First House last night. It wasn't an accident. We knew it would come because the Madam and her allies have been getting too strong, but no one knew exactly when it would happen. We hoped *He* would turn up in time to save us."

Lewis almost asked if *He* meant Azazel, but stopped himself in time. It would be dangerous to show too much knowledge.

"The floor manager took you to see the Madam didn't she? Something happened down there."

Lewis didn't answer.

"You need to pull yourself together, you gutless bastard," the man said and suddenly he had a handful of Lewis's gown. He shoved Lewis back so that he stumbled against the operating table. "We'll be gone before midnight. We're going to try to get out of the Deadside. Fat fucking chance. If Reeder's Enforcers don't get us, the Resistance will. They don't distinguish between Dead and Half-Dead, not that I blame them." The man moved close again. "You've got the key. Don't deny it, though why it's been entrusted to such a craven fucker as you, I'll never know. Get it out to the Resistance. There are enclaves in the city, people who will know what to do." He pushed himself away and walked out of the room.

***

The list, always the list. His life, and the lives of those who worked with him. It protected them and kept them alive. No matter how sick, hung-over or frightened he was, Lewis had to service the relentless snake of Dead who passed through the clinic.

Afternoon stretched towards evening, the list now behind because of the rebel and his wife. There was near silence in the theatre. Melissa quiet, efficient but somehow disengaged, Campbell tense and pale.

Dead skin was sliced, gas-bloated abdomens pierced and pressure relieved, rotting vitals were hauled, writhing and thrashing from decayed body cavities, all re-packed with living tissue. On and on it went. On and bloody on.

Until it was dark outside and the work was finally over for the day.

And all the time there was Anna.

When he returned to his rooms, Lewis stood in the tiny bathroom, staring at the grubby mirror over its sink. He opened his shirt. The child was a misty translucence, stretched over his skin. The hairs on his chest were flattened, crushed between the membrane and his flesh, which was pin-pricked in black and red, where the creature's roots penetrated his chest. Roots that robbed him of, what; blood, nerve-energy, soul-vitality? He ran his hand over the disturbing textures of the child and noticed changes. Smooth contours in the membranous landscape, as if something was forming.

Lewis re-buttoned his shirt and retreated to the constricted space that constituted his living area. He needed food. There was a knock at the door. Melissa called his name.

"Are you okay?" she asked when Lewis let her in.

"Scared, but apart from that...." Then his fear broke

through; shock, delayed reaction, a debilitating panic attack. It didn't matter. He wanted, *needed*, to get out, but knew he couldn't. "She's going to kill us. I don't know what to do. Jesus Christ, Melissa -"

She grabbed his arms, held him tight. Her strength was startling. "It...She's your daughter. She's Caitlin's child. I don't pretend to understand, but you helped create her."

"Those Half-Dead, the ones upstairs. They know. They said I had the key to saving us all. They mean...this." He pulled his right arm free of Melissa's grip and laid his hand on his chest. "What does that make me? Some sort of messiah? Or am I John the Baptist and Anna is the one?" Voicing the child's name was strange, yet, good somehow.

"You're more of a Virgin Mary by the sound of it," Melissa said and Lewis managed a shaky laugh.

"The Virgin Robert," Lewis said as Melissa fetched the scotch from the chipped, damp-bubbled worktop that constituted his kitchen. "I like that." Melissa poured two tumblers and handed one to Lewis.

"I didn't know she was pregnant," he said quietly. "I didn't want a child. I was so bloody selfish. We had a fight. We were still angry with each other when the Dead came."

"She's out there, Robert."

"I know. Somewhere. But she might as well be on another planet."

"Don't give up hope." She took his hand. Hers was warm and steady, too warm and too steady. He didn't want her to let go. "Things are happening. We have to get Anna out of here and to the Resistance."

"So everyone tells me. But no-one has any ideas about how."

Melissa paced again. "I'll think of something."

There was a certainty in her voice that Lewis found both

comforting and disturbing, as if, somehow, she really could wrought such a miracle.

"Who is Azazel?" Lewis asked Melissa as she made to leave.

"A fallen angel," Melissa answered with a swiftness that unnerved Lewis. How did she know that? And was the description figurative or literal?

Lewis needed Melissa to stay with him now, if only to deliver those comforting platitudes all over again. But she was heading back upstairs to Campbell. He envied them their mutual comfort, the seemingly unshakable bond between them. Andy and Melissa against the world. When they had first begun their slavery here, Lewis had hoped that it would be Melissa and him against the world, but Campbell's rough charm had won out. Lewis wanted a drink but he resisted the urge. He needed to be sober and clear-minded, despite the memories, which were crowding back in tonight...

...of when their hoods were removed and they saw that they had been brought to the ruins of a pub. Its windows had been smashed, its furniture wrecked and scattered. Everywhere there was glass, cutting into their knees as they were forced to kneel.

This is where we die, Lewis thought and the idea was no longer terrible...

Lewis stood abruptly, went into the bedroom and was sickened by the sight of the place as if seeing it for the first time. The bed, an examination couch, was unmade, the sheets grubby and stained. The room's expensive flocked wallpaper was peeling in places and its plaster mouldering in one high corner, as the building's ancient walls began to bleed dampness.

...His arms, held immovable behind his back, ached. The flesh of his wrists was bruised and torn by the viciousness of a thin plastic cable tie. He tried to distract

himself from the pain by counting how many Living were being held there. It was impossible of course. Whenever he turned his head to count those lined up behind him he was struck, with an open hand, a boot, a rifle butt. He began to welcome the new and quick pain, it broke the relentless cramping aches that dominated his consciousness.

Counting was impossible anyway, new prisoners were being bundled into the pub all the time, while those who cracked and began screaming or shouting, were hauled away.

Their jailers stood around the walls, blurred by shadow, or they wandered amongst the prisoners, kicking and striking out. They were not natural thugs, they were elderly, they were children, men in police and army uniforms, a nurse, a pretty young woman who wore a badge that declared her to be "Chrissie, Dior Consultant".

The prisoners stank of sweat, urine and excrement, their guards were beginning to stink of decay.

Lewis worried about his hands, the lack of blood flow, the crushed tendons.

Then a new horror walked in. He held a Stanley knife in his slender hand.

"My name is Reeder," he said.

And it got much worse.

The doorbell warbled loudly, dumping Lewis from restless sleep. Then a fist pounded. Lewis heard Rob shout for their visitor to calm down and wait a minute. The bolts were slid across. Lewis got to his feet and stumbled, blearily, out into the entrance hall as the door opened. A slightly built man in his sixties, or perhaps even his early seventies, stood on the front step. He wore a dark blue suit and held a walking cane in one slender hand, Lewis's medical bag in the other.

"My name is Reeder," he said and stepped inside.

CHAPTER FIVE

REEDER

"You left this behind last night," Reeder lifted the bag for Lewis to see. His eyes were devoid of expression, his voice of inflection.

"Seems that way," Lewis managed to say. He was collapsing inside and about to break. He was ready to tell the bastard anything he wanted to know, even give him the child. After all, what was one small non-life in exchange for three real human lives?

"Your assistants?" Reeder said, nodding towards Campbell who had now been joined by Melissa.

"Yes."

Reeder turned to the door and snapped out an order.

Four enforcers came in, huge and bulky in their black, fireproof and armoured suits, anonymous behind their tinted visors. They carried automatic rifles, snub-nosed like the ones Lewis had seen in the hands of armed police before the uprising.

"We're going to search your clinic," Reeder said.

Lewis stepped aside to let the enforcers come in. What choice did he have? "What are you looking for?" He was startled at how calm he sounded.

"Filth," Reeder said.

"No need for searches."

The voice rolled down the stairs. Reeder's head snapped up and Lewis spun round to see the Half-Dead and his wife.

The enforcers paused, halfway across the hall. Reeder's gaze returned to Lewis. "Guests of yours?" he said pleasantly.

Lewis shook his head, speechless, crumbling. A part of him was already resigned to the inevitable. He tried to find the strength needed, to plead for Campbell and Melissa.

"We forced him to help us," the male Half-Dead called down. "He's a fucking coward, he didn't put up much of a fight."

"And neither have you," Reeder said.

"You would have found us. There's nowhere to run."

Reeder nodded to the enforcers. Two of them rushed the couple and wrenched them apart, causing the woman to cry out in pain. Neither of them looked at Lewis as they were bundled past him and out of the door.

"What'll happen to them?" Melissa asked. She sounded angry, defiant. Her courage both frightened and shamed Lewis.

"Burning them would be too kind," Reeder said. "So we'll bury them. It will give them time to reflect on their idiocy. A long time."

He held up the bag. "Now Doctor Lewis, we have to discuss this."

"My...My uh consulting room would be best."

***

Lewis perched himself on the edge of his desk. Reeder took the role of patient. He kept the medical bag on his lap. He was a small, more insignificant looking man than the one who haunted the darker regions of Lewis's memory. Yet his detachment was redolent with threat.

"Found in the First House," Reeder said, meaning the bag. "Why?"

"I left in a hurry," Lewis said. "I didn't know what was happening. There was a fire, fighting..."

"Who did you attend?"

"I'm sorry?"

"Who was your appointment? Doctors are seldom guests at the First House. More to the point, the bag was found in the Madam's chamber. What were you doing down there Lewis?"

"Someone must have taken it -"

Reeder snorted, his first show of bad manners. The sound was contemptuous. "Who would take a medical bag down into the chamber, when everyone else was trying to get out?"

"Okay, all right." Lewis took a deep, steadying breath. "I...I went to see the Madam."

"Why did you go to see the Madam?" Reeder almost sounded like a counsellor of some sort.

"I don't know. I was called, a pass was sent to me."

"And when a pass is received you come running, even to the Madam."

"Yes, to the Madam, and anyone else who calls my name. When I got there, the raid started. I ran."

"Why would the Madam send for you?"

"I don't fucking know." He was sweating, he was on his knees in the broken glass...

...unable to move or fight back, waiting while...while Reeder walked among them. When he tapped a shoulder the jailers, old or young, woman, man or child, dragged the prisoner to their feet, so that Reeder could open then from sternum to pelvis with his Stanley knife.

Just opened them and stood back as the blood flowed

and the vitals peeped through the wound. Watched them fall and writhe and convulse. Watched them for long, long minutes until they died, then resurrected as howling, gutted wreckage that was dragged outside and forgotten.

He walked along the lines to the next and the next. Four, five, eight, ten, a pointless, gratuitous slaughtering of human meat, stopped only when it appeared to bore him and he walked out.

There was a second visit. Then a third, when the prisoners' hunger finally forced them to the floor with lapping tongues...

"Have we met before, Lewis?"

Lewis nodded.

"Did you drink?"

Silence.

"Well, did you? Did you lap the blood and offal from the floor?"

"Yes." Lewis could barely force the word out. He felt shame burn his face.

"That's why you're here, one of those whose instinct for survival drove them to find sustenance wherever they could. That kind of strength can work its way to the surface every now and then. It can also drive a warm flesh to the idiocy you call courage."

Courage? Lewis couldn't think of anything further from his grasp at this moment. Each breath was a conscious act, each word a potential mantrap.

Reeder got to his feet. He let the bag fall to the floor. "Look at me Lewis, come here and look at me."

Reeder was pulling away his tie, unbuttoning his shirt. Lewis forced himself to watch as Reeder pulled his shirt apart. Lewis saw rot, the grey green fungus of decay.

"I've been busy," Reeder said. "Neglected my own needs. Can you help me, Mister Lewis?"

"Yes...yes of course."

"Now."

"I'm tired..."

"Now. Repair me."

***

It was ten-thirty at night and there were two of them in the operating theatre; Mister Robert Lewis, Consultant Cosmetic Surgeon, and Commissioner of Law Reeder. No one knew his first name, or even if Reeder was his name at all. He was naked now, prone on the table, surprisingly scrawny, old and frail looking.

As he checked the chiller for skin and laid out his tools, Lewis found himself thinking of the ancient old men brought to book as Nazi war criminals, their crimes now unimaginable in the face of their fragile dotage. But this man, this Dead, was dangerous even in the face of his everlasting old age.

"I expect your best work, Robert."

Lewis swallowed and picked up the scalpel. He brought it across to Reeder's boiling, stinking necrotic chest and abdomen. For a moment, his mind slid back to the pub and to Reeder's cull, the casual, almost bored movement of his arm, the way he gazed over the top of the victim's head without making eye-contact. The scalpel pressed against the borders where whole flesh met rotting flesh. The blade bit. No blood flowed. Reeder did not so much as wince.

"This new order," Reeder said as Lewis worked. "Suits me well. I was in Wakefield prison when the Uprising occurred. The place erupted. My fellow inmates quickly deteriorated into squealing, shrieking animals. They were trapped. They knew that when the Dead came, there would be nowhere to run. I was too tired to worry, so I simply waited for them. Do you know why I was in prison? I killed a lot of people. Men, women, children, I made no distinction.

"I don't know why I killed other than for enjoyment. Not the thrill of the chase or the excitement of avoiding arrest. It was the act, the moment. I was good at it, and when the Dead finally arrived at my cell they saw something special in me, a kindred spirit perhaps. Once I'd made that short but deep journey, I was singled out and given responsibility."

Lewis pulled at the rotten flesh. Drew it away, dripping in his hands, globules hit the floor and slithered towards his boots. He kicked at them and crushed them under his heel. Reeder's musculature was in good condition. And alive with a mass of fibrous tendrils that waved like plants on the sea bed. The muscles themselves rippled with life, things moved through the tissue, burrowed and swam, dark shapes against the translucence. Vessels were webbed across the muscle surface, thick enough in places to create matting from which the tendrils grew. Lewis was reminded of the root system that webbed the Madam's chambers and its environs.

Something scuttled out of the fibres, momentarily visible, then gone. Lewis turned away, coughing and gagging. It was the same species he had seen in the passageways under the First House. When he managed to return his gaze to the opened regions of Reeder's torso, he saw that it was alive with the things, all scrabbling their way back into the dark.

Lewis crossed to the chiller and lifted a sheet of skin from its cold interior. As he neared Reeder's body the tendrils became frenzied and they stretched towards him like flowers reaching for light. As they brushed the inner surface of the skin they hooked and wrenched it from Lewis' hands before he could set it into place. There was little work to do when the skin was drawn down. Reeder's body was intent on self-repair.

"Why were you at the Madam's chamber last night?" Reeder asked.

That sudden question was a trip wire. Lewis ignored it, able to because of the intensity of the work.

"I will find out. I don't want you hurt. But rules are rules."

Reeder pushed Lewis's hand aside and sat up, a third of the suturing not completed. He pulled on his shirt, buttoned it methodically, top to bottom. "I will leave a few enforcers here to protect you. The Resistance may well call because Hillier, the warm flesh who helped you escape from the First House, is a Resistance fighter. If the Resistance do come for you, they won't be as understanding as me when it comes to ripping information out of a collaborator."

"Now, my last request before I leave you," Reeder continued. "Is for you to show me every room in this building."

Lewis started with the second floor, including the old consulting room in which the Half-Dead had hidden. The place was a mess, a desk still in place, its sheen softened by damp. The plaster had bubbled in places, and peeled from the lath underneath. The couch was covered by a rumpled, stained sheet. The consultant's chair was pulled up beside it.

Next to this one, there were a series of other empty rooms; dusty, cobwebbed, musty. Their curtains were rotten, furniture crumbling to ruin. The whole building was dusty and stale anyway. Cleaning and maintenance were not high on anyone's agenda. The carpeting was threadbare, the paint faded and stained.

"Where do your assistants sleep and eat?" Reeder asked.

"What?"

"Your assistants' rooms. I need to see them."

Campbell and Melissa had taken three rooms. As much as they loved each other, constant proximity demanded as much personal space as possible.

They were in their communal room and stood aside to watch silently as Reeder wandered round, not touching anything, but staring at the worn sofas and coffee table. At the sun-bleached prints and fading wallpaper. Their bedroom was simple, two examination couches lashed together and a drawer unit dragged in from another room. No television of course, but books everywhere, piles of them. Thrillers, horror, crime, literary. Anything with pages and words was consumed voraciously in the compound. Their kitchen was the original staff kitchen; water boiler, cooker, toaster, little else. Small and utilitarian.

Reeder observed it all with the apparent fascination of a sightseer on a guided tour of a stately home. He studied the high ceilings, the walls, nodded and made affirmative noises.

Melissa's own room was relaxed, slightly messy, and contained a waiting room chair, a consulting room table, more books, a CD player and the CDs themselves, stacked untidily and in no particular order. Campbell's room was sparse and neat. His books and CDs were stored in a shelved unit.

As he waited for Reeder to finish his inspection, Lewis was struck for the first time by how unanchored they all were, by the lack of personal ornaments, photographs, or anything else that linked them to their pasts. It emphasised again, how little he knew about these people. And how little they knew about him.

"We've seen the theatre of course," Reeder said. "And the consulting room. That leaves your apartment Lewis."

"Nothing much to see," Lewis answered and was

astonished at how calm he sounded, even though he was fully aware that the request was an order.

"I'm fascinated by the small things, the seemingly insignificant, by what people consider to be nothing."

Lewis led the way downstairs, his strength, his self and the structures that were him dissolving. He felt steadily more detached with each step, resigned to death, which seemed inevitable now. He worked on excuses and justifications. Convinced himself in a fury of half-mad optimism that it would be all right and that Reeder would be satisfied with his vague explanations of his movements and actions of the previous night. There was also an odd relief, no more lies or hiding. They reached the bottom of the stairs, his door.

There were more enforcers now, four of them in the entrance hall, two more on the first floor landing. Lewis suspected that there would be others outside. He glanced at one of them as he brushed past and saw nothing beyond the visor. No hint of face or features.

Lewis gathered the remains of his courage into a semblance of dignity and opened the door to his rooms. Reeder went in first. Lewis followed, exhausted by his dread. He wanted it over now. Reeder stood in the living area, looking for all the world like a prospective buyer weighing up a property. Then he opened the door to the bedroom. Lewis stayed where he was, unable to move, waiting. A moment later Reeder emerged from the room.

"You are an untidy man," he said. "I believe in order. I believe in cleanliness. You don't. A poor trait in a surgeon."

Reeder came close, his breath, hot and stinking on Lewis's face. "There is something here," Reeder said, so quietly it was almost a whisper. "I don't know what it is, Lewis, but I will discover it."

And he left, abruptly, slamming first Lewis's door then the front door of the building. Gone.

CHAPTER SIX

THE OCCUPATION OF
131 HARLEY STREET

Melissa appeared in the doorway of Lewis's rooms. "Has Reeder gone?"

"For now."

Melissa glanced at the door. "We have to be bloody careful, the clinic is crawling with enforcers." She slumped onto the bed and pressed her fingertips to her temples. "God, I thought it was the end." Her voice was broken, almost a sob. Lewis wanted to comfort her, but held back, because he sensed that, at that moment, she would accept his arms rather than push him away. Andy Campbell did not deserve that sort of betrayal.

"But we weren't arrested and we're still breathing. It's a glimmer of hope," Lewis offered.

Melissa uttered a scornful laugh. "Hope? When have we ever had hope?"

***

There was no list the next day. It was Sunday. Although lacking, as far as Lewis could tell, any Christian or other religious leanings, the Dead still granted their vitally skilled slaves a weekly day of rest. The inhabitants of the Harley Street compound were allowed to mingle during those 24 short hours. They visited each other's clinics to eat together, talk drink, argue, rut and occasionally fight. A rough and ready visiting cycle had developed, each clinic taking its turn to play host. Social nicety quickly became a party at which the fear and never-ending tension could be relieved with alcohol, sex and general rowdiness. The Masterson Clinic, five buildings towards Devonshire Road, was hosting this Sunday's fun.

When they met for breakfast in Campbell's and Melissa's communal apartment, it was already eleven am. The sky was immaculate blue, the sun hot.

"I guess we still *are* allowed out of here today," Melissa said.

"I fucking hope so," Campbell answered. "Or I'm going to go insane."

"I have to stay here," Lewis said.

"No, Robert -"

"Melissa, I can't."

"You'll be playing into Reeder's hands," Campbell said. "He's watching us. I can feel it."

"I'll fake illness," Lewis said.

"But you're not ill, and Reeder isn't stupid. He'll come back today, Robert. I know he will. He'll walk in here unannounced and catch you playing truant."

"Everything has to look normal," Melissa said. "Staying here isn't normal

"I'll *make* myself ill."

"No, no, bad idea," Campbell said.

"There's nothing you can do, even if you do stay," Melissa said.

"I can't go. I am not fucking going to the party, not with this...not with the child. Someone will see her. I have to stay here."

Campbell banged his palms onto the table. Cutlery rattled. "This is your bloody fault, you brought this onto us."

Melissa was up, her voice harsh and authoritative. "Shut up, Andy. This stops now! We don't fight among ourselves, ever. Do you understand?"

Campbell grunted. It sounded like a sorry.

"Your mind is made up?" Melissa said to Lewis.

"Yes."

"How are you going to make yourself ill?"

"There's some teriparatide in the pharmacy cupboard."

"Chemo?" Campbell said. "Dangerous, especially as a lot of that stuff in the pharmacy is out of date."

"One dose isn't going to hurt me."

And the child? It...she was feeding off him wasn't she? What would the chemical do to her? To hell with the child, he hadn't asked for this. Lewis was stung by his own callousness, born of fear, yes, but still a brutality that he had not thought himself capable of. There was a risk, but his own destruction at the hands of Reeder was an even greater risk to Anna's well-being.

"It's often given to men to increase bone mass anyway," Lewis continued. The justification seemed dry and weak at that moment.

"Not anymore it isn't," Campbell muttered.

Melissa said nothing, but she looked worried.

Lewis injected himself in the right thigh as soon as breakfast was over. He did it in the consulting room before the other two left, in case there was an acute reaction. The vicious bite of the needle seemed harsher than normal, and the aftermath was more painful than it should have been. He smuggled the spent syringe and ampule up to the theatre to incinerate them and hoped no one decided to carry out a strip search, because the fresh needle wound was plain to see.

Campbell's concerns were justified, and Lewis deliberately avoided checking the teriparatide's date. All he could was wait. Nausea was a common side effect of the drug, but not guaranteed.

To return to his rooms, he had to pass the silent and motionless enforcers, posted on each floor. The black anonymity of their visors, the absence of anything resembling humanity within their flameproof suits, disturbed and repulsed him. There was something merciless, something implacably soulless in that absence. There could be no reasoning with an enforcer, no bended-knee and clasped-hand supplication. When ordered to kill, the enforcer would kill. To Lewis, the darkness inside that armour was a howling wilderness. An entranceway into Hell itself.

Lewis shrank away as he passed each Enforcer. He could *not* touch them.

Once safely behind his own door, he dressed as if for a normal Sunday. The drug was supposed to stimulate the vomit reflexes in his brain within an hour. Nothing was happening so far, except that his leg was sore. He shaved, pulled on one of his handful of faded short-sleeved shirts and even more faded chinos.

He was suddenly hot and shivering. He returned to the living area and sat down, but that didn't help. He paced, then leaned over the sink, breathing deeply. At last it started, that awful onrush as his stomach went into revolt. He only just made it to his bathroom, where he vomited and retched until exhausted. Crouched on the floor, unable to move, he waited miserably for the next attack.

He was only vaguely aware of the pantomime of surprise and concern acted out by Campbell and Melissa when they came in to pick him up. Then, enervated and dizzy, he crawled back to his room and slumped into his tatty armchair.

He must have slept because he woke suddenly and to

see someone leaning over him.

"Lewis."

He sat up, too quickly, and crumpled under a wave of dizziness.

"Reeder..."

The Commissioner stepped back, then dropped to the floor and sat cross-legged in front of him, a position that should have been far too awkward for a man of his years. But, Lewis reminded himself, Reeder was no longer a man.

"You look unwell." A statement of fact, not a display of concern.

"Some sort of sickness bug," Lewis answered.

"So you're missing your Sunday entertainment."

"It doesn't matter, there's always next week."

Was there?

"Something concerns me, something isn't right."

Lewis swallowed. His mouth tasted foul. He wanted to go back to sleep.

"What do you mean?"

"What would the Madam want with a cosmetic surgeon?"

"I don't know. I didn't get to find out." Lewis didn't want to talk. The nausea was coming back.

"So you've told me, several times." Reeder leaned forward. "Your pass wasn't only for the First House. It took you to Kensington first, to Onslow Gardens."

No answer was possible.

"Normally a pass allows a vitally skilled to travel to and from one destination only. Why were you sent to the First

House Lewis?"

"I…I don't know, I can't remember…"

"Your ex-wife, Caitlin, lived in Onslow Gardens and she must have been the originator of the pass. We don't know, we can't read her properly. That's the problem with the Half-Dead, they can block us out. That's why I need you to tell me what happened."

"I went to her house, but she was gone." Careful, so many trip-wires, so many gaping, steel-jawed mantraps.

"You would spare yourself pain and suffering if you told us the truth."

"Why should I care about Caitlin? She's a Dead." Lingering nausea was making Lewis dangerously irritable. He sighed and offered Reeder a morsel he hoped would ease his hold on the noose. "She left a message, for me to go to the First House. So I went. I couldn't disobey a Dead, especially a high level one like her. I had no idea why I was supposed to go there, I just knew I should."

Reeder got to his feet in a fluid motion, as if, for a moment he was liquid, then flesh again. "I don't believe you." He crossed the floor and leaned over Lewis, his face close. Lewis recoiled at his foul breath, and when he remembered the creatures that lived inside that body, felt his nausea-bruised stomach twist into a renewed spasm.

"Tell me the truth," Reeder hissed.

"I have…"

"The truth. All of it. What happened between you and the Madam? What did she tell you? What did she give you?"

"Nothing, I swear -"

Reeder's hand caught Lewis's chin. His grip was strong.

"I will arrest you soon," he said. "Not yet, though. You need to recover fully first. In this state you would crumble to dust before I could retrieve one word of truth out of you." He made to go, then was close again, lips to Lewis's ear. "Your colleagues may know something of course. Remember our first meeting, Lewis, in that dark and noisome pub? Do you recall how I culled the weak and fed the strong?"

Reeder was gone before Lewis could reply, on his way to arrest Campbell and Melissa. They would be taken away and murdered and it wasn't their fault. Lewis needed to do something, but when he got to his feet he almost collapsed. If Reeder was going to follow through on his threat, it would already be too late for his friends. He could call the enforcers in, rip open his shirt, confess and try to keep the others safe.

Lewis attempted to stand again and this time remained on his feet. He stared at the door. All he had to do was step out into the hall and walk up to one of those soulless bags of night. Then it would be over. No more hiding, no more fear and hopelessness. It would be done. He opened the door, struggling to breathe. He took a step.

There would be pain. There would be death, of some kind. There would be Hell.

Brief resolve collapsing, Lewis turned and went into the bedroom. Too ill and wretched to care anymore. He collapsed onto the bed and closed his eyes. He needed a drink, to drown his guilt, but that wasn't a good idea. No telling what a blend of whisky and teriparatide might do to him. Pain pulsed through his skull and painted the darkness red.

Until

He was once more in the house. Light burned bright and the staircase stretched away from him, infinite, distorted and unclimbable. Caitlin was calling him. He tried to shout back to her but his voice was no more than a ragged whisper. "I'm coming," he said, even though his body would not respond to his silent commands. "Caitlin, I'm coming."

"I know." She sounded close now. He smelled her perfume, her skin, her hair, scents he had become accustomed to.

He stopped, looked up. And saw a shadow, a smudge in the air itself.

"I'm sorry," he said. "I'm sorry I hurt you."

"We have a child now. It's all right. You must bring her to me."

He saw her face in features formed from mist. He reached up and felt her skin. She kissed his hand and held it against her cheek. He felt the softness of it, the warmth of her grip. "Bring her to me, Robert. Please hurry..."

She was fading away, the mist dispersing. "No, don't go, Caitlin, don't go -"

The main door slammed and he woke, startled and confused. There were voices. Lewis struggled to his feet, and froze. Caitlin's scents lingered. He drew breath and savoured them, even as they too dissolved. She had been here. It had not been simply a dream. Lewis didn't want to leave the the last, dying breath of her presence. His eyes welled.

He struggled to regain his self-control and went out into the front hall. The first thing he saw were the enforcers, three of them. Then there was Campbell and Melissa. It was late. He glimpsed night as Melissa closed the door.

"You okay?" Lewis asked them, momentarily forgetting the Enforcers.

Campbell looked at him. He was flushed, a little worse for wear, but not as bad as he could have been. Melissa, on the other hand, was sober.

"We're fine," Campbell said. "Why shouldn't we be?"

"How about you?" Melissa asked him.

"Weak, but I think the worst is passed. I'm hungry now."

"Come up to our rooms."

"In a minute."

He watched them ascend the stairs, Melissa leaning in on Campbell, who slid his arm about her shoulders. Thanking God they were safe, Lewis went back into his room. He whispered her name. "Caitlin." But there was no answer.

He opened the bedroom door and was suddenly unnerved by the fact that Reeder had twice been close to him, but had completely missed the child. Did that mean that Reeder had genuinely been duped, or was he playing some game? Lewis sighed. He needed company. He turned to leave.

The window exploded.

A blizzard of glass sliced through the living area behind Lewis. As he spun round he saw plaster gouged off the walls by something he realised must have been a bullet. There was a stink of smoke and swirl of dust. Lewis threw himself onto the floor, clutching at the worn carpet with the same desperation as a man clinging on a rock face.

Lewis forced himself up onto his hands and knees. Crouching low, he headed for his door. He was halfway across the glass and plaster-strewn floor when the door flew open to reveal the armoured bulk of an enforcer. Lewis froze and waited for the hammer blow to fall. The enforcer stood for a few seconds, then toppled inwards and crashed to the floor, face down.

Lewis saw that the Enforcer's suit was ripped open. The edges of the tears were scorched and brown.

Darkness poured out. There was no flesh, no human-shape. The suit was the enforcer's body and skin. Offal writhed and thrashed wetly across the floor, ropes of intestine lashed at Lewis who leapt to his feet, panic overriding his fear of being shot. He stamped on them and kicked them aside. More of it gushed from the fallen enforcer, like an army set free.

A second enforcer filled the doorway. Its weapon swung round to find Lewis, who was now huddled against the wall, unable to move or even cry out. The enforcer was jerked forwards. Holes appeared in its chest. Its visor disintegrated, glass sprayed. It fell like a tree, spewing its parts over the walls and carpet before it hit the floor.

A third, smoke-blurred figure, replaced it in the doorway, someone shouting and waving, demanding that Lewis get up and get out. The figure carried a weapon, a snub-nosed gun identical to the ones carried by the enforcers. The figure was familiar.

Melissa.

Lewis finally got to his feet. The two fallen enforcers blocked his way, their suits now collapsed as what was inside them slithered across the floor. Melissa fired again, the noise deafening. Bullets tore the remains, but did not stop them moving. Lewis ran towards her, jumping awkwardly over the corpses and out into the entrance hall. The ruins of two more Enforcers lay there, one by the front door, and another strewn over the stairs.

"We have to get out, now," Melissa shouted. She carried her weapon with the confidence of a veteran. She knew what she was doing and, Lewis realised in those moments, she knew what was *happening*.

Lewis saw Campbell, crouched halfway down the stairs, above the shattered Enforcer. He looked shocked and confused.

"Andy," Melissa yelled at him. "Come on, hurry up. There are people out there, they've come for us."

Campbell got to his feet, unsteady, clutching at the stair rail. Lewis took a step then the world dissolved in a rage of fire, smoke and splintered wood.

Lewis was hurled against the far wall, his instinct only to cling to Anna. Coughing, ears ringing, he felt someone haul him to his feet. He blinked away smoke-tears and his eyes cleared for long enough for him to see that it was Campbell. Melissa was in front of him, moving fast as they were climbed the stairs. She spun round and fired over Lewis's head. He felt the whip-crack passage of the bullets. Melissa ran up to the landing and when Lewis saw her next, she was holding a bottle with a burning rag jammed into its neck. She threw it past Lewis. He felt a brief flare of heat before glass exploded behind him and flame whumphed violently into life. A second then a third Molotov cocktail arced over him as he and Campbell climbed the last few steps to the landing.

Smoke boiled up the stairs, punctuated by washes of heat. The fire wouldn't hold the enforcers for long, their suits would protect them. But there was shooting down there. Melissa's allies, presumably, trying to fight their way in or creating a diversion. The Resistance then, it had to be, and she, it seemed, was one of them. And she must have also been preparing for a moment like this, rifles, ammunition and ready-filled Molotov cocktails didn't appear out of nowhere.

Melissa led the way along the landing towards hers and Campbell's rooms. Lewis tried not to breathe the smoke-tainted air, but it was impossible. Each inhalation reduced him to a fit of helpless coughing. The firing downstairs suddenly intensified. Then stopped. Lewis heard boot-falls on the stairs. Christ, more of the enforcers were coming. Melissa swung round, called Campbell's name then placed a bottle into his hands.

"Throw it at their visors not their feet," Melissa shouted.

Lewis's last glimpse of the technician was of him fumbling in his pocket for his lighter.

Once in Campbell's and Melissa's communal room, Lewis shut the door behind them. He heard Campbell's Molotov cocktail explode among the approaching

Enforcers. There was less smoke in here. The room was dishevelled, furniture overturned and a handful of floorboards ripped up and thrown aside. Melissa's hidden armoury, presumably. The far wall was broken by a set of French windows which led out onto a rusting, iron fire escape.

Melissa, now laden with a khaki backpack she must have picked up in here somewhere, was already wrestling with the latch.

"Fuck, its jammed," she hissed.

"Let me try."

She turned on him. "Keep back, just look after that bloody kid, okay?"

Where was Campbell? Lewis glanced at the door to the room. Campbell should be back with them by now.

"Got it," Melissa said. "That's it. Robert, let's get out of here." She paused. "Where's Andy?"

"I don't know, he hasn't -"

Then Campbell stumbled in, smoke-smudged and wild-eyed, as if on Lewis's verbal cue. . There were bullet holes in his chest and forehead. Neat round holes.

"Andy?" Melissa said. "Are you all right? Andy..."

"Warm flesh whore," he said and smiled. "Fucking warm flesh bitch." He let out an animal roar and surged across the room, hands bent into claws, slavering and howling.

Lewis met him head on, barged him in a way he hadn't barged anyone since his mediocre performances as a barrel-scraped, school rugby reserve. The impact hurled them round in a momentary, crazed mutual orbit then into a coffee table and down.

Lewis scrambled to his feet, light-headed, aware that things had been damaged, but feeling no pain as yet.

Melissa was screaming his and Campbell's names. She stood in the open French windows, a smouldering Molotov cocktail in her hand. Lewis saw Campbell on his feet and running towards Melissa. Then he was on fire, shrieking and crashing about the room.

Lewis scrambled out through the exit, grabbing at Melissa as he did so. She was screaming as well, primal in her grief and horror. Enforcers burst in and she fired and fired until the magazine was empty. She shattered the visors of the two creatures, ripped open their suits, spilled them onto Campbell's smoking, charred remains.

Lewis wrenched her round and onto the clanging, rickety stairs. She hissed and snarled at him, gouging at his face with her nails. Then she collapsed into his arms and had to be supported down the final steps.

They were in the clinic's small, overgrown and long-neglected back garden. A crumbling brick wall formed the boundary. Beyond it stood a row of derelict houses that fronted a cul-de-sac called Devonshire Mews West. The night was punctured with gunfire, flashes and a flame-painted column of smoke that looked to be rising from Marylebone High Street.

The wall had crumbled at its left end, and there was a gap large enough for Lewis and Melissa to clamber through into the nearest of the cottages. There seemed to be no attempt at pursuit. The Resistance raid must be huge - big enough to divert the Dead away from Harley Street, or at least stretch their forces.

The cottage was dark, a labyrinth of collapsed masonry and other debris. It smelled of dankness and rat urine. Clumsily, and unable to move quietly, they made it to the front. Melissa, silent but apparently in control again, waved Lewis back from the remains of a window. She stood to one side and peered round and out into the street. She waited, then, satisfied, waved Lewis towards the open doorway to her right.

"If we get split up, make for Baker Street and St Cyprian's church, it's at Clarence Gate, near Park Road. Do you know where that is?"

"Yes, yes of course I do. But why there? Surely we have to get out of London -"

"Just do as I tell you. A lot of people have sacrificed themselves for that child tonight and you don't have any say in this, just get her to St Cyprians, okay?"

"Okay."

"I'll wave you out if it's clear. Got that?"

"Yes, I've got that."

Lewis saw Melissa take a deep breath then she was out of the door and gone.

CHAPTER SEVEN

FUGITIVES

A moment later she reappeared, an indistinct figure on the opposite side of the narrow street.

"Here goes," Lewis muttered. As he ran into the road he felt vulnerable. This was the first time he had been out of the compound without a pass to protect him. Outside, *out*. There was too much space, too many enemies.

He made it to the far side and slumped against a wall, panting, unfit from spending too much time in the confines of one building. And smoking too many cigarettes and drinking too much. Instinctively he reached into his pocket for his hip flask. Not there, still in the clinic. The burning, devastated clinic. The flask's absence heightened his need for a drink to near-desperation. Nothing he could do about it now, except grit his teeth and not think about it.

With Melissa in the lead, they worked their way to the cul-de-sac's entrance, which opened onto Devonshire Street. There was smoke from a series of small bonfires scattered along the road and pavement in both directions. The bonfires, it turned out, were burning bodies. They smelled of roasting meat. The stink of it turned Lewis's stomach, still fragile from his self-imposed nausea.

They moved carefully out of the Mews. There was a barrier a few metres from the Marylebone High Street end. They were not going to get far, but what choice did he have but to follow Melissa?

A few moments later he saw that the barrier had been breached. More bodies burned beside the gate house, presumably Dead, but it was hard to tell. There was no sign of any active Dead; enforcer or civilian.

"Just as they promised," Melissa said grimly.

They, must mean the Resistance, Lewis decided.

Keeping close to houses and shop fronts, resting briefly in doorways, they worked their way past the broken barrier and out onto the High Street.

Though a little battle-bruised, it seemed unchanged from when Lewis had last seen it, nearly three years ago, before the uprising. He realised that, close as it was to the clinic, Marylebone High Street had been as distant and unreachable as the moon, for both himself and for every other vitally skilled slave in the compound. The thought made him weep, for himself, his friends and his world. Everything was gone. Everything that had seemed so solid and immutable had been altered, corrupted, ripped away by...what? Why exactly *had* the resurrection and uprising happened? Was it a plague, the result of some invasion? There had been threats and warnings of the imminent demise of civilisation for as long as Lewis could remember; nuclear war, asteroid strike, global warming, but this...

It was the distortion of reality that was so terrible. This was not simply a smoking, post-apocalyptic ruin, this was an inversion of normality. Whatever was alive was now dead, and whatever had been dead was alive, and living – a grotesque parody of 21st Century life. There were shops and cafes, pubs and restaurants. Marylebone High Street was not only lit by the unsteady glare of burning corpses and vehicles, but by orange-tinged, electric street lamps. Power stations were working, no doubt run by slave labour, but working so that the Dead could see in the dark and make their society function.

Did they have television? Radio? Computers? Lewis doubted it, but somehow the image of a necrosis-ridden, nuclear family gathered around a flickering screen to watch the latest soap or reality, while snacking on freshly carved Living flesh, had lodged itself into the wilder regions of his imagination. And was there really any difference? Wasn't pre-Uprising society already deteriorating into media-nourished living death?

"Where the hell is everyone?" Melissa muttered. She shivered. "Is it me or is it getting cold?"

"It's not just you," Lewis said. The air had chilled, the temperature drop sudden. There was also a breeze.

The silence was shattered by an explosion. Then gunfire erupted, off to their right. In moments it sounded like a full scale fire fight. An armoured troop carrier roared past, heading for the battle. It was a British Army vehicle, which meant it was probably full of Dead. Lewis noticed a group of enforcers, a hundred metres or so to the left, working their way slowly along both sides of the street. Their weapons were at the ready. The place was not completely deserted, although there was no sign of any Dead civilians.

"This is our chance."

Melissa ran. Lewis followed before he had time to consider options or consequences. For a moment they were in the middle of a crossroads, once more exposed and visible. Lewis crushed Anna tight, gripped by some instinct he had never experienced before, a need to protect her for her own sake.

He tensed, waiting for a shout, a shot. Out-of-condition, he panted and gasped, but kept running through the pain, eventually stumbling to a halt by the gates of Paddington Street Gardens. Melissa was bent double. She winced, rubbed at her leg. "Fucking cramp. Bad one."

"This way." Lewis took her arm and helped her to a clump of large shrubs inside the Garden where Melissa collapsed. Lewis slumped on the grass and began rubbing her leg.

"Pull your foot back, hard, that's it, stretch your calf."

Lewis helped her by pushing at her toes.

She still wore her dress, her leg poured into a fishnet

stocking, though laddered and holed at the feet, erotic to the touch. No, Campbell was her man and Campbell was newly dead. Dead in the true sense of the word. But there was an undeniable pleasure in the touch and the admission burned shame into Lewis's face. He was glad it was dark.

"Thanks, Robert," Melissa said and sat up. "God that's better." She rubbed at her calf for a while longer.

The fire fight sounded closer, more violent. Beyond the houses on the far side of the street, flame throwers roared and night turned to flickering, orange-yellow day.

"I burned him." Melissa said. Her teeth were chattering. The temperature had dropped even further, but Lewis didn't think that was the reason for Melissa's tremors.

"You had no choice," he told her. "It...it wasn't Andy anymore." Just as Caitlin is no longer Caitlin."

"I know, I know it wasn't him, but...Jesus, Robert... Andy's gone...God..." She wept, an unstoppable flow of grief.

Lewis felt his own control slipping again, as reality began to bite. He pulled Melissa to himself and stroked her hair. He even allowed himself some tears of his own.

"St Cyprian's?" Lewis had no idea of the significance of that particular church, but Melissa had named it as their destination.

A nod. Felt not seen. "We have to get there." Melissa straightened and pulled away from him. She sniffed noisily and wiped her nose with her forearm. "We can't stay out here." She rubbed her leg. "It's still bloody sore."

"Give it a few more minutes," Lewis said. He rubbed his arms and wished he had brought a coat.

"How long have you been in the Resistance?" he asked Melissa after a moment.

"Since before the uprising."

"Before?"

"We saw the signs, Robert. We didn't trust them even though there were three or more years of 'peaceful coexistence' between the first resurrection and the uprising. And it wasn't just paranoid Deadists like me. There were elements in the government, the army, somewhere up in the higher levels who saw it too. They provided the resources and training. We used to go away to camps at weekends, Dartmoor, the Dales, out of sight of prying eyes. My husband, Alan, thought I was overreacting, but he tolerated it, bless him, probably because it meant a weekend of peace and quiet, whenever I disappeared for a training exercise. My teenage daughter found the whole thing one massive embarrassment." She laughed, a rueful, humourless chuckle. "But when it actually started I forgot everything they'd taught me about evading capture, and shooting, and making Molotov cocktails. I was as shocked as anyone else. I didn't even get a chance to escape to my local Resistance rendezvous point.

"I was at work and it all happened too quickly. I was a theatre sister in the burns unit at the Chelsea and Westminster. Mr Rajab was operating on a young woman who'd had half her face ruined by an acid attack, courtesy of her vile, fucking ex-boyfriend. She was in good hands, Mr Rajab was popular. He treated his patients and his staff with respect and never shouted or snapped at us. He always operated to Mozart." Melissa chuckled again, it was a sad sound. "He was complaining about the snow and how it would make getting home difficult, when the shouting started. I thought it was some altercation out in the corridor. We weren't too bothered by it. Security would sort it out. Then theatre door was forced open and a patient came in. He had a drip tube dangling from his arm and he was yelling about the Dead and that it was war. A moment later, about half a dozen other people came in. I remember them, vividly. I want to forget them but I can't. Some were in scrubs, and others were in hospital gowns. There was a security guard and a woman in a fur coat. They had blood on their clothes. Their faces were...broken and they looked wild and angry, like animals. They were armed as well; scalpels, iron bars, a large kitchen knife...All the staff except for Mr Rajab and me were killed - whatever that means these days - Most of them had their throats cut, but that wasn't the worst of it, because, suddenly, my own colleagues, and the woman with the acid burn, were kicking and beating me and bleeding all over me and calling me a fucking warm-flesh.

"I was hooded and tied-up for days," Melissa said. "There were others but I couldn't see them. We were bundled into vans and lorries that took us here and there, we were slapped and shoved and beaten until finally we ended up in a warehouse somewhere. That's when they took off our hoods and I saw that there were hundreds of us, kneeling on the floor. We were kept there for days, eating off the floor like dogs. Mr Rajab was with us, but he collapsed and was dragged away. The thing I dreaded most wasn't torture or even being eaten alive by those fuckers, the thing I dreaded most was seeing Alan or my daughter. I would have gone insane."

She paused, regained control.

"The Dead made a mistake," she continued. "They use too many Living as slaves. People always resist. The Resistance found me; one of the truck drivers who bring the skin to the clinic. He had been given a set of photographs of known Resistance fighters who were unaccounted for. He identified me and made contact one evening. You were drunk in your room and Andy...Andy was sulking. We'd had a row over some trivial shit. The driver asked if I was still willing to do my bit for the Living. I said I was. I was ready to burn anyone or anything that night. Over the next few weeks he brought a short wave radio, this gun and a jerry can full of petrol. It was up to me to find the rags and bottles. There were plenty of those in the compound. I hid them under your noses, Andy didn't know either, you see. God I was taking a risk. We all were, and we still are. The Dead can't stop us. They can arrest the Living and burn us or eat us, or just kill us and make us change sides, but they can never stop the Resistance. It's human nature to fight back.

"I contacted my handler as soon as you turned up with the child and within hours the Resistance were planning the biggest attack they've ever attempted. It wasn't to win territory or take over the city, it's simply a very costly and bloody diversion. Anna is fucking important Robert. I don't know why or how, but she has to be delivered to the Resistance. And it has to be at St Cyprian's. That why the fighting is this end of the town, to give us a chance of getting through. She's important enough for a lot of lives to be sacrificed." Melissa shivered and rubbed at her arms. "Jesus, it's so cold. This isn't right."

The breeze was strong enough to disturb the branches of the trees in the park. It ate into Lewis' flesh and burrowed deep.

"Come on," he said, no longer wanting to stay out here, needing to get to St Cyprian's and whatever refuge it promised.

Icy wind tugged at his hair as he struggled to his feet. Paddington Street was intact but disturbingly quiet. Fighting was still in progress a few streets away, but it sounded sporadic, no longer concentrated.

Another sound, odd, like a moan.

Melissa stopped and looked round.

"Sounds like someone's hurt." Lewis had to shout above the wind, which was buffeting them now, and was so, so cold.

Melissa shook her head. "Not to me it doesn't." She walked faster, Lewis struggled to keep up.

"For God's sake," he said. "We should at least see what it is."

Melissa swung round on him. "We have to get to the

church. We can't let anyone stop us. It could be a trap or a Dead. It could be any bloody thing. We have to keep going."

She had slung her machine pistol over one shoulder by its strap, her bag over the other and was blowing into her hands. Beyond her, Lewis saw ice crystals forming on a shop window. Another moan, closer this time, loud and mournful as if driven in by the wind. Lewis looked round, Melissa grabbed his arm.

"Jesus." Melissa's eyes were suddenly wide. "Oh fuck, run, Robert, we have to get out of here."

Lewis turned in the direction of Melissa's stare. She was tugging at his arm, shouting at him to move. But he had to look. There was a shadow, a figure, too big to be human. A shape running towards them along the far side of the street. Its gait was odd. The motion of its legs and arms, the twists and flexing of its body did not match its speed. Litter and other debris was blasted into a grey, gritty tornado centred about the thing, blurring its outlines.

It was roughly ten feet tall, and vaguely human, but its head was terrible. The thing had no eyes, no nose, only immense jaws, crowded with long pointed teeth. Then Lewis saw its claws that looked like scythes. As he finally stumbled into a run, Lewis remembered the gouges hacked into the walls of Caitlin's house.

Scythers.

The name snapped into his mind and stuck.

Melissa was already jogging ahead of him. As she ran, she struggled the machine pistol off her shoulder, then danced round and squeezed the trigger.

"Christ, Melissa," Lewis shouted as he stumbled aside, bent double, convinced that he was about to become collateral damage. Nothing. No firing, no bullets. She had emptied the magazine as they had fled the clinic.

Melissa suddenly darted left into the lobby of an office

block. Lewis followed, relieved to be out of the wind then realising that they had trapped themselves. There was a dust-greyed desk, and an upturned chair. Melissa motioned Lewis to get behind her then reached into her bag and pulled out a magazine for her gun. She fumbled then swore as she dropped it.

The scyther appeared in the doorway. Melissa was knocked backward by the blast of freezing air that came in with the creature, slamming Lewis against the wall. The monster slashed at Melissa with an immense claw. She rolled and the blade swept the air above her. Lewis acted out of some long buried instinct, grabbed an upturned chair and wielded it, gleaming metal legs outwards. It was an awkward weapon, ineffective, but it had already distracted the scyther which was now moving towards him.

The room became a vortex of ragged, ice-edged wind.

"Come on," Lewis yelled. "Come on you bastard thing."

The scyther was vast, a titanic, dark shape within the swirling tube of debris the hell-wind had gathered up around it. It roared, spraying Lewis with thick mucus. It lashed at him, tore the chair from his hands and hurled him sideways. He fell against the desk, hammering his ribs against its edge, winding him and leaving him gasping like a landed fish. He saw the claw arc towards him, but couldn't move. His anger and defiance collapsed.

Melissa's machine pistol clattered and bullets tore through the scyther's chest and abdomen. Chunks of its flesh were swept into the whirlwind. The creature stumbled, twisted round, arms flailing. More bullets ripped at its skin and bone. The wounds bled light, spewed dazzling white beams that cut the dust-fogged air at crazy angles. Lewis threw himself to the floor. He shut his eyes and clenched his fists, wincing as bullets ricocheted and thudded into the walls and desk above his head. The scyther squealed and howled.

The hurricane stopped suddenly.

Lewis needed to get up. He lifted his heavy, heavy head and struggled to his feet. Melissa stood in the middle of the room, the gun hanging loose in her hand. There was no sign of the scyther.

"The last magazine," Melissa lifted the weapon. "I've got a few rounds left but..." She shrugged.

They emerged onto Baker Street several minutes later. The air remained cold, and disturbed by gusts of wind. The near silence was broken by the moans of unseen scythers, each cry louder than the last. It felt as if the creatures were moving in from every side. Lewis tried to shut them out. He muttered the name of their destination over and over, a litany that distracted him. He focussed on Melissa, a few yards ahead.

They headed towards Marylebone Road. Lewis could see the Underground station. The streets were empty. Even the Dead seemed afraid to come out tonight.

A powerful gust of freezing air ripped along the road to shovel litter and dust and rattle doors and windows. A moment later a scyther emerged from a side street ahead of them. Another appeared on the opposite pavement. Lewis sensed others, close behind them. None of them made a move, perhaps made cautious by the sight of Melissa's weapon. Good so far, but if they all rushed in at once, he and Melissa wouldn't stand a chance.

"We need to cross the road," Melissa said. She stopped walking and stood on the edge of the pavement. Half-obscured by a sandstorm of grit and rubbish, there was a scyther blocking the entrance to Melcombe Street.

Lewis glimpsed movement to their left, squinted against the storm and saw another of the creatures advancing towards them. If they stayed where they were, they were damned. If they tried to cross the road, they were damned.

"We charge the one across the road," he heard himself say and wondered where such decisiveness came from.

"Use whatever ammo you've got left-" *Ammo?* He had been watching too many war films "- to shoot the bastard and perhaps the others will get scared and back off."

Melissa studied him, frowned then smiled. "That is the most stupid fucking idea I've ever heard, but it's the only plan we've got because I haven't got a bloody clue what to do."

She breathed deeply a few times, nodded then ran. Lewis followed, yelling because yelling helped. He saw Melissa plunge into the dust storm, and surged into the howling, excoriating madness in her wake. The blurred shape ahead of them let out a long, aching cry and exploded into motion, arms flailing, head down.

Melissa fired from the hip and stumbled from the recoil. Lewis heard glass break as bullets went wild. But he also saw eruptions of bright, white light. The thing was an onrushing violence of claws and teeth. The thing was punctured and bleeding light. The gun rattled. Then stopped. Melissa was still running, Lewis still shouting. The scyther was a vast stroboscopic, thrashing onrush; light, dust, a brief sun-bright flare.

Gone.

Lewis almost tripped on the opposite pavement and careened into the wall of a shop or house or office block. It didn't matter, he didn't care. They were still alive, still running.

Lewis's throat was raw, his lungs burning. He couldn't run for much longer. Ahead of him, Melissa stopped and bent over, panting, hands on knees. A moan and a fresh blast of cold air galvanised them both into movement. Lewis looked back towards Baker Street where three scythers stood. The air was sucked back towards them, an icy wall into which Lewis rammed his exhausted, burning body.

Melissa darted to the right, into Glentworth Street.

Lewis followed and saw a church at the far end.

Dear God please let that be St Cyprian's.

Light shone from the windows of the church, which was becoming obscured by a swirl of dust. The street lamps were not working, but Lewis could tell that this street was derelict. As they drew closer he saw that everything around St Cyprian's was ruin, as if the Dead avoided the place and had left it to moulder and crumble.

Melissa angled across the road, aiming for the church. Lewis followed, almost tripped, and danced to keep his balance. Debris flew from the derelict houses, tiles, pieces of wood, brick dust. The creatures broke into their strange, disconnected run. Their approach was inexorable.

Lewis crumpled to his knees beside Melissa who was pounding the tight-shut church door with her fist. They were bathed in multi-coloured light, splintered into blue, red and green by the stained glass windows. No one answered, Melissa screamed for entrance. The scythers closed in.

CHAPTER EIGHT

JACK MARTIN'S
CHURCH

They all stopped, halfway across the road, each one shrouded in a swirl of dust and debris. The scythers stood, immobile, moaning. Lewis rose slowly to his feet and still they made no move towards him. It was as if they were afraid to come any closer to St Cyprian's, in the same way that the Dead had not wanted to settle near to it.

After a few minutes the scythers backed away, until they were on the far side of the street. Perhaps it had something to do with St Cyprian's being God's house. No, that wouldn't be the reason, because it would apply to every place of worship and Lewis had seen the Dead using churches as dormitories when he had been let out of the compound on a pass visit. But the scythers weren't Dead, they were something else altogether. They looked as if they had had stepped out of Hell itself.

He became aware that the church door had been opened to Melissa's hammering. Only a crack though, just enough for someone to peer out and make themselves heard.

"Who are you? What do you want?" A man's voice.

"Resistance," Melissa said. "Blue Five Cell."

"And who's he?"

"Robert Lewis," Melissa answered before Lewis could speak. "And he has a child. *The* child."

A pause.

"What are you talking about?" The voice sounded shaken.

"Let us in and we'll tell you."

"I can't, I need to check with -"

"For fuck's sake do as she tells you."

Lewis recognised the new voice. The driver who had helped him escape from the First House. Not much of a friend, but familiar enough to make him feel better.

Another pause. Then the door opened fully.

"Okay, okay, get in and hurry up." The doorman was in his sixties, a short, stocky character, topped off with a set of dreadlocks. He scanned the street and flinched when he saw the scythers. "What the hell are they?"

"I don't know and I don't care," Melissa snapped as she brushed past. "Just thank Christ they're not religious."

The driver laughed. "Spiky bitch."

"Piss off, Hillier."

The driver, Hillier, gave Lewis a rueful smile. "And you're still alive. That's the biggest fucking surprise of my week."

The door slammed shut, the sound loud and reassuring. All detail inside the church was smudged by the shadow-rich illumination of a thousand candles. A crowd filled the nave. All ages from early twenties to middle-age were represented. No children, and few elderly. Each face was chiselled to its raw landscape by the uncertain light. There was fear here, Lewis could smell it, feel its pulse, hear it in the subdued drone of conversation. The air was hot and close, tainted by odours of unwashed flesh and smoke from the candles.

Lewis was unnerved by the sight of so many Living in one place. This was something he hadn't seen since those few nightmare days after the Uprising. There must be many more still out there, the rebels, the willing and the enslaved, the labour force and food stocks of the Earth's new masters.

Many of these people possessed firearms and wore pseudo-military clothes, Resistance fighters fresh from the battle, seeking refuge and respite in the church. They sat around, exhausted. Some trembled, their faces blank with shock. There was a low murmur of conversation, which died as Lewis was led into their midst.

There was another group, men and women, who were moving amongst the fighters and other refugees. They wore blue armbands and were handing out plastic cups of water and bowls of hot food. There was bread too. Lewis felt a pang of hunger. The deadlock doorman wore one of the armbands.

All attention was focussed on Lewis. What he carried, was the object of their efforts and sacrifice tonight. The realisation made Lewis uncomfortable and ashamed, although he had no reason to be. He had hidden her from Reeder, brought her here safely and even fought against the scythers. But he was also a collaborator.

He became aware that the Living were roughly divided into two groups; the heavily armed Resistance fighters, and the other 'civilians' who had found their way here. Many of those were armed with crude weapons, lengths of metal pipe, knives and pieces of wood, some with nails driven through them to turn them into savage-looking maces. But these people too, would be seen as cowards, Living who had chosen to serve the conquerors, rather than resist and die, until now, when the Resistance assault had given them a chance to escape.

Someone recognised Melissa and called her name. It was a woman with wild, black hair and a freshly carved scar sliced diagonally across her face. They embraced. Melissa's welcome into the Resistance camp, further isolated Lewis.

Dreadlocks grabbed Lewis's arm. "We'd better take you to see the Rev, though you look like you need some sleep my friend. I'm Tommy by the way. Not my real name, but I like it better." He offered a hand to Lewis who was glad to return the welcome. "Sorry about the rudeness at the door, but we have to be careful, not that the Dead are ready to take us on yet."

"Why is that?" Lewis asked.

"You don't know? I thought everyone knew. This place is built right over a source, one of the ones taken by Azazel himself. He's here, Doc, the great angel is right here and no Dead is going to set foot in this place until they've gathered their strength. They'll come, but not yet." He looked back at Lewis, frowned, then offered a wry smile. "You still don't know what I'm talking about, do you?"

"Not a clue."

"I'll leave it to the Rev to explain."

As Lewis was led through the church, he became aware of a third group, quiet, separate and half-hidden in the deeply-shadowed north side of the nave; Dead. Here? Surely they must be Half Dead rebels. For a moment, Lewis wondered if Caitlin was among them. But no. No one called out to him, none of them ran into his arms, weeping with joy.

Tommy guided him into a warren of narrow passages to a small office Lewis took to be the vestry. The door was closed. Tommy knocked, firmly.

"Rev," he said.

"What is it?" The voice was male and sounded ancient.

"You need to see this, Rev."

A moment then the door was opened by an aged, but sturdy-looking character wearing a worn set of clergyman's vestments.

"It's the child, Rev," Tommy said before anyone else could speak. "This is Doctor Lewis and he's brought the child."

"Child?" the old man seemed puzzled. He stared at Lewis, then understanding dawned. Understanding and shock. "Caitlin's daughter? You've brought Anna?"

"You know Caitlin? My wife?" A glimmer, a spark of hope, Lewis knew that he was being foolish, but the hope wouldn't stop. "Is she here?"

"I'm sorry, she isn't with us and I've never met her, although her name has become precious to us. The Madam sent us a message, telling us that we had a survivor here in London. There are so few, Doctor. Most died in the womb, others are...monstrous, terrible creatures for whom life itself is a cruelty. This child, your child, is a miracle and a saviour." He gestured towards Lewis's chest. "Show, me, please."

Lewis sighed then unbuttoned his shirt. Instinctively, he laid his palm on the child, and was startled to note that she was no longer a flat, second skin. Contours had formed, starting to take on the familiar features of a human baby. She moved under his hand. There was no detail, her face, hands and feet still melded into his flesh. Her skin though, was becoming mapped with a web of delicate blue and red blood vessels.

"A miracle, Doctor Lewis, and our salvation; a child with no soul, a truly empty vessel. Thank you."

Lewis re-buttoned his shirt.

"Tommy," the Rev said. "Fetch some coffee and some food, will you."

"Yes, Rev." Tommy withdrew.

The vestry was a simple cube-shaped room, furnished with a modern-looking, though chipped and battered, desk and four chairs. Three of them were ranged about the front of the desk, the fourth behind it. The Rev took the latter and indicated that Lewis should sit opposite him. The room was warm, probably too warm, but Lewis was still cold from his encounter with the scythers, so the heat was more luxury than oppression. He sat, gratefully, and realised how exhausted he was.

"I'm the Reverend Jack Martin," the clergyman said. They shook hands. Martin's grip was firm, his accent precise and neutral yet holding a trace of some London past that was much tougher and street-forged than Lewis's. "And this is my church and congregation. A flock made up of those who fled here for sanctuary on that awful Sunday afternoon, and those who attended this house of God, before the Uprising. People like Tommy."

"Those with the armbands?"

"Yes, although others have joined since, people who escaped slavery. St Cyprian's is also a refuge and supply depot for the Resistance. We look after them, they look after us. So, Doctor Lewis, would that be doctor of medicine or science?"

"Medical."

"Which branch of the profession?"

A pause then; "Reconstructive surgeon."

Martin didn't respond.

"At least, that's my specialism," Lewis said hastily. Why all this self-justification? What was it about Martin that had reduced him to a babbling child within a few seconds of meeting the man?

"From the Harley Street Compound I presume?" Martin answered.

"Yes, what's left of it. There was a lot of fighting in that area tonight."

"There's war in the Deadside, a huge resistance operation supported by an insurrection by the Half-Dead. This evening's bloodletting has brought us a lot of wounded to care for, which means that we can make good use of you, Doctor Lewis. You won't be alone in your work, we have another surgeon here, same branch of medicine." Martin regarded him carefully. "There are Half-Dead here as well. They are as welcome as any war-weary Resistance fighter. I do not allow feuds within these walls. I do not allow reprisals on so-called collaborators. Anyone who comes in is cared for and sheltered and treated with as much dignity as we can manage."

Tommy returned and placed two mugs of hot, fragrant coffee on Martin's desk. There was a bowl too, and some bread that looked as if it had been ripped off the loaf rather than sliced.

"Is she the one, Rev?" Tommy said. There was wonder in his voice. "The kid, is it *her?*"

"We can't be sure Tommy," Martin said. "But you must play it down, do you understand? The fewer people who know, the better it will be."

"Sure, yeah."

Martin chuckled ruefully when Tommy left them again. "My request for discretion is probably too late. Tommy is my right hand man, his enthusiasm keeps me going, keeps me believing, but it can get us into trouble. Be careful, Doctor, there are a lot of people interested in Anna. She is the focal point of many agendas."

Lewis wanted to eat, but he needed some questions answered first. "I don't understand any of this. I don't know what is so special about this church or my daughter. And I don't know who you are, not really. You're obviously brave and compassionate, but I can't believe you're just a heroic priest, caring for the wounded, and hiding Resistance fighters."

"I am disciple of the great angel."

"Azazel?"

"Yes. Satan's general, the lord of the legions of the damned, the fallen angels who revolted against God."

"*Satan's* general? So why is this angel helping you? Aren't you his enemy?"

"Once yes, but Azazel has repented of his rebellion. He is seeking atonement, forgiveness, a way back into heaven. I've been a disciple of his for a long time, since before the Uprising. This church you see, was built over a source. A lot of churches are, it wasn't a conscious decision on the part of their builders. It was a sense, a feeling that it was the right place to build." Martin sipped coffee.

Lewis finally allowed himself to eat, too tired and hungry to interrupt with questions. He would have to take all this at face value for now.

"Source is not a particularly good name," Martin said after a moment. "But then neither are angel and devil, demon and God, or even Heaven and Hell for that matter. A source is a...gateway, I suppose you could call it, a place where realms, planes, dimensions merge.

"The energies that power the Dead came out through these Sources. Azazel has taken control of some of them and his legions are ready to break through and help us defeat the Dead. It is his atonement, the act that he hopes will restore him to Heaven."

"So Azazel could break through here, in St Cyprian's?"

"Yes."

"So why doesn't he?" Lewis certainly felt a rush of hope at the thought of some shining, supernatural army burning away the corruption that had blighted the world. Was it false hope though, based on the delusions of an old man he had only just met? But others appeared to believe in this as well, including Hillier, who didn't strike Lewis as being gullible. And wasn't the idea of the Dead returning to the life a crazed idea in and of itself? If the resurrected Dead, why not a repentant fallen angel?

"Azazel can only break through for moments of time. The bonds that tie him to his home are strong."

Ah, of course, like all supernatural saviours there was always promise but never action, the time was never quite right, the omens never auspicious enough.

"Doctor Lewis, you look exhausted, the night has been traumatic for you. I suggest you get some sleep and we can talk again in the morning."

"I need to know, Reverend. Anna has something to do with this, doesn't she?"

Martin nodded.

"Then I have a *right* to know."

"As I explained, Azazel can reach through, like any of his kind, for brief moments. He can come to our aid and fight our enemies, but then he is drawn back. Spiritual beings cannot live in this world. They require flesh. The Dead for example are corrupt flesh, but flesh none-the-less. Souls long fled, mere carcasses and ripe for habitation by malevolent spirits. Demons I suppose you would call them."

"Extremely vain and sensual demons."

"Indeed they are, Doctor Lewis, creatures who glory in the five new senses they have inherited, along with new and corporeal ways of sating their appetites."

"Why Dead flesh? Why not possess the living, haven't demons always supposedly tried to take over people's bodies and souls?" Lewis asked.

"Yes they have, but full possession isn't possible if the shell, the vessel, is already inhabited, hence the physical torments and contortions of the possessed. They are the signs of inner struggle. The Half Dead are another example, souls who managed to cling to their bodies after death and are in constant struggle with the invader."

"A waking hell."

"Absolutely."

Caitlin...

"Okay, so you're telling me that Azazel also needs a vessel, an empty body to inhabit before he can truly break through into our world."

"Exactly."

"So why doesn't he use a corpse?"

"He could, but as you well know, corpses deteriorate quickly. They are fine for hordes of lowly demons, Satan's foot soldiers. Azazel needs something else, something durable, and symbolic."

"A living body with no soul, if that isn't a contradiction in terms."

And wasn't Anna just such a contradiction?

"Yes. A rarity."

"An impossibility I'd say, although the concept of soul is somewhat dubious in my belief system."

"How much of your belief system has survived, Doctor Lewis?"

"Good question. I cling to as much of it as I can, like a survivor from the *Titanic*, clinging to wreckage. As for souls, I see them as sparks of consciousness, created by the electrochemical reactions that power life itself. Even insects have this. You can't separate them, until death of course."

"Nevertheless, such creatures do exist," Martin said. "Living beings without souls are a reality."

Suddenly uneasy, Lewis placed a protective hand over the parasitic monstrosity that was his daughter.

Lewis found his own way back into the body of the church and, after a brief search, located Melissa. She was settled among the Resistance who seemed even closer knit than ever and were grouped in a huge, inward facing circle that blocked out everyone else. They were loud in their banter and laughter. Proudly smoke-smudged, they wore their injuries like medals.

The other Living were quiet, shocked and huddled into arbitrary clusters, as if gaining comfort from anyone with a heartbeat. Lewis headed for the nearest of these rag tag groups. A member of Martin's congregation caught up with him and gave him a bottle of water and a blanket.

"Hey, Doc we've saved a space for you." It was Hillier. "A nice soft floor slab."

Melissa spoke up. "It's all right, Robert you can come over here with us." She made it sound like a privilege and the tone irritated Lewis, though only for a moment. He was too tired to care.

"The Doc, here, fought one of those scythe-handed bastards out there with nothing but a chair," Hillier said as Lewis sat down. "And saved the lovely Melissa's life." He clapped a big hand on Lewis' shoulder. There was mockery in his voice, but, perhaps a little grudging admiration too. "That's the story anyway."

"It's the truth," Melissa said with a flint-edged firmness that indicated an on-going dislike for Hillier. "He gave me a chance to reload this bloody pistol." She laid a hand on Lewis's arm, her voice softened. "I never thanked you for that."

He shrugged. "I...I wasn't thinking, I just..." It sounded like false modesty so he stopped.

"That's how it is most of the time," another of the fighters said. He was a middle-aged man, his accent clipped, his hair short to the point of crew-cut. He had a grubby bandage wrapped about his right wrist. "Confusion and gut reaction."

***

Lewis was awakened from his usual dreams, in the early hours of the morning by the sound of the scythers outside. Their mournful wails came in from every quarter around the church, which meant that there were more of them out there now. The door rattled in its frame, trees creaked and hissed beyond the big stained glass window above the altar. It sounded as if June had been transformed into January. Coughs and snores were replaced by murmurs of fear. Forces were gathering.

Late in afternoon, after managing to go back to sleep on the unyielding, and cold, stone floor for the remains of that first night, Lewis was put to work in, what Tommy described as the field hospital. The wounded and ill were laid out on the chancel floor, between the choir stalls and, somehow fittingly in Lewis's mind at least, in front of the altar.

His first patient was a woman called Marion with a face-wound that had opened her left cheek to her teeth. It had been hastily repaired with Sellotape and a now-filthy, dressing. He cleaned then stitched the wound and she told him, in a muffled, wet voice, that he was a miracle worker. Then she kissed her own fingertips and laid them briefly on his chest.

"I love you, Anna," she managed to hiss through the dressing.

Everyone had a job to do, whether it was preparing food, filling empty bottles with petrol, hauling crates of ammunition and other supplies up from the crypt or breaking up the chairs, pews and any other expendable wood to make fire traps under the windows and in front of each door. It was a risk, almost suicidal, but the general belief seemed to be that the fires would not last long under sheer weight of numbers of the Dead as they poured into the building. Lewis was uneasy about this, but he was a newcomer, a foot soldier, albeit the bearer of a precious cargo. His job was to look after Anna and the wounded.

Despite his vow to look out only for himself, the vow he

had made to Lewis during that crazed car journey away from the First House, Hillier was a dynamo of organisation and morale-lifting, and led regular patrols out into the streets. There was a feeling that an attack was imminent, despite the Dead's reluctance to come anywhere near the church.

The other doctor in the field hospital was a thin, fragile looking man with thinning hair, an ashen complexion and the red-tinged eyes of exhaustion. He brusquely introduced himself as Fuller and gave Lewis a quick rundown of the more serious causalities in their care.

"I was based in the Wimpole Street compound," he said. "I was out on a pass, a consultation with one bloody High Level or another, when I got caught up in trouble amongst the Dead. One minute I was walking towards Charing Cross station, the next all hell broke loose; guns, and flamethrowers, even a grenade. I hid in the National Gallery, or what's left of it - place is a wreck, most of the paintings have gone. A group of Half-Dead found me. They'd been fighting and were on the run. They brought me here with them. Reeder seems to be clamping down. I hear he burned the First House. Unbelievable, that building has been standing for almost two hundred years and the bloody Dead have to destroy it.

"Last night the Resistance decided to wade in. They picked an uneven fight. Look at them." He nodded towards his patients. Lewis counted at least thirty of them, suffering mostly from bullet wounds, burns, and vicious looking cuts. "Thank God you're here, Lewis. I'm absolutely exhausted and need some sleep. Do what you can. The Resistance have stored a lot of medical supplies here, so their wounded can be treated before they get back to the ghettos after their raids. God knows where they get the stuff from. The important thing is that if any of them die or look as if they're about to, shout, so the body can be cremated straight away. We missed a couple the other day and there was hell to pay when they resurrected right in the middle of us."

His lecture complete, Fuller moved across the church towards one of the non-Resistance groups. Lewis surveyed the patients, trying to work out who needed his attention first.

"Need some help?"

Lewis looked up from the unconscious, sweat-slicked face of a gut-shot young man and was relieved to see Melissa. There was an older woman with her and a young man who looked to be barely out of his teens.

"Thanks." Lewis said and meant it. He knelt beside the casualty. "Fuller's done a good job, but a lot of these people are suffering from infections. We need to keep an eye on this poor bastard." He indicted the gut-shot victim. "I don't think he's going to last much longer."

The young man wordlessly took on a watching role. He was pale and he trembled. The older woman shook her head and told Lewis that she had found the lad wandering outside a burnt-out restaurant. "I think he was livestock and next on the menu, when some sort of raid took place," she said.

"What about you?" Lewis asked her as they set about changing the dressing on a wound that had opened the torso of female fighter. It had been neatly sutured but there were signs of infection. The patient was hot, restless and murmuring incoherently.

"Bridget, that's my name. Make-up artist would you believe. I worked in the theatre before the uprising. That made me Vitally Skilled apparently, not because I was a brain surgeon or nuclear scientist, but because I was a bloody face-painter. The Dead put me to work in their brothels, prettying up the girls and boys." She chuckled, a throaty smoker's laugh. "I've made handsome and beautiful actors look like zombies, but now I was trying to turn zombies into sex goddesses. Trouble is…" She lifted her right hand and Lewis could see a tremor. "Parkinson's? Old age? I don't know, but what I do know is that it wouldn't have been long before I was on the menu at the Savoy or just another Dead in need of some lipstick and strong perfume. I was scared out of my wits, going mad with fear. Then, a few nights ago I was sent on a job at the First House. That was terrifying. I mean you have to be very, very good to work with First House girls. I'd only been there an hour or so when Reeder appeared and the place was suddenly on fire and everyone was running for the exits. I slipped away, headed here, and picked up a few strays, including Jimmy over there. Don't know if that's his name, but it fits -"

"Robert! Quick!" It was Melissa, crouched beside the wildly thrashing, gut-shot casualty. Bloody foam spewed from his mouth, his back arched impossibly and his heels drummed the floor. There was a final stiffening of his entire body then he relaxed and his breath left him in one long, final gasp.

Appalled, Lewis straightened and tried to remember what it was he supposed to do. He saw Melissa glance at Bridget, tried to think. It was Bridget who acted first. "Dead!" she shouted. "Someone's just died."

In a moment three Resistance fighters appeared and, without ceremony, picked up the body and hauled it towards the side entrance and into the maze of passageways that led both to Martin's office and out into a small courtyard. Even though the cremation took place outside, facilitated using both petrol, and flamethrowers stolen from defeated enforcers, the stink of roasting flesh seeped back into the church and hung in the air for the rest of Lewis' long night.

***

Somewhere around midnight there was a pounding at the door.

People woke and the atmosphere tightened. Hillier and Tommy moved to the door. Still on duty in the Field Hospital, Lewis reached for the iron bar he had chosen as a weapon, Melissa went for her machine pistol.

"Who is it?" Tommy called out.

The answer was inaudible to Lewis. Hillier peered through the spyhole that had been drilled into the wood. He nodded and the door was opened just wide enough to admit a fresh band of beaten, bleeding and bruised Resistance fighters.

There was an immediate Resistance huddle, expressions turned grim. It looked like bad news. Tommy and Hillier set off for the vestry, accompanied by two of the new fighters. Food and drink was organised and the wounded were brought over to the chancel.

The worst of the new casualties was a middle-aged woman, slender, and fey, who had lost a leg. Blood loss and shock had drained her of any vestige of colour. One of her comrades sat down beside her and grabbed her hand. He was a big man with long, salt and pepper hair and a fearsome beard. He wore a leather biker jacket overlaid by a badly frayed denim waistcoat.

"I'm not leaving her." There was threat in his voice.

"Of course, it's all right," Melissa answered. "She's in good hands, Doctor Lewis here, is a top consultant."

Thanks, Lewis told her silently. *That grizzly bear will expect a miracle now.*

Lewis did what he could. He cleaned the wound, tied-off ruptured blood vessels and trimmed ragged flesh and muscle tissue. He bandaged the stump, injected antibiotics and sent Melissa to fetch his blanket and any others she could scrounge. It was oven hot in the church but the patient was ice cold. Her breathing was ragged, her skin ran with sweat. And all the time the big man with the beard sat with her and gripped her hand. He was battered, smoke-smudged and tired, but he would not rest.

The woman died just as the dark was greying towards

dawn. Lewis stared at her, appalled, then at her companion and understood that the man didn't realise that she was dead. Lewis knew he should shout for a cremation party, but he was afraid of the biker's reaction. Instead, he crouched beside him, put a tentative hand on his shoulder and said; "I'm sorry, she's gone."

The man turned slowly to glare at him. He frowned then, silently, scooped the woman's body up in his huge arms and carried her away. When he returned, half an hour later, he smelled of smoke.

"Doctor," he growled.

Lewis looked up from his work to see a huge hand, extended and waiting to be shaken. Lewis hesitated then accepted the gesture.

"You did what you could," the biker said. "Name's Nick by the way. Her name was Lynne. I uh...I loved her. Can you believe that? A big fucking lump like me and a skinny streak of loveliness like her. She was a primary school teacher before the fucking stenchers came." He sighed, rubbed at his eyes with the back of his hand. The gesture was rough and impatient. "I was the same as I am now; fucking trouble." He laughed. "She was kind and gentle and the kids probably loved her. But Christ, she was like a fucking maniac in a fight. She hated those stenchers more than the rest of us put together. Fuck knows what the stenchers did to her family or kids, but there was no way she was ever going to let them forget how much it pissed her off."

Nick attached himself to the Field Hospital. He was a tireless fetcher and carrier, and lone cremator of the freshly dead. Eventually he simply fell asleep while kneeling beside a casualty, holding a cold wet cloth on a patient's forehead.

Fuller appeared at lunch time and Lewis was, at last, able to get some rest. He ate the usual broth and rough bread, drank coffee then collapsed into sleep.

It was almost dark outside when Melissa shook him awake. Lewis' first thought was that the Dead were attacking the church. People were awake and on the move. He reached for the iron bar and struggled to sit up. "What's going on?"

"I don't know," Melissa said. "Martin's made an appearance."

Lewis clambered to his feet and saw that the church's inhabitants were forming themselves into a rough arc around front of the pulpit and looking up, expectantly. There was a murmur of conversation, an atmosphere of nervous anticipation.

A moment, then the Reverend Jack Martin appeared. Tommy and a couple of other blue armband helpers were with him.

"Friends." He did not shout or proclaim, yet his voice carried across the nave of the church. "St Cyprian's is surrounded and cut off. Reeder's forces are closer than the Dead have ever come before. There's no escape. Anyone is welcome to try but I fear you'll not get far. Our best hope is to make a stand, here in the church. With Azazel's help we will create enough mayhem and confusion to give as many of us as possible a chance to break through and flee to the Living ghettos."

The murmuring grew louder. Fear had entered the atmosphere. Lewis saw it in the pale, haggard faces of the people around him, heard in in their voices and their quiet weeping.

"Remember this." Now Martin did proclaim. "We are not alone. We have a powerful ally, the Great Angel Azazel. He has promised to bare his arm against the Dead and decaying armies of Satan." He paused, surveyed his flock. "He has promised to come to our side when the last battle starts."

A chant began, the language alien, guttural. Tommy

stepped to the front of the pulpit and took the lead. Voices were raised, fists were raised. Slowly the bruised and battered army gathered in St Cyprian's church took up the words. Always suspicious of the mob mind, Lewis rebelled against joining in, but couldn't stop himself. The rhythm, the coarse, incomprehensible phrases boiled from his throat. There was comfort and strength in numbers, of being part of this.

The candle flames painted fist shadows on the walls. Their voices slammed off the brickwork. They were a mob, they were a unified, desperate, angry, stencher-hating mob. They wanted blood. They wanted to burn and smash and flay the fucking stenchers. And he, Mister Robert Lewis FRCS (Plast), Consultant Reconstructive Surgeon, was one of them.

Energies danced electric on his skin, the roar of the crowd thrummed against and through him, the verbal beat synchronised with his heartbeat. The atmosphere tightened like the moments before a thunderstorm. The candles flared and flickered, their dance adding to the disorientating, confusing swirl of sound and movement.

Something entered the church.

Difficult to define, a feeling, a sense, a presence. The hot, close and humid atmosphere dipped towards cold. The congregation's breath became steam. Lewis shivered and hugged his arms about himself. The longer the song went on, the lower the temperature dropped and the more uneasy Lewis, and many others, became. But no one could stop singing and, despite the growing restlessness of the congregation, there was also a sense of euphoria.

The floor in front of the pulpit shook, people screamed and stumbled back. Waves of fluidity rolled through the slabs and momentary turned each one to liquid.

Martin yelled, his head thrown back, the muscles of this neck, snakes against the inside of this flesh. He choked out animal sound, yells and groans.

The crowd began to howl and scream in response.

Light leaked from the joints between the flagstones, liquid light that crawled across their faces. The light lapped Lewis's feet. He jumped away from it but it was all around him, cutting him off from the rest. He spun wildly. He was alone, the floor under him ablaze with runnels of gold light. A wall of shouting, howling faces pressed in on him from every side. He wanted it to stop.

The veins of light suddenly flared and erupted into a roaring, loudly hissing column and Lewis felt himself torn from his feet and lifted above the heads of the congregation. He cried out, but his voice was lost. He clung to Anna. The light felt solid under him, spread out like the palm of a huge hand. It closed over him and everything became bright and gold and voices.

Something entered him, pushed through his flesh and eyes and mouth. Vast and terrible, it drove into Anna through the fibrous roots that bound her embryonic body to his. The thing was titanic, a monstrous engine of wheels and pulsing organs and tissue. Its borders were lost in all directions, its structure and sense was too gigantic to orientate, one moment glimpsed and imagined, then seen and felt.

It spoke, in a voice that was soft, but neither male nor female.

"I *will* have her."

Lewis fought against the pressure on his skin and against his ears and eyes. *No you won't*. And filled her himself. He was crushed into a small, dark place of black and red, of pulsing heart and whooshing blood. At its centre, there was a spark, a glint of life. Of *self*.

The floor slammed into his back and he couldn't breathe or move. The pressure grew unbearable, he felt himself crumble. From somewhere he managed a scream. The cry was *his* voice. It came from *his* self.

Then, suddenly, the pressure, the monstrous presence was gone.

People were all over him, helping him up, hugging him, with awe in some of their faces.

That thing, that blaze of glory was the great angel, their ally. Yet Lewis had heard threat in its voice. And that threat had strengthened whatever shreds of resolve he had left. Azazel would *not* have Anna.

***

Lewis took the night shift in the field hospital, as he had on the previous day. Nick the Biker remained a tireless orderly and general helper. And now he seemed bigger and more frightening than when Lewis first met him. He called himself the Ghoul, his own name for the job he had volunteered to carry out.

There could be no more cremations outside. It was too dangerous. Instead, any patient who died was taken down into the crypt where they were dismembered and cut up into as small pieces as was possible. The bloody wreckage, with its own semblance of life, was scooped up and locked away in one to the small, dank rooms down there. The gaps around the door were sealed with petrol soaked choir gowns.

Few people knew about the new disposal method. To preserve morale, death among the wounded and ill was no longer announced with a shout. A hand signal or whispered message to Nick and the corpse would be dealt with. The biker's eyes were fixed, haunted. A storm brewed in that rough, sword-edged soul of his. Thank God there had only been three deaths that day..

Not that anyone was paying much attention anymore. No one slept. The church was being fortified, rudimentary training in weapon handling carried out by the Resistance fighters, and more fire traps prepared. All through the night Hillier and a few volunteers disappeared on regular scouting forays. They were never gone for long, which meant that Reeder's forces had to be close. The ring was tightening.

Lewis knew he should be terrified, but he felt nothing.

***

Once again darkness turned to grey but this morning, it got no further. Not long after dawn, rain began to lash against the windows, wind driven and winter-like. Lightning flashed and thunder bellowed. The sound shuddered through the church. Tense silence was punctuated by loud squabbles.

Fuller arrived for his shift. He was dishevelled and, like most of the men in St Cyprian's, sporting the first stages of a beard. We probably stink too, Lewis thought, and then wondered why that mattered? He was supposed to rest now that the other doctor was on duty, but he knew he wouldn't sleep.

He was still shaken from Azazel's attempted invasion. Anna was afraid too, her fear transmitted like electric shocks into Lewis' own nervous system, further proof, perhaps, of the presence of some form of embryonic soul.

He ate and drank then returned to the field hospital. Melissa, Nick and Bridget were there, each of them locked inside themselves, trying to lose their fears in the work, but all the time waiting for the hammer to fall.

Sometime in the middle of the storm-tainted gloom there were shouts from outside. Fists pummelled at the door. Tommy and a knot of heavily armed Resistance fighters formed a defensive arc. "What do you want?" Tommy called out. The church collapsed into silence. Someone began to cry.

"It's...it's Hillier, let us in for Christ's sake, hurry up!"

Tommy worked the bolts, the door crashed open and two figures stumbled in. Hillier dropped to his knees, panting, exhausted. The other fighter was a gangly teenager. He stood, face blank.

"They're on the move, closing in," Hillier told them breathlessly.

A murmur grew in volume. Lewis finally began to *feel*, and what he felt was panic and desperation. The same emotions were rolling through the ranks of the St Cyprian army. Lewis could sense imminent collapse.

Quietly and unannounced, Jack Martin appeared in the pulpit. Despite his physical solidity, he seemed frail and old. The congregation fell silent and Lewis was ridiculously comforted by the sight of him.

"Reeder is coming," he said, then commenced the chant. This time he chanted alone.

Hillier and other Resistance fighters began to shout and order and organise. Lewis snatched up his iron bar and faced the stain glass window above the altar. Nick took his place on his left, Melissa on his right. Both were armed with machine pistols. Bridget was there, and Fuller. Others joined them, including the Half Dead who swelled their ranks. More defensive clusters were forming in the nave. Bottles clinked as crates of pre-prepared Molotov cocktails were rushed out of the choir stalls. Two crates were delivered to the chancel. There was nothing anyone could do for the patients.

Martin repeated the chant, his voice clear and strong. Others joined in. Lewis simply stared at the window. Wind rattled the glass in its frame, rain beat at the flanks of the building. The chant grew louder as more and more Living joined in. *Come on Azazel*, Lewis urged silently. *Hurry up.*

Something slammed into the church and the stained glass window exploded inwards in a tinkling waterfall of blue, red and green.

CHAPTER NINE

STORM

People screamed. Another impact shuddered through the church, another, a fourth. Dust swirled and plaster fell. Smoke billowed in through the smashed window, immediately shredded by a hurricane of freezing air as the first of the scythers leapt into the empty frame and down onto the altar. Two more followed, moaning and howling, from within their cocoons of whirling dust and debris.

Lewis pressed himself back against the tight packed group behind him. He couldn't fight, not those things, he had to get away. Now, away -

He saw a fiery bottle tumble end-over-end towards the piled wood and blankets arranged round the altar. It burst open as the first scyther crashed into the heap. Liquid fire erupted outwards then caught on the petrol-soaked wood. The scyther disappeared in an explosion of flame. The other two tried to scramble back but were defeated by their momentum and tumbled into the bonfire.

Heat seared Lewis' face, and he felt the press of bodies behind him yield as the chancel defenders backed away from the inferno. There was a loud detonation. The main door was blown inwards and Dead poured into the church. Dead civilians, the sacrificial front rank, armed with home-made weapons. A moment later they were engulfed by a wall of flame as a second Molotov cocktail ignited the barricade protecting the entrance.

"Enforcers!" Melissa's yell. Lewis spun back towards the chancel in time to see the fireproof-bulked shapes stumble out of the altar fire. They looked invincible. Nick appeared, shooting from the hip, his shouts lost in the din. Enforcers staggered back, suits bullet-ripped, their slushy essence pouring from the wounded fabric. Some caught fire, oils transmitting the flames back into the suits.

Melissa joined him, spraying the attackers as they burst from the flames, which were already dampening down into thick, grey-white smoke. Behind them, the nave erupted into battle, a crescendo of voices and howls. More Dead careened out of the smoke of the dying altar fire. Nick threw his machine pistol aside and ripped a machete from his belt. He surged forward and Lewis found himself caught up in a charge. No turning back now, rushed forward by the momentum of the screaming, roaring mass of Living.

The impact was shattering. Lewis was driven into a large, round-faced Dead. He felt something give way under the Dead's clothes, then he was gone and he was in a swirling, pressed-in chaos of bodies and flailing arms and weapons. Lewis kept his left arm protectively around Anna and wielded the iron bar as best he could in the press.

Lewis was trapped in the heart of it, trying to stay on his feet, unable to fight, shoved against Living and Dead. His head was full of Anna's raw terror as the Dead piled in. Sheer weight of numbers forced the Living back through the chancel. More scythers appeared at the smoke-blurred broken window, unable to get through to the battle, howling and moaning.

Stroboscopic lightning flashed rhythmically over the melee. The distance-delayed thunder drowned by the roar of the fight.

Then something broke open and the Living stumbled and fell under the sudden onrush of Dead. Lewis saw blood and hacked flesh. A body slammed to the floor beside him, eyes wide. Bridget. He scrambled free and got to his feet in time to meet an oncoming Dead, a young man in a suit, dark hair, grinning with bloodlust.

Lewis swung wildly and felt the iron pipe connect with the Dead's skull. Gobbets of flesh sprayed outwards. The Dead staggered to one side. Lewis was on him again.

Swinging and swinging. Beating and crushing and breaking until the Dead was a crawling slithering thing at his feet. He glimpsed Nick again, huge and berserk and still alive. He couldn't see Melissa. Couldn't see anything but the smoke-stained madness of bodies and violence. This wasn't some rosy-hued Hollywood version of war, this was the hot, stinking, befouled reality.

And all the time, Lewis and those around him were being forced back, further into the nave where the other half of the battle was raging. The Living slowly coalesced into one, desperate mass. Then Lewis saw Martin standing in the pulpit, alone, shouting but unheard.

Lightning flashed and thunder rolled and it was as if the storm was being performed for the antagonists' benefit.

More Dead poured in, wielding clubs and machetes of their own, as well as handguns and rifles. Young, old, men and women, some in uniform; police, soldiers, nurses, their mouths open, unblinking eyes wide and fevered.

There was a seemingly endless stream of them, their huge numbers both boon and bane. They were unstoppable, but were now in each other's way. All was punctuated by the explosive "whoomp" of Molotovs as the next line of fire traps was ignited. Lewis lashed out, sometimes making contact, angry, terrified, and utterly disorientated.

Scythers and Dead fell or staggered out of the inferno - flaming, writhing trees of burning limbs and blistered flesh. Others, glimpsed and shimmering through the flames, milled in terror and confusion. Heat seared the skin of Lewis's face. A shot, something flicked through the air, cracked into the wall to his left. A scyther barged through, and fell to its knees, its flesh blackened, screaming out its agonies. The barrier was breached. Lewis snatched up the club, something rose in him, something greater then fear. Rage, a need to lash, to hurt and damage and kill.

Another scyther stumbled towards the defenders, then squealed and staggered back. Lewis saw light bleeding from the cracks between the floor slabs. Other Dead and their allies broke through the burning chairs, but none of them seemed able to step onto the floor under which Martin's god stirred

Then the enforcers came, bursting through, dropping to their knees and raising their weapons. Guns flashed, bullets snapped through the air. Someone fell to Lewis' left, another to his right, close. They fell forward, their blood mingling with the pools and runnels of gold light.

They would soon be the enemy.

Emboldened by the Dead's reluctance to step onto the strip of glowing, shuddering floor slabs that separated the two armies, the Living broke into a charge. The two lines crashed together. It was confusion with no sense of individual, just a dark landscape composed of frantic, moving things.

Driven by sheer panic and terror and a lust to destroy, Lewis swung hard at the raging face of a Dead and felt the impact. Mouldering flesh was torn to the bone, its necrosis-brittle jaw shattered. Lewis barged past him, slashing at another. Shots were fired, muffled by the crush of bodies. He lashed out, slashed and rammed at flesh with the iron bar. The light was in him, enraging him, giving him strength and a little courage, but below the berserker surface he was screaming in raw terror and revulsion.

Lewis saw people go down, stabbed, cut, beaten, bloody and torn, faces contorted in pain and fear. The fresh corpses twitched and convulsed and Lewis knew that they were changing allegiance.

And still Martin sang, up there in the pulpit, exposed.

Lights arced through the air, Lewis glanced up at them and saw the glint of glass tumbling over and over. The bottles shattered, flame erupted in the close-packed and swollen ranks of the Dead. The pressure eased for a moment and the congregation fell back, blindly crashing into one another, keeping their eyes on the enemy, hurling the fire bombs into the advancing mass.

Massacre threatened as the gun-armed Enforcers cut loose a ragged volley. Lewis heard shrieks and cries, saw people go down, crumpled, lifeless, but only for a few moments

There were newly reanimated Dead in the congregation's midst, lashing out at their own friends. That's when Lewis saw Bridget again, rushing at him as the last of the Molotovs erupted among the attackers and the Enforcers broke into a charge. The Living were pressed against the wall. People broke away to flee down the passageway, from where Lewis heard more firing and screams.

Bridget held a machete, her eyes locked with Lewis's.

Lewis brought the iron bar round in a furious lateral arc. His arm shuddered as the machete blade slammed down onto the bar, sparks flew. The blade slid off and they slammed into each other. Lewis fell to the right, hit a pillar, the impact bruising but probably his salvation because Bridget slipped on blood, In that moment Lewis was able to bounce back off the pillar and bring the bar round to slam into the side of her skull. The action was self-preservation, but the hate and rage dissipated as she went down, head ruined, brain and blood and torn flesh flailing.

The floor heaved and Lewis fell. He slithered over the slabs, among shafts of light, his body bucked and rocked by the floor's increasingly violent convulsions. Then Martin was flung backward out of the pulpit, a hole punched into his chest. The chanting stopped.

The Half Dead broke through and they met the Enforcer assault. Lewis saw them clutching candles. And almost as one, they self-immolated, charging through the oncoming ranks like fire ships against the armada.

Hillier grabbed him and yanked him back. "Get to The

Hill, the ghetto." Then he was gone.

Lewis found himself next to Marion, who was bleeding, barely able to stand and beating at Tommy who was now a scuttling, broken limbed Dead. Lewis coughed on smoke and the stench of burning flesh. He saw the fiery chaos of the Half-Dead attack, flare and fade within the Dead ranks, which quickly recovered and reformed. Scythers were among them now, pulling back like a great wave then hurling themselves at the Living once more.

There were familiar faces appearing among the enemy including the Reverend Jack Martin, howling from the pulpit, eyes wide, spewing drool and rage.

The floor bulged and stretched, distorted like the flanks of a balloon, then it shattered. Light gushed out. The Dead charged straight into it unable to stop. And something vast and terrible burst upward. Lewis saw Azazel's wings, and machineries once more. Dead dissolved under the sheer onslaught of noise and light and fury.

Then Azazel was gone, a brief flare of glory, a momentary glimpse of unutterable beauty and incomprehensible monstrousness, then silence, stillness and devastation. Dust hung in the air and fogged out detail, before settling like snow on the blood-wet floor of the church. There were no Dead, no scythers or Enforcers. No sign, even, of their remains.

Lewis sat on the debris-strewn slabs, his strength gone.

He became aware of the murmur of the surviving congregation and turned to see them, wandering aimlessly, or huddled into tight groups, all as shocked as he was. A few were making for the door, hoping, Lewis supposed, that the destruction wrought by Azazel had extended out onto the streets.

There was no sign or sound of further Dead attacks, so perhaps they were right. Even if the Dead came charging back into St Cyprian's, there was nothing Lewis could do to fight them. If he could get to his feet, he would join the slow bleed of stunned survivors outside and make for the ghettos, or as close to the ghettos as they could before the Dead hunted them down.

He felt tiny impacts on his head. When he looked up he saw that holes had been ripped into the church roof. The sky beyond boiled dark grey and it was raining.

A figure emerged from the dust fog, indistinct, then recognisable. Melissa. Lewis saw that her eyes were empty, her face ashen. For a moment he thought...Lewis grabbed his iron bar and struggled, dizzily, to his feet. Melissa stopped, frowned then blinked. Instinctively Lewis dropped the makeshift club, reached out and drew her to himself. She collapsed against him, and he crushed her tight. She said nothing, didn't cry, was completely, frighteningly silent.

"We have to get to The Hill," Lewis said, not that he knew what or where the Hill was. He said it because he didn't know what else to say.

"I know." Melissa answered. Her voice was small, hoarse.

She took Lewis' hand and led the way out through the burned and broken remains of the church doors. Others followed, there were more survivors outside, many of them milling around, aimlessly. Lewis guessed that any Resistance fighters had already slipped away.

The streets were quiet and empty. The hordes sent against St Cyprian's did not appear to be backed up by any reserves. A fact that puzzled and unnerved Lewis. Where was Reeder? Had he been destroyed in the church? Lewis couldn't recall seeing him there and surely he would have led from the front. He didn't strike Lewis as a coward.

Melissa, Lewis and a ragtag band of followers reached a silent, deserted Marylebone Road unhindered. That was when the sheer size of the city, the distance to be traversed, seeped into Lewis' consciousness. But what other choice did they have?

CHAPTER TEN

THE SEVEN

At least the air was warm, despite the rain and grey skies.

Lewis studied the group for the first time. As well as Melissa and himself, there were three others; Nick the ex-biker, a middle-aged woman with long, salt and pepper hair, the uniform of an ageing hippie and who called herself Indigo, and a woman who had introduced herself as Rachel Gold. They were dusty, smoke-stained and exhausted. All of them were battle-shocked. None of them had slept for two days.

The rain eased, leaving the air humid and close, and the road and pavements strewn with puddles and runnels of dirty-looking storm water. They walked. The road stretched out ahead, bordered on either side by huge buildings. No traffic, no Dead, no Living.

Melissa stopped and slumped against a wall. "Rest," she said. "A few minutes."

No one argued.

Indigo looked round nervously. "Where are they?"

"Perhaps Azazel frightened them off," Nick said. "I mean, he wiped out the whole Dead army didn't he?"

"I don't think so," Indigo said. "I think something's going on."

Lewis was inclined to agree with her and was relieved when Melissa got to her feet and suggested they move. He could feel watchers, from the windows around them, from the dark spaces between buildings.

Indigo tripped and stumbled. The incident was somehow more disturbing than it should have been. Lewis glanced round, distracted. He saw her bent double, hands on knees, hair hanging over her face. "My ankle." Her voice was a hiss of pain. "I've twisted my bloody ankle." She looked up. "You have to leave me, go on. I'll be okay. Please, leave me."

As he took a step towards her, meaning to help, Lewis saw more movement. Then figures poured from the same shadowed side-streets that had unsettled him a moment before. Enforcers.

Lewis struck out at the nearest of them with the iron bar, but the Enforcer was fast, dodging aside and slashing back at Lewis with a knife. Suddenly Lewis was in the church again, raging and destroying, hate-driven. The Enforcer stumbled back and Lewis brought the iron bar round to slashing its jagged end across its belly, which opened to pour writhing, thrashing entrails onto the pavement.

Lewis would die fighting. There was no question of the fact in his mind, no fear. He would die tearing the Dead apart. Fuck them, stencher bastards! He laughed. Once started the laughter was difficult to control. His opponent was coming at him again. Intestines slithered over Lewis's feet, entwined themselves around his leg.

Melissa appeared, colliding into Lewis's opponent, sending the two of them crashing onto the road.

Lewis saw her roll then dance onto her feet, breathing hard. Then something hit Lewis on the back of his head. The pain was sudden and shocking. Bewildered, he staggered back, his ears ringing, limbs weak. Things buzzed, louder and louder; in his ears, in his head. Lewis broke into a desperate run. He pushed himself on and on, gasping for breath until the buzzing drowned the whole world and every part of him gave way. The pavement rushed up to slam into his knees. He pitched forwards and waited for the dark.

There were Dead on the street now. As he lay on the wet tarmac, Lewis watched them move in. Shapes in the gathering grey, any sound they made lost in the roar and hum that ratcheted though his skull. They were angry and they were hungry. Lewis waited, his strength and will to fight were gone. So this was it. Odd that there was no longer any fear in him.

He stared at their faces, at the drool hanging from their lips, there was a woman, heavily made-up, hair suspiciously blonde. Jewellery glinted from her neck and wrists. There was a fair, lank-haired man, lips soft and plump and wet with saliva, there was a wasted teenager, his head caved in and out of shape and hairless on the injured side but long-haired on the other. Necrosis marbled his pale skin, his biker jacket was immaculate and new enough to creak as he moved.

Lewis saw the fire in their never-closed eyes, the energy, the *life* that burned there, the engine of their reanimation. The pain would be immense as they tore him apart with their teeth. He waited, time suspended, barely able to draw what he knew to be his last breath.

"Stop! Enough!"

The Dead stumbled to a halt, scattered across the road according to their position in the race. Some turned, others glared at Lewis, lips drawn back, growling softly. A gap was made as they cowered back to allow a figure to pass through them. The figure was tall, aged and neat. He walked with a stick.

"You might as well let them do the job for you, Reeder," Lewis said and marvelled first at his ability to form a coherent sentence, then at his own defiance.

"Oh come now," Reeder said as he crouched beside him and reached out to examine the back of Lewis's head. Pain lanced in through the numbness. "You'll live. The blow didn't even break the skin. You don't think I would let others do what I would so enjoy doing myself. He changed position and Lewis felt his hand on his shirt. There was a tearing sound, a tugging sensation.

"Ah," Reeder said, the utterance more breath than speech. "The Messiah. The vessel."

Enforcers appeared, and rolled him onto his belly.

"Careful," Reeder snapped. "Don't damage the child."

Lewis's arms were wrenched behind him and his wrists jammed together with a thin, skin-breaking cable tie. He caught a last glimpse of Reeder's immaculate, gleaming shoes before a hood was dragged over his head.

And then there was darkness, pushed close into his face. It clogged his nose and mouth, pressed at his eyes, muffled any sound, and all of it redolent with pain. But the worst dread of all, was the fear of not knowing...

...There were days of it, starting in his snow-covered front drive on the afternoon the Dead came. His name was shouted by a neighbour, who also knew his profession. The warning caused momentary confusion among the newly Dead, then a decision.

"He'll be needed alive."

But what about Caitlin? She's a doctor too? Please, Christ, please don't hurt her...

But she was not the right sort of doctor, not a doctor of vanity.

Bound, lying in the snow until the van came, its white metal interior the last thing Lewis saw for, days, weeks, months. There were others, dimly glimpsed shapes, huddled in the back, men, women, sobbing, pleading; slave labour, vitally skilled, fresh meat.

On arrival at whatever destination they had reached, the Dead blinded their prisoners with hoods. Then there were more journeys; vehicles, buildings, rooms, warehouses, Lewis couldn't tell, couldn't see. Cold hard floors under his knees, eternities of kneeling, of aching, agonising stillness, of stinking confinement, crushed in darkness with a thousand others. Food and water was lapped from bowls on the floor.

Lewis dreamed, perhaps sleeping, perhaps awake. Dreams that became nightmares that became hallucinations, a world in the dark, surreal terrifying, paradise, and hell. His stimulus-starved mind beginning to fragment. Then, suddenly, without warning...

The pub, the glass strewn floor under his knees, hood off but too many shadows and too much gloom for details, other than the presence of unnumbered Living, all bound and kneeling beside in front and behind him. Meagre rations, endless waiting, no speaking or moving, pain, then came Reeder, with his Stanley knife and the salty taste of blood...

Light.

Too much light, filled with images that were hard to comprehend. For a moment Lewis was convinced that he was back in the clinic, back in that first moment when they untied him and told him the place was his and offered him clean clothes and warmth and food and whatever else he wanted in return for their beauty.

Yes, Lewis had sobbed, any-fucking-thing, just no more darkness.

"Mister Lewis." The voice was male, friendly and charming. Lewis looked up from where he knelt on a spotless, stone-slab floor and saw a dining table, white-draped and laden with gleaming cutlery, spotless crockery, and candelabra. There were people, four men, two women, the former in black tie and evening jackets, the women splendid in black dresses and glinting jewellery. The men were square-jawed, handsome, smiling, the women, one blonde, the other dark, but both radiant and beautiful.

Lewis rubbed at tie-bruised wrists, and was helped to

131

his feet by a tall, distinguished looking man who may have been a waiter.

"Sir," he said. "Your place is laid."

Lewis let himself be led to a vacant chair, and sat down, dazed and as cautious as an animal. He stank, his clothes were dirty and his shirt torn open. Anna was plainly visible.

The fair-haired woman smiled and offered a hand across the table. Lewis shook it. The woman's grip was firm, the skin warm. "We've been waiting for you. We can start now," This last was directed at the waiter. "I'm absolutely famished." There was a general chorus of agreement.

There was a slight awkwardness, people on their best behaviour, over-polite, laughing too loud and showing too much interest in anything anyone said. This was familiar territory to Lewis, who had been to his share of stiff and difficult dinner parties in his time. And why didn't they notice his clothes, his beard, his filthy, matted hair? Their indifference to his bedraggled state, and to the embryonic child-shape clinging to his chest was dreamlike and unsettling.

Lewis became aware of his surroundings; pews, columns, a tomb, a vast, black-and-white, chess-board floor. This was another church. For someone who had barely set foot in a house of God since he was at school, Lewis had visited an awful lot of them in the last few days. This church was familiar, awe-inspiring. He realised it was St Paul's cathedral.

"Great place for a dinner party, don't you think?" said one of the men, who was tall, balding and younger than the others. "Quite surreal really. That was why we chose it."

"Oh come on, that's not the only reason," said the dark haired woman who was, Lewis had to admit, very attractive. Her cheekbones were high and pronounced, her eyes deep, dark, chocolate. She stared at Lewis, frankly and he saw a hint of desire.

"No, no of course not. These churches, you know," said the balding young man, "they're built on special ground. Not Hallowed ground, as priests would have us believe, but entrances, gateways, weak points between worlds, but then you know that already. The Reverend Jack Martin would have enlightened you. He did, didn't he?"

"Yes, he did."

There was, Lewis noticed, another empty seat.

"Oh that," said a portly man with a grey beard and silver, leonine hair. "Rather fell out with the woman I'm afraid. It upset us all, I can tell you."

Lewis nodded, compelled to speak by the innate good manners his father and his school had beaten into him. "It's difficult when you fall out with friends," he ventured.

"Absolutely," said the bald one.

The bearded man humphed his agreement.

Dark Hair lifted her glass. "To absent friends."

The toast was murmured enthusiastically. Lewis joined in because he was afraid not to.

The soup arrived, tomato and basil by the smell of it. Lewis tentatively spooned some into his mouth, and found it to be delicious. This was comfort food, winter night food. He fought to restrain an urge to shovel it down his throat. His hunger roared loud and demanded his attention. He managed to restrain it enough to spoon and sip until the bowl was empty.

"Good?" the blonde asked. She had a bright, open face, blue eyes that danced and sparkled.

"Mmm," Lewis nodded "Yes."

"So, Mister Lewis," the bearded one said. "You have something of a reputation."

"A good one I hope."

"Oh yes. You deserve it too, your work is incredible, people made as good as new, death and age forced back into the shadows."

"I don't feel my job is to fight death -"

"Well, you do," the man said, friendly, matter-of-fact. "Ah, the fish."

Trout mousse, a perfect shining mound garnished with a sprig of parsley. It tasted like heaven. Lewis felt his strength return. Despite his unease, he began to relax. Wine was poured, he drank thirstily. He noticed the others watching him. But there was no disapproval, only friendly, understanding smiles.

"Seems you've got yourself into a bit of trouble lately though," said another man, a handsome square-jawed devil who had not spoken before. "Forced on you from what I hear."

The wine glass stopped a few inches from his lips.

"I'd love to meet the child's mother," the bald man said.

"Yes," Square Jaw agreed, and there was a hint of something lascivious in his voice that Lewis did not like. "Do you know where the young lady is?"

"No, I...I don't know."

Square Jaw raised his craggy brows. "Don't know? How on earth could you misplace such a lovely creature?"

"She's a Dead..." Why was he telling them this? He should keep his mouth shut.

"Was the child involved in this trouble?"

"Yes...No, she's too young." He should shut up, he was babbling, confused by the fake politeness.

"Really? You are very careless, Mister Lewis, getting

yourself mixed up with bad people and fighting, especially when charged with nurturing someone as precious as Anna."

Dark Hair leaned into Lewis and held him with her soft, soft eyes. Her glistening red lips melted into soft smile. "Would you like to be with her mother, Robert?"

Lewis made to speak, but some voice, some shrill persistent warning, choked off the name. "I don't know."

"Such a shame," breathed Dark Hair. "Losing the one you love."

"Ah, main course," said the Beard.

Lewis saw no sign of the waiter, no trolley no silver-domed platter. Instead he heard the clank of a chain. Something dripped onto the gleaming white cloth. Dark fluid, gruel of some sort. It hissed and stank. Something bore down on them. Lewis glanced up and saw a huge, shapeless bulk, descending towards them, blood dripping like rain. Hooks were embedded into the thing's flanks, torn into its flesh. The thing struggled weakly, made deep, agonised mewling sounds.

Oh Christ...the Madam.

The pulley was released and her quivering, bloodied bulk allowed to crash onto the table which shuddered under the impact. Crockery, candelabra, were all smashed under the weight of her. Lewis scrambled to his feet, appalled, horrified by her ruined flesh, by the way her arms and legs had been hacked off down to bloody stumps.

"Is she safe?" the Madam breathed, the act of talking, a terrible agony. "Have you looked after her for me?"

Lewis dropped to his knees, strength gone.

"Not hungry?" said bald man. "Steak, rare, as much as you can eat, and you're not hungry." He shook his head and stabbed his meat knife into the Madam's flank. He sliced and hacked and finally tore off a dripping, quivering hunk of flesh, which he rammed into a mouth that was far too wide. He was suddenly wrenched into the air.

For a moment Lewis thought something had taken him, a giant snake, a worm, but then he saw that the long, sinuous limb was a tentacle, and it was part of him.

The bald man's dinner jacket split and folded in on itself, his head expanded, lost all its human features until it was a smooth, fleshy sphere, with only his mouth remaining. The mouth was covered with a thin membrane, just as the Madam's had been. Dark hair was next, soaring upward as her body lost definition and transformed. In seconds, all six diners were hanging over Lewis, like vile flowers on the end of glutinous, translucent stems. Each tentacle ended at a claw-like mass of roots that spread across the church floor and broke through the stone flags and into whatever lay beneath. Each one was almost identical to the quivering convulsing hulk of the Madam.

Lewis saw that one tentacle had been cut, and was a feebly writhing stump. The Madam's tentacle. She had been one of the Seven and these monsters were the remaining six.

"Give her to us." It was no longer possible to tell one diner from the other.

"No." Christ, Lewis didn't know how he managed to get the word out.

"You stole something, Lewis," said the voices. "Although you're not the first thief in the line. The Madam, as the treacherous bitch calls herself, was the first. Our Lord is not pleased."

Their Lord? Satan, Azazel's former master, and now enemy?

"But, unlike The Madam, you can atone, Lewis. You can make things right again. Caitlin belongs to our Lord. Therefore the child is his too."

"No...she's an unformed child, she doesn't belong to anyone -"

"Yes, she does." It was the waiter. He was unchanged, tall and elegant. He smiled coldly and crouched beside Lewis. He was assailed by the scent of the man's aftershave, which was almost clinical in its precise, scalpel-edged tang. He touched Lewis's face. Lewis flinched. "She is my vehicle," the waiter said. "The temple of my spirit."

My spirit? He knew this new claimant on Anna's flesh would not be Azazel. The waiter's fingers were still splayed over his cheek.

"Yes, my spirit."

Then there was pain as his fingers sank deep into Lewis's flesh.

The waiter poured into him and he was cold and dark, like a river of shadows. It was as if Lewis was drowning. He saw nothing but a swirl of foulness. At its core, pulsing, expanding with each beat, was something even darker.

Lewis felt himself rammed back towards the edge of the room that was his soul. Slammed against a door which must remain shut. A child cried from the other side, the sound fearful. Lewis couldn't breathe, his strength was failing, but he pushed back. Voices gibbered and raged at him. Whispered words into his ears that almost took the last of his strength.

In a distant place, his body shuddered and shook with a violence that threatened to dislocate joints and tear muscle. He had to push back, to keep the black, night-coloured wolf from the door, because that was what the dark thing was. It leapt from the core of the shadow, jaws wide, drooling and slavering. It claws, raked at him. Somehow, he grasped its forelegs and managed to fight back. The wolf-thing's fangs tore at his face. Flesh was sliced away and the agony of it was fire. He tasted his own blood.

On his knees, his head filled with the child's cries. The

wolf ripped and tore, and suddenly the pain and ruin was no longer important. The wolf leapt again. Lewis met it and the impact knocked them both sideways and he found himself on top of the beast. It bucked and thrashed under him and tore at him but he held on. Lay on its heaving, ice-cold carcass and howled out the last of his strength.

"Fuck you!"

He gasped for air, bewildered and disorientated. He was on his back, on the chess board floor of the cathedral, looking up into the vast curves of the dome. He was panting for breath. But not bleeding. He was whole. Alive. A face appeared in his field of vision. The waiter, who was angry, viciously so.

A vast, all-but imperceptible blackness shimmered about his outline, like a dark aura. It gave the impression that the waiter was merely a front, a mask worn by something too vast and terrible to comprehend. And trapped, like Azazel, in its own realm, able only to break through for a limited time, then snatched back.

"You are a stubborn cunt," the waiter hissed. "How dare you?"

The waiter slapped his face, the humiliating sting of it, somehow worse than the spiritual battle he had just endured. The face came close. The aftershave was gone. Replaced with the sweet-vile stink of dead tissue. "Don't think I admire that, because I don't. You show such disrespect that your flesh should be peeled from your body and fed to you, and your fucking bastard."

The waiter stood. Elegant, poised.

"Reeder," he snapped. "Break him. Then I'll come back for the child."

Lewis rolled over and struggled onto his hands and knees. He managed to stand, wavering, dizzy. He was not going to be on his belly or his knees in front of Reeder this time. He wondered at his own courage. Sadly, he could feel it running out fast.

He saw Reeder approach, flanked by a handful of Enforcers. The party was dwarfed by the Six who hung over them, each at the end of its arched tentacle. There was no sign of the waiter.

"You look tired," Reeder spoke in a conversational, almost concerned tone. "You need rest, sleep and comfort. Sadly, I can't give you the privilege of a quick Death, even though you deserve it." He paused, tapped the end of his stick against the floor, as if spiking imaginary litter. He concentrated on the task for a moment. Then said; "Even if you open that door, let our Lord in, give up the child. Even then you can't die, at least until the child has matured and can be separated from you. So, you are in an awful predicament, Robert. I'm glad I am not in your position."

Reeder struck the cane against the floor, hard this time. "Now, you lazy pigs. Hurry."

Living stumbled into the cathedral's chancel; mostly men, mumbling and groaning, not speaking. Lewis saw that their lips has been sewn together. The flesh about their mouths was puffy and blackened. They carried crowbars, and used them to lift slabs from the floor. Their work revealed darkness and a stench that brought on another fit of gagging and heaving from Lewis. He bent over, gasping for breath, but only tasted the foulness from the pit they had revealed.

A moment later the enforcers had him, his hands bound with ties again. They dragged him to the edge of the hole. Ropes were slung under his arms and secured at his chest. The chain gang were given the rope's free end. He saw them wind it about their wrists and arms, for improved grip, then he was thrown into the darkness. The pain was unspeakable as the rope tightened and took his weight. The rope cut into his armpits, bit flesh and crushed his chest.

The rope creaked as he was lowered me into the stinking, reeking hole.

A ladder was slid down beside him. Two Enforcers, followed by a half dozen or so of the Living slaves, used it to descend into the pit and wait for him at the bottom. The pit was about twenty feet deep. Black and lit only to grey by the light from above. It was full of coffins. Lewis heard cries, moans and screams, muffled, because they came from inside the boxes. Two of the Living began work on one of them, unbolting its lid.

CHAPTER ELEVEN

LOVERS AND ORPHANS

The darkness was complete. It was a physical force that bore in from every side. It tightened his lungs and sucked away his breath. He lay on his back, the coffin sides pressed hard against his arms, which were bound behind him and immovable. He was trapped, pinned in place. There was nothing but the dark, and the coffin sides, and the hard floor, and the lid, and the inability to move and see.

Panic rose, a huge black wave that swept through him and he began to scream for help. He shouted, demanded, pleaded to be released. Just for a moment, to see some light, to break open the complete and everlasting blackness. A moment in which to suck fresh air, move, stand, sit, walk, kneel, anything but lie there.

But it wouldn't happen. No one came.

Throat too raw for any more sound, Lewis subsided. He wasn't buried. He was in a box, and, unless it had been moved and dropped into a grave somewhere, there was no earth above his face. That would be too much. That would completely destroy whatever sanity he had left. No, they had forced him inside, sealed the lid, and then there was silence, no movement, nothing, which meant that it must still be on the floor of the vault beneath St Paul's. There was space around the box, other coffins, yes, but space between them and, somehow, that gave him a moment for relief.

His breathing slowed.

He let himself feel the pain in his wrists and shoulder. He had survived darkness and helplessness before. He had survived the hood and the ruined pub which had become Reeder's personal slaughterhouse. He had survived and been freed and been able to see light and to move again. So he would survive this one.

Unless they left him here. If they did, this would go on forever. When he eventually died of suffocation or thirst or starvation or a heart attack, his eyes would open again and he would still be in here. Here until the wood rotted away and the moon crumbled to dust and the sun turned to ash. And he would experience every single, eternal second.

No. He managed to stem the breech in his control, managed to steady his breathing again. And listen to the voices. A relentless background cacophony of maddened screams, gibbering, and sobs. The sounds of the other residents in this place. All locked away and forgotten in their coffins. Who were they? The Half Dead, Resistance fighters? Slowly the voices began to grind into his skull. Now he wanted them to stop. To shut the fuck *up*.

***

Someone was calling his name, mocking him, driving him crazy with its rhythm. "Robert, Robert, Robert," it went. On and on, a woman's voice that was too familiar to bear; that wouldn't go away.

A woman's voice that was suddenly an explosion of blinding light.

"Caitlin."

"Oh God, no." Her voice was different, gravelled, as if her mouth was filled with mud. Lewis could hear the beast in her, but he could also hear his lover and wife. "Robert, is that really you?"

"Yes," he answered.

"You sound close."

"Reeder's idea of a joke," Lewis said then cursed his

clumsiness. Suddenly he was talking with the woman he loved and thought gone for ever and he was uttering sarcasms. He tried again. "Are you all right?"

What a monumentally stupid question. Of course she was all right. She was fine, why wouldn't she be, locked in a coffin, eternally awake and aware? And Dead. Lewis groped for something better to say, something profound or comforting.

"How long have you been here?" he managed, which was as good as asking her if she came here often. Or was it that he wanted some reassurance that they were only here for a short while, that somehow, knowing this would make the ordeal easier? "I thought you had escaped."

"Almost. I almost made it." Her voice broke, then she seemed to recover. "Don't think about time, Robert, there's only now."

"Are you..." *What? Okay? Enjoying life? Making new friends? Settling in?*

"I'm still sane. I'm still Caitlin...."

"Be Caitlin," Lewis heard himself say and relished the new strength he found in helping her. "Hold onto her."

"Are you still a warm flesh bastard, Robert? Are you?"

Her sudden vehemence shattered his new found strength. "You are Caitlin," he ground out. "You are Caitlin."

"Fucking warm flesh."

"That's exactly what I am," he shouted back. "I'm still alive, Caitlin. I don't know why they haven't killed me."

"They have. This *is* your death Robert, slow and terrible, worse then you could ever have imagined for yourself."

"They haven't, not yet." Defiance was strangely invigorating. "*My* heart's still beating, Caitlin." Keep saying her name, drag her back to the surface.

A moment then Lewis heard another sound, Caitlin's voice but deeper, angry, a growling which increased into a rage of pain. Then it faded to a laboured panting.

"What's happening? Caitlin what's wrong?" No answer. "I'm sorry, I'm sorry that I made you unhappy on our last day. I was a shit. I still love you, I always will. I don't care what they've done to you, you're still *her*."

"Robert." She was back. Lewis almost wept at the sound of her torn voice. "I'm tired. I can't fight it for much longer."

"What is it? Tell me what you're fighting."

"It's like being a child, alone in a dark house. There's something in here with me and all I can do is lock myself in its empty rooms and hide and shout out of the window. Then it breaks down the door and I have to run again. The rooms are made of my memories and feelings. There aren't many of them left."

"What is it? What's chasing you?"

"No, you don't want to -"

"I do. I need to hear. I want to know and I want to hear *your* voice, Caitlin."

"Tell me about Anna. Is she safe?" Now Caitlin sounded animated, there was a desperation that Lewis had never heard in her voice before.

"Yes."

"Where is she? Is she in there with you?"

It took a while to answer. He was unsure whether she should know.

"Yes, she's here."

"She'll die."

"I'll look after her," he said, a vain promise. How could he look after anyone or anything in here?

"You can't."

Perhaps, Lewis thought, it would be better if Anna actually did die. She was not a child. She was a creature, her soul was a tiny spark. Surely she had no awareness. But would her death be final? Would she come back? A grotesque, parasitic thing that would feed on him and suck him dry?

Caitlin was crying now. The sound grew in intensity then collapsed into growling and raging. A battle, the bogeyman bounding through that shadowed house, slavering and hungry and wanting to tear her soul apart.

"Caitlin. Caitlin!"

Slowly, the rage subsided.

"Caitlin, what happened to you that day? What happened, tell me. Talk to me."

"You know what happened."

"I couldn't get back into the house," Lewis persisted. "I wanted to get to you but there were too many of them."

"I went upstairs to get dressed. But then someone pounded on the front door and I thought it was you. It sounded urgent, as if you were desperate to get in, so I ran down. There were three of them..."

One of them was wearing a police uniform, riot gear, you know, one of those big vests, Kevlar, that's it, he was wearing a Kevlar vest, but no helmet, and he had a knife.

It made no sense.

Because there was a hole in his forehead, a little black hole centred above his nose. The skin was charred where the bullet had burned into his flesh before smashing its way through his skull and into his brain. Caitlin knew it was a bullet wound because she had treated two gunshot patients, long ago as an exhausted and overworked junior A and E doctor. She knew also that the back of his skull was probably completely torn away and that he should be dead.

There was a moment, absurd in its way. The two of them close, face-to-face, staring but neither moving. Then the man made a grab for her and she stumbled back out of his reach. She spun round and tried to run, but he was fast. She felt an arm round her neck, was jerked back and off her feet. The two of them crashed into the big vase by the bottom of the stairs and fell to the floor in a waterfall of legs and arms and shattered ceramics. The destruction of the vase was awful, more awful somehow than the dead police constable now laying on her back and the icy cold blowing in through the front door and Robert's shouts and screams from outside. The vase was precious, and it was a physical, immutable fixture in her house. Now it was broken which meant that this was real.

She crawled, carried the Dead on her back and hauled both of them towards the stairs. He grabbed her hair and yanked her head back. She screamed and snarled and writhed. She kicked and rolled over and lashed out with her hands. Others appeared, help, salvation. But they took her ankles, her wrists and now she could barely move at all.

The police constable with the ruined head reappeared. He was swearing and his face was contorted into the rage of a beast. Spittle sprayed her face as he slammed the palm of his hand down onto her forehead. The floor slammed the back of her skull, a shocking, sudden pain, superseded almost immediately by a quick, deep sting across her throat.

The wound was unthinkable. She choked, tried to cough but everything was disconnected. Air rushed into her lungs, her neck and chest and shoulders were warm and wet. The world retreated from her, spiralled away.

The pain eased, and a red-tinged dark swept in. The dark promised peace and an end to fear. She let herself fall and welcomed it and for a moment it was good. She laughed, mocked her attackers as she fled away from them.

The dark didn't come.

Something had followed her. The encroaching dark was ripped apart. Energies tore through her like an electric shock. She felt her body lifted from the floor and twisted back on itself. She felt the invader's smothering presence flood into her.

And fought back. She held onto her self. She ground out her own name. She filled her mind with Robert, with their lovemaking, with the house, the snow, with the child she suddenly knew had begun to form within her. She pushed outwards, she held on.

Even when she was helped to her feet and followed the others out into the thickening, wind blasted snow, because her body couldn't help but follow. Even when she saw Robert, a hunched, figure being hauled away towards a waiting van. Even though she was naked but for her blood-stained cardigan which was now hanging from her arms and trailing on the white, hidden ground, naked but feeling no cold, feeling nothing.

She was a passenger, clinging to the wreckage, hanging on, unable to exert any control. She was an observer, but she was alive. And she was going to remain that way.

"We walked into London. I wasn't tired. We just kept walking and whenever we found any Living...We were hungry. I can't describe just how hungry. But it wasn't me, you have to understand that. I was waiting, gathering my strength. I didn't really understand that my body was dead.

"When we got to the city we broke into whatever buildings we could and rested and waited."

And were given food; animals, people, screaming helpless, screeching all-but insane human beings. Thrown

147

into the lobbies and lounges and concert halls and churches where the Dead were gathered. Some were bound and quickly overpowered, others able to run and fight, but always beaten down and torn apart and squabbled over and gorged on. The Dead were filthy and bloody and broken. The Dead were insatiable in all their appetites, were decaying, stinking beasts.

Caitlin survived. She hid, deep in the darkness that inhabited her body. It knew she was there but it was too primal too raw and hungry to hunt her down. She tasted flesh in her mouth, she felt the needs and let them in because she didn't know how to fight them.

High levels came, along with Reeder and his enforcers. The high levels wore good clothes, were clean, glossy and polished. What was inside them was fierce and powerful and cowed the darkness inside Caitlin. The hierarchies of Hell, it seemed, were enforced with more brutality and rigour than any dictatorship on earth could begin to attain to.

They stood, aloof as the sorting began, sheep from goats, wheat from chaff. The mangled and dismembered in one group, the drones and workers in another. And Caitlin, inspected like an animal then ordered to a small cluster formed in a far corner of the hotel lounge in which she had made her home. The group consisted of men and women, though mostly women. All below forty, not badly damaged and as physically good looking as it was possible for a corpse to be.

They were left until the others had been moved out to take up their roles in the new world order. The last group were taken upstairs to the hotel rooms and instructed to shower and attend to themselves as best they could. Caitlin did so and for the first time found herself relishing the physical again, the touch of warm water, the sloughing of dirt. Water flooded into the neck wound, filled her lungs but it didn't matter. She dressed in the hotel's complimentary dressing gown and waited as ordered.

"I was cleaned up and repaired by a Living surgeon named Fuller. I was given clothes, good clothes, the best, and a house in Kensington. I was a high class whore, a speciality for high level Dead who liked women with a spark of a Living soul in them. I was privileged. I had access to surgeons, I was able to authorise passes for them to visit me. I even had a Living servant. Jemma, that was her name. I treated her as well as I was able to. She was so traumatised she could barely speak."

And it was in that sumptuous, luxurious house that the war began.

Something else was growing inside Caitlin's body. A child, a cluster of Living cells, energised by the life currents coursing through her mother's Dead flesh, by the electricities of the unknowing invader and by the fierce glow of Caitlin's persistent self. The child was alive, she understood, because it was a repository for her soul. It didn't grow as an ordinary child, but stayed unformed, dormant and hidden. Nine months became two, then three years.

Caitlin began to fight for possession of her own body, clawing and tearing at the invader, pushing back the darkness until it was only the energy that gave her movement and physical life. It snapped at her heels, flooded her dreams, slithered back into the hidden spaces, slowly, regained lost territory.

"I took her back, you warm flesh fucker," Caitlin snarled. "And I've got her now, although there isn't much to see. Her body's rotting away, all that lovely red hair falling out, all that lovely pale creamy skin running to ruin. She can't afford a plastic surgeon anymore. Even if she could, he can't come here can he? So I've let herself go. You'd like to see that wouldn't you, Robert? Mmm? You'd like to see her now." There was a burst of laughter, soil-gruff, sodden with juices.

"Caitlin. Caitlin come back. Come on, please, come back."

"Fuck you, warm flesh...fuck you..." The thing began to growl then howl and roar, the wet snarling of a carnivore at bay. It went on and on. Then there was silence, followed by a small, small voice.

"Robert?"

"I'm here." Where else would he be? Because he couldn't move, because his neck burned with pain and he could barely endure the hot agony of turning his head once more. Reality came back, he wanted to roll over. He wanted to sit up, stand up –

"I'm here. Talk to me. What happened? You were pregnant? What did you do?"

Exhausted, she stood on a bridge and stared down at the night-splintered rush of the Thames as, all around her, the Dead made their noisome way towards the First House. She knew she couldn't jump and even if she did it would solve nothing, for her or the child.

So she choose another suicide. She closed her eyes and imagined her own soul being sucked out into the freezing night air. And as she imagined her own evaporation. The darkness rushed in and forced a howl from her throat, the animal noise the final expulsion of her.

Caitlin felt the invader drag her to her feet and throw her at the orgiastic maelstrom that lapped at the skirts of the First House. She was touched and she touched. She kissed and ate and swallowed and laughed. And screamed, inside.

When it was dawn, and she was lying on the roadside with other strewn survivors of the night, something shook her gently awake. When she opened her eyes she almost screamed in fright. The thing was all teeth and claws and long, coarse hair. It didn't speak but helped her to her feet with a gentleness that belied its brute alien appearance. It led her inside the First House, past the Living security guards who simply stepped aside and let them through, then along grand and elegant corridors, also strewn with spent and satiated Dead as the streets outside had been, and down to a chamber deep underneath.

Where she met the Madam.

"She warned me that Reeder was about to purge the Half-Dead because we were seen as a threat."

"And you...come closer, Caitlin, that's it, don't be afraid of me."

It was hard not to be, but Caitlin did as the Madam asked.

"Touch me, with your fingertips, please, you have to touch me."

Caitlin held back. She glanced at the creatures in the chamber. None of them were threatening her but she sensed that obedience was required down here. So she reached out and touched the soft, pulsing flesh of the Madam.

The darkness inside her erupted and splintered and squealed and shrieked. Caitlin was thrown backwards. She stumbled but retained her balance.

"You're pregnant," the Madam said. "And the child is Living. You have to care for the thing, look after it. A Living child born to a Dead is more important than you could ever know.."

"She sent me home, in the care of one of her creatures. Its name was Eve. She was there when the purge started, when the demons came."

Eve knew. She sensed their approach long before they were anywhere near the house.. She gave Caitlin time to send Jemma out with the letter to Lewis and to prepare the book, and its message for him. Then Caitlin heard the windows rattle in their frames, the door shudder. She looked out and saw debris and dust whipped into tornadoes by some freak wind. The dark in her hammered at her soul, she could feel the invader's terrors.

Good. Be frightened you fucker, she told it silently.

But when she saw the first of them, huge and scythe-handed, her own courage all but failed her. She rushed to the back of the house, in time to see another of them clambering over the wall, its huge feet crushing the overgrown, neglected garden, its eyes hungry.

Her body knew what she had to do long before her mind caught up. She was in the kitchen, she had a knife, its blade rusting because no cooking or chopping or carving ever took place here anymore. Half Dead as she was, Caitlin could find sustenance only in the charnel houses frequented by her kind.

She lay on the floor, stared at the ceiling. The dark tried to stop her. Eve grabbed at her, but the blade sliced down and without looking she sliced open her own belly. The stench was terrible, but there was no pain. No sensation whatsoever. Her body trembled as some form of shock tore through it. Eve reached inside the bloody mess and drew out the child.

Caitlin managed to weep. Enough of her remained to feel something resembling love for the limp, formless creature in Eve's hands. She reached out, took it and crushed it to her breasts.

"Anna," Caitlin whispered.

Then the front door burst open and Eve tore the child from Caitlin's arms and was gone.

"They tried to make me tell them what I had done and why, but torture doesn't work where pain doesn't exist." Caitlin paused. "I did all I could. I tried to save her. I have to let the dark in now Robert. And if it comes to you, let it in too, don't be a Half-Dead. Don't send yourself to Hell. I love you Robert. I...love..."

"No," Lewis shouted above her silence. "Caitlin, no. What if they let us out..."

She was gone. He knew she was gone. Whatever had hounded her through the house of her soul had won.

Christ, Caitlin was gone.

Lewis forced his eyes closed. What he couldn't see could not hurt him. And the press of the coffin walls, the pressure of its tightly screwed-down lid, the dark and increasingly stale air was replaced with an odd light. Suddenly he was back at the Christmas Ball at St Thomas's hospital where the women were beautiful while the men were portly and laughing, hazed with cigar smoke and mellow with beer, wine and port.

The woman caught his eye, cream-skinned, red-hair, green, green eyes. He stared at her and didn't know her name. Then she came to him, and he was terrified of her wry smile, of just how beautiful she was. She stood next to him at the bar and said that as he was never going to ask her for a dance, she would ask him instead, before giving up on him completely.

God, she was so light in his arms, so fragile and sweet-scented and gorgeous. Without thinking, without even knowing her name, he drew her to himself and held her close. Then she fell apart and bled and leaked and collapsed and he screamed and tried to put her together again.

He shrieked and pleaded into the close, muffled, physical dark of the coffin.

"Caitlin."

Nothing.

"Caitlin! Caitlin! *Caitlin!*"

Just the background wails and cries of the tormented. He tried to call her name again but his throat was tight against sound. Then there was another noise. Scratching which became pounding, impacts that shuddered through the coffin. Lewis cried out. The coffin shuddered and became an inferno of vibration and snapping and splintering. Then light.

CHAPTER TWELVE

LIVESTOCK

His rescuers were indistinct, shadow-laden, a fast moving dance of hands that clamped round his arms and dragged him free. He was hustled away, from his own coffin, from Caitlin's.

Not Caitlin anymore. Caitlin was too dead.

Lewis's wrists were still bound behind him. He didn't understand if he was a prisoner or being rescued. No one spoke, though there were growls and grunts enough for Lewis to understand that these people were probably Half-Dead. They carried battery operated torches that sent mist-softened beams skittering over the crypt's stone walls and low arched roof.

He couldn't tell where he was or how many of these people there were - a half dozen perhaps, less, more. They were movement and sound, glimpsed silhouettes in the restless torchlight.

The important thing was that he was able to move, and breathe, even though the air was dank and humid. The crypt became a tunnel, and though it was rough and cramped, it felt as good as a vast open space to him. He slipped and slid over the rough ground and noticed that stone block walls had been replaced with soil. Water dripped from the low roof, dirt fell. Lewis became aware of the millions of tons of rubble and masonry bearing down on him. There was no reinforcement, no props, nothing but the self-supporting earth that formed the sides, floor and roof of a seemingly endless passage.

They reached what looked to be a hole, chopped through a brick wall. Lewis's rescuers manhandled him through the gap and his feet met with a solid floor. As the others clambered through, their torchlight revealed an arch of algae-covered brick. When he saw the watercourse, Lewis realised that they were in the sewers. He was surprised at the lack of stench and when glimpsed in the dancing light, the apparent cleanliness of the water. Of course, there was no longer any sewage to speak of. The Dead didn't defecate, instead they absorbed everything they devoured. No waste. The sewers had become redundant, and rain had washed them out. The place still held lingering odours, but no doubt mild compared to the pre-Uprising perfumes that would have filled the place.

Although easier to negotiate than the earthen tunnel, the sewer was still a hazardous obstacle course of fallen bricks and broken concrete. The place was no longer maintained and rapidly falling into ruin.

The air was cold and damp. Patches of mist curled about the sewer's corners and floated above the water courses. At least Lewis hoped it was condensation and not some sort of gas. He was tired, his legs and arms ached. He wanted his hands to be freed but no one made any effort to free them. There was no choice but to trust his uncommunicative Half-Dead rescuers.

Two of them, at least, were women, one statuesque and possibly blonde, the other more elfin, and short-haired. They wore jeans, trousers, the elf buried in an outsized combat jacket of some sort, the taller woman, in a mouldering knee length cardigan. The rest of the group included a stocky, completely bald man in the remains of an evening suit, complete with bow tie.

Their silence could have been a security measure, it could equally have been the result of that inner struggle with the dark that Caitlin had described. Lewis guessed that they were physically degraded. It was possible that they could barely speak at all as a result of damaged vocal chords and other decay to their speech hardware.

Despite their own tirelessness, they stopped regularly so

that Lewis could rest and drink from a bottle of water held to his lips by the elf.

The journey became a trial. Lewis was cold now, shivering, ill. The damp air made it hard to breathe. When they reached another side tunnel, its entrance yet another hole smashed into the brick wall of the sewer, he needed to be lifted through. Once inside the rough-hewn, dank tube, he dropped to his knees and wanted nothing more than to stay there and be left alone. He was forced back to his feet by the realisation of what hung above him, more unsupported earth, and rats. A constant stream of them, scurrying through the torch beams, buffeting his legs, slithering over his feet.

The stink of mud and stale air twisted Lewis's already empty stomach, he was dizzy, sick. He wanted to stop and curl up and sleep, but he also wanted to forge on, to get out of the dark and away from the rats. As with the other tunnel, soil and filthy water continually dripped onto his head and down his neck. He could taste it, gritty and foul on his tongue.

Then finally there was light, other than the restless strobe of torch beams. Yellow-orange and straight ahead, it defined the end of the tunnel. A spark at first, then a tiny disc until it became everything Lewis lived for as it grew and he pushed himself towards it.

More hands were there to haul him through the hole. Something was wrong with those hands though. They were gloved, heavy. Too late to question, too late to fight back.

He slithered through and dropped, belly-down, on a rough concrete floor. Panting for breath he looked up. The lighting was harsh and bright. The walls were brick, the roof arched and low.

The figures looking down at him were Enforcers.

***

He sat, shivering, in the corner of a cage. He was not

alone, although at this moment, he didn't care about the others. Three of the walls were concrete, the floor covered with filthy straw. Through the bars of the fourth wall, Lewis could see more cages. He could tell that there were others on either side. The foetid air was torn with the moans of the damned, with howls and shrieks, peppered with short, fierce squabbles.

He was angry with himself. He had been duped, subjected to one of the oldest forms of torture in the canon; a glimmer of hope given, then snatched away and replaced by even darker despair and agony.

It was hot down here, a damp, close heat. He shivered because he was afraid. He kept himself apart, knees to his chest in an effort to protect the child.

The last remaining shred of Caitlin.

The one thing that stopped him being alone.

Everyone else was gone; Andy Campbell was truly dead, Melissa, Nick, Hillier, the only people he knew in this Hell-spawned fucking world. Alive, dead or Dead?

He looked up at the knot of humanity in the cage. Some stared back at him with eyes filled with raw animal terror, others with the vacancy of the mindless. All adult, thank God. There were no children in there.

No one asked him who he was. Some of his cellmates huddled together in the shadow-ridden corners of the cage and held private, murmured conversations. Others sat and rocked, or stood at the bars and screamed for release. The light was harsh, its white brutality painted shadows everywhere.

Lewis slid his hand into his soiled, filthy shirt and laid his palm on the child and was sure he detected the first knobs of a spine. Anna was warm and moved under his touch. He felt the tug of her roots, and though uncomfortable and even painful, was glad of it. He also felt half-formed thought, like a bright, beautiful flame that uncurled in his mind. Caitlin was in the flame, along with something tiny, yet strong. Lewis whispered the child's name. The flame flared brighter for an instant, then faded to a dull glimmer. But it was still there. Anna's proto-soul. Growing.

"What you got in there?"

Lewis looked up to see a tall, gaunt-faced and balding, middle-aged man. He wore the remains of a boiler suit. There was no threat in his voice. His accent was Polish, perhaps, or East European.

"Leave me alone."

"Of course, but we all need to be friendly in here. It helps. My name is Aron." He offered his big, workman-style hand. Wincing, his shoulder aching from his confinement in that coffin, Lewis accepted the gesture. It was good to shake hands and to feel some sort of living, human touch.

"It is easier for me than for the rest of them in here," Aron said. "I am dying, you understand, yes? Which is why I'm here. Cancer." He shrugged. "At least this way I won't come back. I am a train driver, for the London Underground. Well, I was, until the coughing started. I am not much good to them now."

Lewis felt a knot of dread form in his belly. "What did you mean, when you said that you won't come back?" He thought he knew the answer, but part of him was vainly hoping it was the wrong one.

Aron frowned, looked surprised. "You...You don't know what this place is? Maybe I shouldn't tell you, maybe it is better for you not to know."

"I want to know," Lewis said. "Where are we?"

"Down on the farm," Aron replied. "Doesn't look like a farm to me. There are no fields." He chuckled grimly. "Plenty of livestock though." He sighed, closed his eyes. "I just wish they would hurry and get it over with." The last word collapsed into a fit of coughing, which quickly became a violent hack.

Lewis felt his bowels liquefy. He had been expecting this ever since he was locked in the Harley Street compound, ever since he had understood the way of things. And now he could not grasp its reality, or comprehend his own fear. There was a numbness, a total loss of hope and energy. He felt as if he were already dead.

Aron's cough became increasingly violent.

"Shut the fuck up," someone snapped.

"Leave him alone!" Lewis shouted back, shocked by his own careless aggression.

The speaker rose to his feet. He was big, shaved head, tattoos that unfurled from his neck onto his cheeks, but unlike Nick the Biker, there was little intelligence, humour or compassion in this character's face. He was also younger than Nick

"You up for it then, you little tosser?" The giant chuckled and the sound was startlingly childlike.

"Sit down," Lewis said.

"Fuck you."

The giant was standing over him now, fists clenched. Lewis looked up at him. "Ignorant fucking pig," he said. The insult, and the reckless disregard for the obvious consequence of it, gave him a moment of crazed release. It was if he had been set free.

The giant seemed taken aback. He growled and snorted. Then recovered. By now Lewis was on his feet, his own hands clenched into unaccustomed fists, his breathing, fast and hard.

"That is enough, friend," Aron said. He sounded breathless and was still sitting, probably too weakened by his coughing fit to get up.

"You shut your fucking -"

"All right, go on, kill him," Aron said. "Then what? We will have a stencher in this cell with us. You can't kill a stencher, can you? But it can kill you."

The fact that the stenchers were going to kill them all anyway, did not appear to compute in the giant's mind. He hesitated. Then a revelation came to him. "I'm not going to kill him. Just shut his fucking mouth for him."

Lewis saw the blow forming, changes in the giant's expression, a slight tensing of muscles.

"Don't you dare hit him, you stupid oaf!"

The new voice was a slightly built man. That he had once been neat and dapper, was apparent, despite his beard and bedraggled hair and clothes.

"I know him," he said. "We fought together. That's right you idiot, the man you are about to beat up was one of the heroes of St Cyprian's." Why would these people know anything about the battle? It had only taken place a few hours before - a day at the most, and how many of them had already been locked-up in here, while it was going on, and unlikely to know what was happening in the outside world? "I don't recall seeing you there." The man continued. Astonishingly, the barb seemed to work. The giant's anger dissolved into confusion and something resembling shame, although his absence from the battle was undoubtedly not his fault. For most of its participants, involvement had been as much chance as design. "There's more," the man announced and swung round to address all the cage's occupants. "His name is Doctor Robert Lewis, he has the child and he is going to save us all."

Lewis tried to protest, but the babble of voices and questions drowned his protests. He was surrounded in an instant, by people demanding information, and how he was going to save them.

"I can't save you, I'm sorry. I don't know what he is

talking about, it doesn't work like that. Please leave me alone."

He sat down again, beside Aron, and slumped back against the wall. Someone tugged at his shirt, Lewis beat the hand away. "I said leave me alone!"

His rescuer managed to push to the front and force himself between Lewis and the others.

"You heard him, leave him alone. Please. That's enough. Everything will be explained in due course."

Astonishingly, the crowd quietened and moved back to their original spaces within the confines of the cage. "I know you're angry with me for telling them, about the child," the man said. "But they need hope, we all do, to endure this."

"I have no hope to offer anyone." Lewis said. "I'm sorry."

"At least, let me introduce myself." The man held out his hand. "Kingsley Whyte. I'm an actor, *was* an actor. I went on the run as soon as the Uprising broke out, and hid in the church." That was when Lewis noticed the threadbare blue armband. "It was the only thing that saved me. I don't think us theatricals count as Vitally Skilled." He paused, then said; "Show them the child."

"I can't. It's no one's bloody business -"

"Yeah, show us, come on. We have a right to see it," someone said.

Lewis instinctively wrapped his arms about himself and shrank back. But there were too many of them. The inmates pressed in once more and someone managed to rip open his shirt.

Silence fell again.

Until the giant spoke. "What the fuck is that?"

People recoiled. Others moved closer, staring. Someone

made to touch. Lewis slapped the hand away.

"You have all seen it. Now, piss off and leave us alone," Aron snapped. "And you." This to Whyte. "Thank you for helping, but keep your mouth shut in future, yes?"

The inmates seemed to lose interest. Most turned to shuffle away, many cast black, hostile looks towards Lewis. One woman, however, remained behind. She crouched in front of him, tears streaming down her face. "Please," she said. "Please help us."

A commotion outside the cage put a stop to the fight. Two, big, shaven-headed men in overalls appeared. One of them pushed a cart, the other scooped the cart's contents with a shovel and scattered it into the cage. The occupants went into a frenzy, as they scrabbled at the scraps littering the filthy floor. Bread, fruit, chicken thighs and wings. None of it looked appetising, or fresh.

Lewis's stomach rebelled at the sight and smell of it. The others fought over the food, then scuttled to their corners to eat. Some, like Whyte and Aron, held back until their hunger became too urgent to ignore.

This was a master class in dehumanisation. The feeders were Living, slaves no doubt, survivors. The lives of those crammed into these cages was worthless. They were meat, nothing more.

Lewis stood, to stretch his cramped legs. He was hungry, but could not bring himself to eat the slop that had been thrown to them. He knew that in the end, if he was in here long enough, he would be on his hands and knees, fighting for scraps with the rest of them. His own body would see to that.

"Hurry up and fucking do it!" he yelled and realised that he was clutching the bars of the cage. Further down the passageway, the two Living feeders, glanced back. Neither spoke. Their faces were haunted and empty.

"Robert, don't." He felt Aron's hand on his shoulder. "It

will happen when it happens."

***

At some point the lights went out, which meant presumably that it was night time. Real night, or fake night, part of some forced cycle like that foisted on battery hens. Whichever it was, the occupants of the cage settled into restless sleep, punctuated with moans and cries. Someone, a man, sobbed.

Exhausted, Lewis lay back on the straw, curled himself into a foetal position and tried to sleep.

"Comfortable?"

He started, lifted his head and saw Reeder, standing outside the bars. He wanted to tell the bastard to fuck off but even here, in the depths of despair, when nothing worse could happen to him, he was still too afraid to do so.

"You don't have to endure this Robert. You can walk away. Just accept what we offer. Give Anna to our Lord."

He tried "Fuck off." It had no impact, sounded weak in his own ears.

"No, I'm not going to do that. I want you to give in Robert. I want you to plead with me to let our Lord have the child."

"I'll die first, Reeder." Even speaking the words was an act of courage. And, no doubt, his last one.

"They will come for you in the morning. They will take you to the Savoy and you will scream in agony as the guests there rip you and the child apart with their teeth, while you are still living. It won't be quick, and it will be far from clean. Think on this Robert."

He walked away.

Lewis folded himself back into the straw. His teeth chattered. He was facing death now, real death, horrible death. This was his last night, his last few hours. He tried to comprehend what was going to happen; the pain, the sheer unutterable horror of being devoured by another being. Man's worst fear, someone had once told him.

He pissed himself, he couldn't stop it. He cried and moaned and tried to find Caitlin. He laid his palm on the child. Felt it stir.

"I'm scared," he whispered. "Caitlin...I'm going to die."

Don't be scared. I'm with you, I'm here. I can feel you Robert. I can feel you darling...

And that other life stirred.

Can you feel her?

He nodded, murmured yes.

I'll be with you tomorrow. I love you. I...

Darkness flooded in.

"Caitlin...Caitlin, please..."

She was gone. Never there. He was alone. Then the lights came on and it was morning.

***

He waited, hunched in the corner of the cage. The others were silent, either staring at him, or away from him as if he was a pariah. There was a tension in the cage. The air taut. Aron woke and coughed for a few minutes. When it was over, he didn't speak, but seemed lost within himself.

Lewis waited, every sound magnified and terrible as unseen and unknown time passed. He yearned for the Harley Street compound, and what now seemed like a sun-drenched, golden era of confinement. He had Campbell then, and Melissa, and those wild Saturday nights of orgiastic madness. He wanted it back. He did not want it to be *now*, he wanted to live.

He clenched his teeth against the panic, against the pain in his limbs, the rawness of his skin.

They came.

Five of them. Two were Enforcers, three of them were Living slaves, big, tough, shaven headed ones in stained and faded overalls. Two of them held baseball bats with nails protruding through the business end.

The door swung open. Lewis stood and tried to keep his head up. He clawed at his dignity, determined not to collapse into blubbering, desperate pleading. He looked the closest of the warders in the eye.

One of the Enforcers stepped into the cage, flamethrower levelled on the inmates. The other Enforcer stood in the doorway. The Living slaves came in.

Christ...

One of them grabbed Kingsley Whyte's arm, hauled him to his feet and shoved him towards the Enforcer at the entrance, who moved aside and indicated that Whyte should step outside. Whyte looked at Lewis and smiled bravely. "You will save us," he said, quietly and with courage Lewis could only marvel at. "I know you will." He went out with his head held theatrically high.

A second man was dragged from the cowering, huddled knot of inmates. He was lean, sullen, and ashen. He ran a shaky hand through his unruly mop of sandy hair and snarled a defiant *fuck you* at everyone concerned. The Enforcers made to grab his arm but he shrugged it off and walked out on his own terms. He was shaking though, close to breaking, but hiding it well.

My turn then, Lewis decided and stood, straight, teeth clenched, hands balled into fists. Blood roared in his head, his heart crashed painfully through its rhythms.

The Living caught his eye but turned away and selected a woman. It was the woman who had pleaded with him for help. She was in her late thirties, brown hair, hazel eyes. She almost collapsed. The Enforcers stepped in, held her up and all but threw her from the cage. The lean man caught and supported her. She looked back at Lewis, her face grim, determined. Tears cut white lines through the dirt on her cheeks. The Living slaves, and then the Enforcers backed out of the cage. The door clanged shut. And the party moved away.

Lewis collapsed onto his knees, trembling so violently he could barely breathe or move his arms and legs.

Another trick, another shock, to unnerve him and gain his cooperation.

Fuck you Reeder.

They had chosen Whyte and the woman deliberately. There was a camera in here, there had to be. They chose those whose selection would affect him. It would be Aron next. It would be all the people in this cage before Reeder tired of the game and they came for him.

He looked up at his fellow prisoners and saw their fear and desolation. Even the tattoo-ridden, giant was sitting with his face in his hands, shoulders shaking as he wept.

I will save you. Christ, I am going to save you or die trying.

He went to the bars of the cage and shouted. "If any of you stencher bastards are out there, get a message to Reeder. Tell him, I'm ready. I can't take anymore."

CHAPTER THIRTEEN

DESPERATION

"Fucking coward!" someone shouted from one of the other cages.

The voice was shockingly familiar, but before Lewis could work out who it belonged to, the whole place was in uproar. Everyone, it seemed, had decided to join in the abuse, with an outpouring of yells, screams and threats. His own cage-mates did their part, though tempered by an odd caution, as if no one wanted, or dared, to touch him. Perhaps it was because no one dared to touch Anna. Their voices beat at him. They pounded his ears and nerves, and sent the child part of him scurrying to a dark, safe place deep inside. Then someone spat at him. He flinched as a shower of spittle sprayed against the side of his face. He did not react, instead he bit down on the humiliation and held his peace. He must not make any enemies in here, or they were all lost. He tried to convince himself that it was not personal, but rather that the frightened, cowed prisoners had been given a scapegoat against which to unleash their tension and fear.

He gripped the bars, eyes closed, focussed on his plan. It was crazy and unworkable, but was all he had. It depended on the others in his cage reacting quickly to his actions. Lewis knew that he should forewarn them, so that they would know their part when the moment came, but he was convinced there was a camera in the cell. This had to be unexpected and shocking. Its purpose was to stimulate the others into revolt and breakout. Beyond that, Lewis had no idea what might happen next.

What he did know was that he was terrified.

Having Reeder here was vital, because it gave them a

hostage.

The problem, the gnawing, nerve shredding, mind-screaming fact, was that Lewis was no action man. Until the last few days, he had never even been in a fight. He might freeze. He might not be able to go through with it when the moment came.

And it was Reeder who was at the centre of his plan.

Christ, *Reeder*, his nightmare made flesh.

The din was dying down now. The inmates, exhausted by their sudden eruption of energy, slowly returned to their accustomed postures of demoralisation and despair.

Except one.

"You hear me, Lewis. You're a coward. I knew you were a fucking coward the first time I met you."

Hillier. The voice belonged to Hillier!

Which meant that the Resistance Fighter was a prisoner down here. Lewis ignored his insults and thanked God, even though he was no longer sure who, or what, that was. Hillier would be a huge asset when the proverbial hit the fan, provided any of them lived long enough to unlock the other cage doors

"You hear me Lewis?"

"Shut up," someone shouted.

"Fuck you" Hillier replied, then quietened, despite his defiance.

"Doctor Lewis?" It was Aron, who seemed to grow frailer and more ashen with every passing hour.

"Yes?"

"You are not a coward. Don't listen to them. You're doing what is best for the child, yes?"

"Thanks," Lewis said and he meant it.

Lewis turned his attention to the giant, who was glowering in his direction. He scowled, sniffed and rubbed his arms with huge, tattooed hands. He was the key. The giant would be Lewis's greatest ally, until they could set Hillier free.

Footsteps. Voices. Lewis once more grabbed the bars of the cage. His body was stiff with tension. He was exhausted by it, barely able to draw breath. The last of the noise in the cages died completely as three people appeared in the passageway between them. Two of them were Enforcers, flamethrowers in their fists. The third was Reeder.

He stopped at the cage door and peered in at Lewis. His expression was inscrutable. "You wanted to talk to me?"

"Yes, about the child, about..." Lewis made a show of looking around. "I can't talk here. I have an offer."

"*You* have an offer, to make to *me*?" Reeder seemed amused.

Lewis could feel the tension rise, energised by the hatred of his fellow prisoners.

"I want to talk to you," Lewis said.

"Then talk."

Lewis licked dry lips. "Not in here. I need to talk privately. They'll tear me, and the child, apart. I've already been threatened. Please." Lewis forced himself to hold Reeder's stare, to endure the scrutiny of whatever shared Reeder's flesh with his spirit.

This was not going to work -

"All right Robert, we shall talk." Reeder nodded to the Enforcer on his right. The Enforcer unlocked the door.

It swung open. The Enforcer stepped aside. Reeder paused in the open doorway. For a moment. A second. He raised his brows. *Well?*

Lewis tensed.

He couldn't. He could not *do this. He was finished.*

The moment was passing, the chance crumbling to dust.

Now! Fuck it, now!

He threw himself at Reeder. He saw the Commissioner's expression change, from smug to bafflement. Then Lewis had the Dead's jacket in his fist and, driven forward by his momentum, slammed him against the opposite cage. The impact jarred through them both. Lewis swung Reeder round, until his own back was to the cage, and oh how light Reeder was, what a fragile bag of bones.

"Idiot!" Reeder croaked. "You can't -"

"Fuck them! Kill the bastards! Kill them!" Lewis screamed, because something had burst inside him. A rage, a fury that took away his fear and made him crush Reeder's neck under his arm. He squeezed and squeezed, the sensation and expenditure of strength was oddly, horribly joyous. He felt something yield and collapse. Reeder groaned.

The Enforcers raised their weapons, but seemed uncertain, confused, obviously afraid to injure their leader.

It was working, it was bloody working!

The giant hurtled from the cage, the others streamed out in his wake and the Enforcers, were suddenly overwhelmed. Reeder snarled and began to thrash in Lewis's arms. He was strong, far beyond his age and build. Lewis wrestled to keep his grip on the Dead's throat.

Someone had found a key. Cage doors slammed open and more prisoners poured into the narrow passageway, milling aimlessly, clawing at each other in an effort to escape, but not knowing which way to run. The giant reappeared, now armed with a flame thrower, ripped off the remains of one of the Enforcers.

Reeder erupted into another fit of wild struggling. He became slippery, his broken body impossible to hold. Then he was free, and it was if he had flowed from Lewis's grip like sand. He spun round, Stanley knife in hand. Lewis stumbled back, dancing clumsily away from the tight sweeps of the blade. He fell, and saw Reeder hesitate, then launch himself at the confused rabble of escaped inmates.

Screams were added to the confusion. The giant appeared and grabbed Lewis's hand. Exhausted, shocked, Lewis allowed the thug to drag him through the chaos. There was no sign of Reeder, but Lewis saw someone on their hands and knees, deep slashes across their back. Another sat, staring at hands, bloodied by a wound that had stretched his mouth into both of his cheeks.

Reeder was nowhere to be seen.

"This way! Come on, Doc!" Hillier shouted. He was filthy and bedraggled. His eyes were wild, as if he had been driven half-mad by his ordeal. He beat his way through the press. Lewis followed. The giant was beside him, a self-appointed bodyguard

Footsteps, heavy. A roar and blast of heat.

Enforcers, bearing down on them from behind. Lewis didn't turn around.

The passageway ended at a wall. A hole had been broken through the brickwork, the hole by which Lewis had been brought into this hell. A knot of escapers were trying to claw their way through, jamming the exit in their panic. Hiller wrenched at the nearest of them and threw him aside, the jam cleared, there was a gap, Hillier scrambled through and disappeared. Trapped in the tangled surge of yelling, crying, shrieking prisoners, Lewis could do little but wait his turn. The giant tried to beat a path through but was hampered by the flamethrower and its fuel canister. What blows and kicks he managed to deliver, were rendered ineffective by the press. Aron appeared, as if washed up against Lewis by a wild sea. Now Lewis played body guard, grabbing the man's wrist and hanging on, even as the melee buffeted and tore at them, seeking to rip them apart.

The Enforcers were coming, Dear Christ, everything would be ended by a rush of awful heat. Any second now. Panic rising, Lewis renewed his efforts to get to the hole in the wall, no longer able to resist his headlong rush into raw desperation.

Then he saw in front of him, a disc of blackness, its edges ragged with broken and loose bricks.

Another roar, another wave of heat, and shrieks of pain this time. Smoke billowed, oily and scented with the stink of roasted flesh.

Aron had to go through first. Against very instinct, against every voice yammering in his head, Lewis pushed the man in front and shoved him into the gap. All the time yelling go, go go, as if the word itself would provide the motion and energy for the action. Aron scrambled and wriggled and was gone.

Lewis followed, and found himself crawling in mud. Only when his eyes turned the pitch-black to grey, did he comprehend that he could stand and run.

They ran along the earth tunnel, blundering through the dark, a disorganised, ragged stream of Living flesh. The stronger shoved the weak out of their way in the scramble for freedom, and distance between themselves and the Enforcers. Lewis kept Aron close, and the amorphous, shadowy form of Hillier in sight. The giant was right behind him, out of breath. What air there was down here, was thick, barely breathable and tasted of soil.

Shouts and screams, then the roar of flamethrowers and blasts of heat and smoke signalled the presence of the pursuing Enforcers in the tunnel. It wouldn't take them long to burn their way through the stragglers and catch up.

Lewis didn't know where the idea came from, but he knew it was the only way to buy them more time. He stopped. The giant blundered into his back and almost sent him sprawling. Immediately people began to protest that he was blocking their escape route, threats were made, but the presence of the giant discouraged their translation into actions.

"The roof!" Lewis yelled as people clawed their way past, buffeted him, and jammed him against the wall of the tunnel.

The giant frowned. "What?"

"We have to bring the roof down on them. Block the tunnel."

"How?"

"We use the flamethrower."

"It won't work," Aron shouted back at him. "It has no uh, push, no force."

"Are you sure?" Lewis asked.

"Yes, yes, of course I am sure. Unless...yes, yes, give it to me." Aron said.

The last of the escapers wriggled past. There was little space. Lewis began to doubt his own plan. The idea was dangerous, it might bring the whole tunnel down on them all.

"Nathan," Aron snapped at the giant. "There is only one way to make it work. And I have to carry it out, yes? I have bad cancer. It doesn't matter anymore to me. Hand over the flamethrower and go!" He collapsed into convulsive coughing. "Go on. I'm dying anyway. You must run. Fast. Now."

The Enforcers had to be close, moving steadily and

inexorably along the tunnel.

"Nathan," Lewis said and noticed that his voice was shaking. "Do as he says."

A moment, then Lewis heard the giant pass the flamethrower and its tank to Aron, who took them awkwardly; "Go, please, save yourselves."

Before Lewis could protest, Nathan had grabbed his arm and hauled him away. Lewis looked back. He saw a brief flare of light, of flame. Within that instant he saw Aron, right arm raised, holding the canister against the low earth roof, left hand gripping the flamethrower nozzle as it spewed fire at its own fuel tank. He also glimpsed the Enforcers, only a few metres beyond Aron, lit by the flame-thrower's brief glare.

All was frozen for less than a second.

The canister exploded. The detonation threw Lewis forward and a moment later he was engulfed in a searing tornado of smoke and dust. His ears rang, the world slanted. Great clods rained down on his head and his shoulders. He clawed himself to his feet and ran, sobbing out of fear of burial.

Led by Hillier, a ragged knot of escapers who had stayed together and not ran off into the black like terror-struck rabbits, finally scrambled out of the earth tunnel and into the redundant sewers. Here, the unrelenting darkness was alleviated by shafts of grey light from air vents and from gratings at street level. It was impossible to establish exactly how many prisoners had managed to escape. As they passed through the beams of light, Lewis caught glimpses of Hillier, the giant, Nathan, and a handful of other familiar faces from his own cage. Everyone was filthy with soil and smoke.

Hillier set a brutal pace. People were falling behind. His plan, which he explained as a series of barked orders, was to find a set of steps or a maintenance stairway to the surface. To Lewis, the plan seemed as vague as his own escape strategy had been. And God knew where they were or what they would find when they pushed open a manhole cover and stuck their heads out into the Deadside.

After the explosion, once Lewis and Nathan had caught up with him, Hillier had chuckled grimly and said; "I was wrong about you, Doc, you are a fucking hero."

"I was desperate." Despite his modesty, Lewis was surprisingly pleased with Hillier's grudging praise. The warm glow, however, was quickly dissipated by the grinding effort of their trek. Lewis was thirsty and weakened by hunger and shock.

In an effort to distract himself from his cravings, Lewis caught up with Hillier again and grabbed his arm. "What happened to Melissa? Did she...Did she get away?"

Hillier shrugged. "After they took you, we all ran like hell and scattered. That's the last I saw of anyone I knew. It didn't take long for the stenchers to chase me down. Those fuckers never run out of breath. And, no, Melissa wasn't in any of the cages back there, I'm certain of that. Maybe she made it out."

Or she could be a Dead, or burned by an Enforcer flame thrower, or on the run, lost and desperate. The thought drove panic into Lewis and he was surprised by its intensity. Yes, she had been a part of the close-knit, Harley Street family. A fixture in his life. But there was more, something deeper in his concern for her.

"Hillier, when I first met you, you spoke about free communities, out in the country."

"It's a rumour, they may not even exist."

"But you're going to try to find them?"

"Fuck knows," Hillier sounded agitated. "It's a fantasy, a dream, okay? So, don't count on it. We need to get to the ghetto and get the child to Azazel."

Lewis almost told Hillier that he had no intention of giving Anna to the angel, but he held his tongue.

He was lonely. He could trust no one. He could talk to no one.

"I was thinking of afterwards," Lewis lied.

There won't be an afterwards, he knew. Until the child was fully formed, he would be forced to carry both the child and the angel. Then, when Azazel was done with him, he would be discarded. What happened when an angel discarded you? He had already experienced the might of Azazel. There had been strength and power but precious little compassion.

The sewers were endless. There was no sign of a way out. Even though he knew that the water that could be heard running through the channels beside them, was filthy, Lewis wondered if thirst would eventually drive them all to drink it.

The air down here was hot and stale. The shafts of light through which they walked, tantalised them with the fact that there was fresh air and space only a few dozen feet above their heads, but was as unattainable as the moon. The brightness of the light meant that it was probably a cloudless, hot day. The Dead would be off the streets, taking refuge in shadow and coolness and waiting for twilight when they would emerge for their fleshly entertainments.

No more First House though.

Lewis wondered what had taken its place, if anything at all. Perhaps the destruction of the First House had brought an end to the Dead's pursuit of the carnal. Perhaps some sort of martial law had been established. The crushing of the Madam and the resulting violence must have changed everything.

A gentle, cool breeze wafted out of the darkness up ahead. Lewis relished the feel of it.

What breeze? There shouldn't be a breeze, not down here in the stagnant heat.

He felt it again. And this time there was a sound, a distant moan, from somewhere ahead. Lewis felt his heart stop.

"Did you hear that?" Hillier snapped. There was a note of panic in his voice. "We have to get out of these fucking tunnels."

Another moan. A fresh gust of air, cold, chilling Lewis to the bone.

"Fuck," Hillier uttered under his breath. "It's one of those bloody scythe-handed bastards."

"What are they?" Nathan had caught up. He was a different character now, more childlike, vulnerable even. And he was frightened.

"Something new and not very nice," Hillier said.

Lewis stopped. He saw a shaft of light illuminate the water ahead of them. "There's a side tunnel over there," he said.

"We might as well try it," Hillier said. "That scythe-hand bastard is in front of us somewhere, we might lose it down there."

And ourselves.

Shouting for everyone to follow him, Hillier ran into the water and the shaft of illumination. When he stopped to wave the others on, he looked for all the world like a performer in the spotlight.

Lewis sensed movement behind him, sharp, quick. Others must have seen it as well because some of the group froze, someone whimpered, someone uttered a prayer. Another gust of wind, stronger this time. But escape was blocked by a second shape, that scuttled in and out of view; silent, light-footed and too fast for detail or identification, other than the fact that the two creatures were human-sized. That made them too small to be Scythers, too fast to be Enforcers, but fast enough to be Dead. Lewis called out; "Who's there? Come on, who's bloody there?"

The escapers instinctively drew together, their combined unease palpable.

A third figure, ran up onto the wall, and crouched, spiderlike, in a shadowed niche in the mouldering brickwork. Lewis felt someone take his arm; a woman, sobbing. She sounded very young, the praying voice grew louder.

Then one of the creatures darted into the light and dropped into a crouch on the far edge of the channel. It opened its jaws wide in a cat-like snarl and displayed rows of needle teeth. Its body was long limbed, pale, almost human, its hair was coarse, long and black. Lewis recognised the thing.

It was one of the creatures, the Madam had called her sucklings. From his reaction, it didn't seem as if Hillier had ever seen the creatures, despite being part of the Madam's rebellion and working as security guard at the First House.

"It's okay," Lewis said. "They're on our side."

The other two creatures came out of the shadows to join the first. They did not look like allies. Instead, they snarled and tensed as if to attack. Perhaps, Lewis thought grimly, they had only been held back from their natural, feral state by the Madam herself. Now that she was gone...

Only one way to find out. Lewis gently removed the woman's hand from his arm and stepped forward. Facing the sucklings across the water, he pulled open the tattered wreck of his shirt.

CHAPTER FOURTEEN

DOWN STREET

The station's name, *Down Street*, was burned into the chipped and mouldy remains of its familiar white London Underground wall-tiles. Its long abandoned platform was lit by crudely wired electric lights and guarded by a handful of Resistance fighters, who supplied Lewis and the other escapers with water, then coffee and finally hot food. The coffee was poured into military-style, metal mugs and was black and strong. The food was the same unidentifiable broth and rough bread that had been served to the people taking refuge in St Cyprians.

A thousand years ago, or so it seemed to Lewis.

He sat against the curved wall, facing the rusting tracks and ignored the awkward questions scratching away at his mind. Where did the food and coffee actually come from? How could there be a Resistance stronghold right under the heart of the Deadside? If his memory served him correctly, Down Street was not far from Hyde Park Corner and had been the headquarters of the railway command during the war, then abandoned.

Questions could wait. He needed the moment, especially as he seemed to be suffering from some sort of reaction, delayed shock or something similar. He was wracked with tremors, nausea, and was exhausted. His mind a restless loop of questions, and bright, savage memories.

He was dimly aware that Hillier had identified himself immediately as a fighter and been absorbed into some mysterious Resistance business back in the depths of the station proper. Nathan had accompanied him and Lewis could only assume that the giant had volunteered to join their ranks.

The three sucklings, who had led the escapers here, were crouched at the far end of the platform, sleeping, watching, more feline than ever while at their ease.

"Doctor Lewis?"

He started and looked up to see an energetic, slight-built young man, who introduced himself as Li. He helped Lewis to his feet and guided him back through the station's eerily empty maze of passageways and frozen escalators to a dusty little room lit by an oil lamp and furnished with a handful of camp beds.

"Wait here."

Hands laced behind his head, Lewis stretched out on one of the beds and wondered, briefly, at how his perception of luxury had changed since the Uprising. He felt movement on his chest and pulled his hands free to check Anna, The child was restless. She calmed under his hand and Lewis felt light flare in his mind. Was that her awareness, sensed through some telepathic or neurological link between them, or was it her soul? In which case, the faster it grew and established residency in her tiny body, the harder it would be for Azazel to take full possession of her.

He murmured a wordless, calming sound. The child stilled.

Li returned and sat himself down on one of the other camp beds. He leaned his rifle against the wall and lit up a cigarette. "Smoke?" he offered. He was a lean, tough-looking Chinese man, with short cropped hair and the beginnings of a beard. Lewis realised that his own beard was fully formed now, beyond the itching stage but, like the rest of him, filthy.

"No, thanks."

"You're a sensible man," the fighter said. "You must be pretty important."

Not me. Lewis answered him silently, my child.

"Do you know what happens next?" Lewis asked.

"Me?" the fighter laughed. "They don't tell me anything. I'm just trying to get home. There are a lot of us trapped in the city after the big attack. Me and my unit couldn't get to St Cyprian's so we came here. Thank God for abandoned Underground stations. That attack was a waste of good lives if you ask me, I don't even know why we did it. We all knew the stenchers would wipe us out, but orders are orders eh?"

"You're right about that." Lewis said. He hoped his guilt at being the cause of the near-suicidal uprising, didn't show through the threadbare mask of his self-consciously rough-and-ready affirmation.

Lewis drained the last, cold, dregs of his coffee. "Maybe I will have a cigarette after all."

The two of them had been smoking long enough to be on first name terms, the fighter now knew Lewis as Robert, when the door of the room opened to admit two more Resistance fighters; one was Nick the biker. The other, Melissa.

Nick's smile was warm, his huge hand crushing in its welcome. "Glad you're still alive ,Doc," he growled.

Melissa held back. "Robert," she said. "Thank God..."

Lewis got to his feet and he held her tightly. Her hair was matted, her body frail and thin in his arms. "I thought you were...I don't know what I thought."

She pulled away, sniffed loudly then said. "We're getting out of here tomorrow, once it gets hot and the Dead go inside."

"How many of you are there?" Lewis asked. He felt oddly shy in her presence, as if his new and unexpected feelings had surfaced and tattooed themselves on his face.

"A dozen or so, about thirty with the people you brought, although a lot of those are in a poor state. Not exactly an army." She seemed nervous and Lewis wondered if she felt the same away he did.

Christ, I need to stop this. I'm acting like a 16 year-old.

Melissa glanced at Li and Nick. There was meaning in the look. "I want you to meet someone, Robert."

"Okay."

"I want you to listen to what he has to say."

Lewis shrugged. "Do I have a choice?"

"No," Nick said.

Puzzled, Lewis shrugged his compliance.

Melissa nodded to Li and Nick and the three of them left the room. A moment later, the visitor appeared.

"Christ," Lewis muttered and dropped back onto the bed.

"Hardly," said Reeder.

"Are you sending me back to St Paul's?" Lewis said and found himself oddly resigned to the possibility. "Does the torture go on?"

"No," Reeder said quietly. "I would not have gone to all this trouble just to put you back in that coffin." He was a mess, a filthy, bloody wreck. A flap of skin hung down the side of his face. One eye glared from raw, necrotic muscle and meat. "I was wounded in that explosion you engineered as I pursued you into these tunnels. My Enforcers recaptured most of the escaping cattle, by the way."

"Cattle? They are people, Living. Never call them cattle you bastard." The dynamic had changed. The fear dissolved the moment Lewis had Reeder's throat in his hands.

"Living no longer, I'm afraid. Those who were rounded-up were sent straight to the kitchens."

"What are you doing here, Reeder? Am I supposed to trust you? You put me into a coffin, for Christ's sake -"

"And I got you out."

"You..." Lewis slumped into himself, disorientated, confused, angry, and exhausted. "I can't even try to understand anymore," he said.

Reeder sat on the bed beside Lewis. His presence, the stink of him, no longer hidden by scents, turned Lewis's stomach.

"You've forgotten something about me. You've forgotten that I am also Half-Dead." He paused. "It was why the Seven used me, because they wanted enough of Reeder's soul to remain, to provide the spark for the work I had to do. But they misunderstood me Robert, as has everyone, the police, back in the before, and my own defence council."

"I bleed for you," Lewis said, unable to curb his hatred.

"Not a good offer to make to me," Reeder said and there was amusement in his voice. "But no one ever bled for me; not your compatriots in that ruined pub, nor those who died beside Melissa in her own side street in hell. Those who died in those and many other places, died for the rest of you, they died to feed and sustain you.

"And as for the others, those I took before the uprising, before I was caught and imprisoned, I was no psychopath, no serial killer driven by some deep malady of the mind or soul. I was a student at the feet of seekers and explorers, Crowley, Benvenuto Cellini, John Dee, Julius Evola. I consumed their works, subsumed their beliefs and communed with fallen angels. There were rituals to be followed, offerings to be made. I wanted to find the soul, Robert. I wanted to explore beyond the physical convolutions of the inner machinery. I was intrigued by the moment of death, I wanted to see it over and over again and I did, but it still made no sense, it is still a blurring rather than a crossing of a line. I became convinced that one began before the other was complete. I wanted to know how long the soul, call it what you will, lingered after the heart stopped beating and all response was gone. There was no unwholesome pleasure in my work. I was no torturer, as the press would have you believe. I inflicted terrible suffering, I'm aware of that, but it was in the interest of research, that's all."

"Fuck you, Reeder."

"You have a filthy tongue, Robert."

"As filthy as your hands." He could not hold back his contempt. "Are you trying to tell me you're on my side? That you're a member of the Resistance?"

"I'm a disciple of Azazel and his allies are my allies. Don't be so quick to judge, Mister Lewis. Where did all that Living skin come from which kept you in business and alive? Have you any concept of the suffering of those who donated that particular organ to your practice? Do you know how much of their flesh is carefully cut away before they are good only to be eaten alive? The Dead consider them to be delicacies by the way. So are *your* hands so clean?"

"No, they're not," Lewis said. "And that's what gives me the right to judge you, because we're the same, we're both cowards and traitors to our own kind."

"I was never enamoured of my own kind, as you called them, just as I'm not enamoured of the Dead, or the Seven, who I serve so faithfully. My loyalties are complex. The Seven rescued me from a prison cell, they allowed me to live, or a part of me at least. They have shown me, first hand, the hinterlands between life and death. Not intentionally of course, there is little subtlety or spiritual appreciation with the Seven. They were not sent to carry out this task because they are sensitive souls or brilliant minds. Hell, Pandemonium, the Devil, call it what you will, wanted ruthless military leaders to create and lead an army of minor demons against Azazel. That's what the Dead are, cannon fodder, an immense horde designed to keep the Great Angel at bay. There's a lot of trouble down there, Robert...Azazel commands the legions of fallen angels. He is a very powerful being. He wants to defect, and that would upset the balance of power considerably." Reeder snorted, scornful now. "The Seven were a bad choice. They even lost one of their own to Azazel. Appropriate I suppose since the Madam secreted herself at the heart of the biggest whorehouse in England.

"My treatment of her was terrible, but the illusion must be maintained."

"So you're a double agent."

Reeder chuckled, the sound disconcerting when it came from him. "Yes, yes I suppose I am. And because I'm Half-Dead, the Seven can't read my thoughts. I'm on your side and firmly so. But now, I have been found out, my cover is blown. I am a fugitive, like you and the others in this place. Ah, how the mighty have fallen, eh Robert? You need me."

"Need you?" The concept was a bad taste in Lewis's mouth.

"The Enforcers are mine. Now they are yours too. Though, sadly, most are being hunted down by the scythe hands. Don't weep for them, they feel nothing, they are blow-by's, constructed of what was broken after the Uprising, and the results of my own experiments in the bonds between flesh and soul. I'm offering you my personal bodyguard, those and any other Enforcers who can find their way to your side." He stood, abruptly. "In return, I want absolution. The Dead are foul and dirty. And doomed. Once Azazel is in this world they will be annihilated. It won't be shining beings with wings and flaming swords, Robert, it will be an apocalyptic unleashing of energies we simply cannot comprehend. The Dead will be gone in a moment. And our souls, the souls of the Half Dead will be free. Caitlin, she'll be free, gone to her rest, waiting for you Robert, up there, in heaven."

Lewis couldn't answer. He was consumed by Reeder's presence, crushed by it.

"So what do you want?" he asked at last. "I don't believe this is altruism."

"Once he has broken through and destroyed the Dead, Azazel will need to take flesh or his essence will wither and die in this dry and arid world. The shell he inhabits will become a figurehead, a messiah, an Angel incarnate. And a rallying point for the remnants of humanity as they pick themselves up and try to rebuild their world. In short, Robert, Azazel is waiting to rid you of that parasite clinging to your flesh."

***

"Do you see me as a traitor?" Melissa asked later.

"I don't know what I see." Lewis was halfway through his second mug of black, coffee, which Melissa had brought to him on Reeder's departure. Melissa sat, cross-legged on the floor. Lewis paced, tired, but unable to remain still.

"Like I said before, we have to trust him, we don't have much choice. We have to get to the ghettos. It's a long trek and we're not exactly an SAS battalion. So, not good odds. And Reeder let us go. I think he simply wants what he says he wants."

"A seat on the right hand of Azazel?"

Melissa was on her feet in a moment. Lewis found himself staring into her eyes, her hands on his face, holding him still. "Yeah, on the right hand of Azazel, which is a lot better than where we thought he was. It's why he didn't find Anna at the clinic. He knew she was there, he must have done."

"So why did he attack the church? That was one hell of a

risk, Anna could have been killed."

"He's playing a dangerous game and anyway, we agree he has no loyalties to the Living or the Dead, so what's a few hundred casualties to him? How many people has he murdered in his life, and in his death for that matter?" Melissa calmed. She released Lewis and sat down on the floor again. "I was captured an hour or so after they caught you. They trussed me up and hooded me and threw me into the back of a van, I think there were others from St Cyprian's. I was more terrified than the first time. I thought I would lose my sanity. Started crying and calling for my mum. I couldn't take anymore. I just wanted to die, *really* die.

"Then the van was attacked. The next thing I knew I was out and being dragged into a side street by a bunch of Half-Dead.

"Reeder let it happen. He arranged my escape, but it had to be convincing. I think the others were killed. I heard screaming." Her voice was hollow, dulled. She looked up and there was utter desolation carved into her face. "All to save me, Robert, so I can help get you to Azazel, which means that Anna is worth as many deaths as it takes." She broke down again and Lewis went to her. She collapsed against him and was warm in his arms.

***

Later, Lewis woke and found himself on one of the camp beds. Melissa was curled beside him, naked. She moved in his arms, a simple stirring, which aroused Lewis instantly. He nuzzled and kissed her hair. Then understood what had happened and also that there was someone in the room with them. He turned over, almost rolling out of the tiny bed and saw Li. The fighter was standing awkwardly in the doorway.

"We have to go now," he said, then left abruptly.

Lewis sat up, feeling hot and stale, his head ached.

"Time to move out," he said to Melissa, and found he couldn't turn to look at her.

"Okay." She sounded as awkward as Li had looked a moment ago.

They dressed in silence. Suddenly, Lewis wanted to clean himself up, to at least wash his face. He was sick of filth, of his own stink, but there were no facilities. Li returned about fifteen minutes later to deliver more broth and coffee.

"You all right?" Lewis asked Melissa as they ate.

"Mmm." She nodded. "What about you?"

"I... we needed comfort, we...ah bugger it, it was good."

"You don't have to say anymore, Robert, but you're right. It was good. I'm glad we did it."

"So am I."

"I know that Caitlin is still alive -"

"No, she isn't. There's no Caitlin anymore."

"I'm sorry, Robert." He felt her hand on his arm, and told her, about the coffin, about Caitlin's surrender.

"And us?" he said. "The whole bloody world has changed, which means that different rules apply."

Melissa nodded.

There had been other women for Lewis, in the Harley Street compound, but that was when he had believed Caitlin to be Dead. This was different. Wasn't it? Caitlin had let the darkness in. There could be no marriage anymore. What happened last night had happened and that was where it would have to stay for now.

***

Down Street station was a place of mouldering walls and

floors, of strange changes in air pressure and the ghost roar of Underground trains along the neighbouring Piccadilly Line, each proceeded by the hum of the transformers which powered the signals.

The Down Street group consisted of Lewis, Melissa, Hillier, Nick, Nathan, Li and six other Resistance fighters as well as fourteen escapers from the cages. The sucklings prowled at the rear. Their presence reassured Lewis.

Less reassuring were the dozen or so Enforcers, standing by the burn-scarred black woman who, it turned out, was named Katherine, and served as leader of the somewhat rag-tag Down Street Resistance group.

Reeder was making his own way north-west, towards the nearest of the ghettos. He considered himself to be too high a risk to travel with the rest.

"Very bloody magnanimous of him," Lewis had muttered, when he was told just before they set off.

Paint peeled from the metal stair rails. The ceilings and walls were blistered with mould and damp. At the top of the frozen escalator, there was a door. Li produced a key from his pocket and in a moment the door opened.

Li went through the exit first. He was gone for what seemed a very long time and when he reappeared he waved the others on. He looked shocked. When it was his turn to emerge onto the street outside, Lewis saw why.

CHAPTER FIFTEEN

SCAPEGOAT

It was early morning, the sun barely risen and not yet visible above the roof tops. The air was chilled but promised later warmth. The sky was a deep, clear blue.

The exit from Down Street Underground Station was an innocuous, heavy door set into the frontage of a large, brown-red building; unmistakable Underground Station architecture when viewed carefully, but camouflaged by the conversion of its frontage into a newsagents. The shop was abandoned. The Dead, it seemed, had no use for tabloids and broadsheets. These were glimpsed details, registered but unimportant. It was the street itself that sucked in most of Lewis' awareness. It was the sheer impossibility of what he saw there.

Down Street was full of Dead, on the pavements, in the road, scores of them.

His first reaction was panic. They were outnumbered, finished before they had even attempted a breakout.

Then he understood that all the Dead were motionless, all facing north, eyes open and fixed on some distant point, and apparently unaware of the Living party as they assembled in the lee of the station building.

"I walked right into the middle of them," Li said. "None of them saw me, or knew I was there."

"What the hell is going on?" Nick growled. "Do you think something's happened? Do you think they've gone?"

Lewis took "gone" to mean that the demonic force that energised the Dead had dissipated, that the invader had left.

Melissa shook her head, "I don't think so. Empty corpses don't stand up. And there's life in their eyes."

Before anyone could stop her, Melissa stepped off the pavement and into the road. Wanting to rush out after her yet too afraid to move, Lewis could only watch, and will her to come back safely.

Melissa moved cautiously between the scattered figures; men, women, children, old and young. No movement, no twitch, nothing. At ease Melissa stepped up close to one of them, an elderly man with a pronounced hump and not a scrap of hair left on his scalp or face. She stared into his eyes, made to touch him, but flinched back, as if unable to bring herself to actually make contact.

She straightened. "It's okay. They really are out of it."

Katherine led the way down the street, Melissa behind her then Lewis, Nick, and Nathan, who had acquired a rusty looking iron bar as a weapon and had adopted the grim, determined, though world-weary persona of the veteran soldier. The sucklings prowled along their flanks, the Enforcers guarded the rear. And all the time the wide-open eyes of the Dead followed them like the eyes of a thousand painted portraits, but not one of them moved. It was both bizarre and nerve-wracking, like moving through a forest of sleeping predators.

The party took a weaving path, negotiated almost on tip-toe because everyone was afraid of touching the Dead. Lewis wasn't sure if it was revulsion, or fear of waking them. Probably both. Their smell began to permeate the rapidly warming air, a stench Lewis had become accustomed to, but found hard to endure this morning.

The party emerged onto Park Lane and the full extent of Dead paralysis began to dawn on them. The road was as still and silent as the smaller streets had been, but so crowded that it was almost impossible to negotiate a contact-free path through the stinking, frozen crowds.

The Dead were not stiff in their inertia. Their arms hung loosely, their shoulders looked relaxed. There was life hidden away behind their eyes, or at least the demonic spark that passed for it. Lewis could feel their latent violence, as palpable as the heat-shimmer that glistened on the endless road stretched out between the Living and the ghettos.

Lewis was assailed by waves of panic. If the Dead awoke, this unnerving tableau would turn into a vast, raging, hungry mob. Survival would be counted in seconds.

Oxford Street looked to be impassable further down. Fortunately the park end Dead were more scattered, which allowed awkward, nervous progress. Lewis had not been to this part of town since the Uprising and was surprised by how unchanged it looked, even down to the motionless crowds of Dead who resembled a real-life photograph of a normal Oxford Street day. The shops were well-stocked with clothes, although whether they were the remains of pre-Uprising stock or there was some form of manufacturing in existence, he had no way of knowing. The styles were certainly pre-Uprising, the relentless shifts of fashion frozen on that violent, snow-grey Sunday afternoon. As it would be, Lewis knew, until this ended.

And it was going to end, in either a burst of glory from Azazel or the cataclysmic extinction of Living-kind The former apocalypse would, of course, mean the sacrifice of Anna to the great angel; the destruction of one, embryonic soul for the salvation of uncountable others. It was, it seemed, his duty to offer her up as a flesh-carriage for the saviour of the world.

He brought his attention back to Melissa. She had made no attempt at real communication since they had left the station. If he was honest with himself, Lewis was relieved about that at the moment. Sex was a line in the sand. Once crossed, it changed the personal universe almost as much as the Uprising had changed the external one. Their journey was perilous enough, without emotional hazards to clutter their progress. That familiar tension was there, however, as old as nature itself and not to be denied. Lewis could feel it in the heavy rhythm of his own labouring heart and taste it in his dry, dry mouth. He could also see it in the set of Melissa's shoulders and her careful avoidance of eye contact.

When they reached Baker Street, and began retracing the last journeys he and Melissa had made together, Lewis felt a pang of sweetly mournful nostalgia. That had been a moment when they could be at ease and talk and fight side-by-side, when the burgeoning sexual tension between them was not advanced enough to stifle their friendship. It had made each other's company not only bearable but pleasurable, even in the midst of the hell that had broken out around them.

It also meant that the ruins of St Cyprian's church were close by. Lewis fancied he could smell smoke beneath the ripe perfume of the Forest of Dead.

***

Marylebone Road again, which was as far as they had got last time, during the unsuccessful escape from the battle of St Cyprian's. This time it was far from deserted, but not a trap. This time it was awash with paralysed Dead.

"What scares me," Melissa said suddenly, the first person to speak since they had left Down Street. "Is that we don't have any Molotov cocktails. If they do wake up, we really are fucked."

The fighters all carried guns, but bullets, Lewis remembered, were of no consequence against the Dead.

"We can do them some damage," Nick said. "Punch a few holes in them before we go down." He seemed to almost relish the prospect of a heroic last stand. Lewis didn't answer. He wanted to keep walking, and remain utterly and ludicrously optimistic that nothing was going to happen.

"What about the Enforcers?" Nathan said, sounding a little reticent to put his head above the parapet. "They've got flame throwers, haven't they?"

"He's right," Katherine said and Nathan grinned, basking in the approbation of his leader.

"And you trust those fuckers?" Hillier, of course.

"I don't." It was the young girl who had hung onto Lewis's arm when the sucklings had made their appearance down in the sewers. "How do we know it isn't a trick?" She was a little wild-eyed. Her long brown hair was matted and unkempt. She moved close to Hillier. "Reeder is a murderer. He's on their side."

"She has a point," a pale, scrawny, hatchet-faced individual added. "Reeder killed..." He collapsed into a fit of coughing that doubled him over and quickly left him in the Living's wake. It was only when the Enforcers themselves caught up with him that he managed to jog back into the main body of the group, taking refuge beside Nathan, rubbing his mouth with his sleeve.

Katherine raised her arm and stopped the column. She turned to face them and spoke, clearly and without rancour. "We have to trust Reeder. He came to us with an offer. He's given us the only weapon that can help us if these...these things come back to life. If the Enforcers had been sent to kill us we'd be dead by now. If you can't bring yourself to walk with them, then you are free to go your own way."

A moment. A shuffling, awkwardness. Then Katherine resumed her steady, careful progress and the group followed. All of them.

***

The air warmed quickly, and as the temperature rose, so did the stink of the Dead, many of whom looked to be in a bad way. Necrosis disfigured virtually every one. Even high levels, denoted by black tie and cocktail dresses, were not immune from the physical realities of Dead-state. Things had changed, even before this mass paralysis. Civil war and the clampdowns rigorously enforced by the mercurial and oh-so-slippery Reeder, made vanity much less of a priority.

Something was being prepared. Something was about to be unleashed. The Dead could communicate on an almost telepathic, level. Theirs was a hive mind and at this moment, Lewis decided, the hive mind was thinking things through and coming up with a plan, waiting for the music to re-start the dance.

The Living group moved out of the shade of the imposing architecture that bordered Marylebone Road, and up onto the flyover. It arched over Edgeware Road and gave sight of Paddington Station to their left and a huge swathe of the western edge of central London to their right. Every street they could see was clogged with Dead. Not one of them moved. All faced north.

The further the Living moved onto the long, arching bridge, the more exposed Lewis felt. The road here was as crowded as the streets below. Halfway across Lewis wanted to hurry, to run even, knocking Dead out of the way as they went. Anything, just to get off the flyover and to where there were at least side streets and houses and places to hide. With a hundred metres to go, a breeze tugged at his hair and for a moment, Lewis was glad of its cooling touch. No, not cool - cold, icy. His relief dissolved into confusion. The air was hot, but he was shivering.

Christ, not now...

A sound, familiar, yet so distant it could have been his imagination. He caught up with Melissa and grabbed her arm. She spun round, surprise then annoyance on her face.

"Can you feel it?" Lewis said.

"What?"

"Scythers."

She glanced round. "Where?"

"I heard…"

She didn't believe him and neither did the others, who had all stopped, here, in the middle of an uncountable mass of Dead.

Lewis shook his head. "Okay, okay, let's keep going. Please, let's get off this flyover."

They moved on. Then Melissa shivered. "God, you're right." She began to shout, suddenly urgent. "Move, come on. Robert's right, there's something coming."

As if on cue, a loud moaning erupted from behind them. Lewis spun round and for a moment could see nothing. Then, on the far side of the flyover, he saw one, two, no, at least half a dozen scythers, weaving through the Dead. They brought with them a hurricane of icy wind that tugged at the Dead's clothing and at the remains of their hair

"Run," Katherine yelled.

Lewis glanced over his shoulder and saw Nick in the middle of the road, weapon raised; time, it seemed, for his heroic last stand. Then Katherine was screaming at him not to be so fucking stupid. Her voice was drowned by the loud, mechanical stutter of Nick's machine pistol. Chunks of flesh were torn from the nearer Dead, but the scythers kept coming. One of them stumbled as light erupted from its chest, but it didn't stop. Enraged by pain it hurtled towards them, mouth open in a cold-hurricane shriek.

The magazine ran out and the abrupt silence of his gun seemed to startle Nick into awareness of their situation. He swung round and began to run.

Lewis stumbled and his knees and palms slammed against the tarmac. There was a moment of pain which blotted out everything else, until he felt the cold blast of the scyther's vortex on his neck and twisted round to see them veering off and making for him.

Him.

Their attention was on *him*. The creatures were ignoring the others. They were an irritation, but not the problem. Instead they were bearing down on Robert Lewis. If he died then Anna would die and Azazel would be deprived of at least one stepping stone into this world.

A burst of liquid fire from the enforcers broke up the scythers' advance. Two of the creatures erupted into pillars of oily, malodorous flame. The others stumbled to a halt. The scyther-borne wind blew smoke across the flyover. Lewis felt the heat of their burning on his face. The enforcers had formed into a loose arc across the road, and were now fighting a rear-guard, giving the rest a chance to escape. Nick and Li grabbed Lewis's arms and hauled him to his feet then bundled him away to where Katherine, Melissa and Hillier knelt, ready to provide covering fire if the Enforcers were overwhelmed.

"Katherine," Lewis was almost too breathless to speak. "Katherine, listen, it's me they're after, not you. It's me, and Anna."

"Let's get off this bloody flyover," she said. "Come on!"

She led the way over the final stretch of the bridge. As he ran, Lewis looked back to see, glimpsed through the smoke, that the Enforcers' flamethrowers were beginning to fail, which meant they were running out of fuel.

The Living ran into the first side road they came to; a residential avenue, lined with rusting cars and unpruned trees. Li and Nick took up guard at the entrance to the street. Lewis noticed that there were very few Dead in this particular road. Perhaps a dozen, mostly older people, fixated, like the rest, on some invisible point far to the north.

"It's me they're after," Lewis repeated. The group were seated by a low wall, breathless and shaken. The sucklings waited nearby, inscrutable, a welcome presence. "If I could lead them away you could set up an ambush." He realised that he sounded braver than he felt. The idea ranked high with the other lunatic plans he had dreamed up over the last few days.

Katherine shook her head. "No, we have to stay together -"

"Then we'll all die. They want me. I'm the only one who can save Anna."

There was doubt on Katherine's face now.

"Hurry up," Nick shouted. "Those bastards are getting close."

"Shut up and just let me think."

"There isn't time to think," Lewis said. "And I'm not asking permission, I'm going to draw them away."

"Okay, okay," Katherine said, showing the first signs of impatience she had so far, managed to contain. "I saw a BP sign further up the main road. Lead them there. That's where we'll be. Got that?"

"Yes, okay, lead them to the petrol station."

"Hide in the toilet, we'll find you."

"The toilet, yeah." The scythers would certainly not follow him in there, especially if he slid the bolt to "engaged".

"Robert," Melissa said.

"What?"

She grabbed him and kissed his mouth. "Good luck." She sounded upset.

Before he could change his mind, or lose his nerve, Lewis spun round and ran back past a startled looking Nick and Li and out onto the main street. The scythers were frighteningly close now, the Enforcers, nowhere to be seen. Lewis pounded the road. Despite his tiredness, he actually felt fitter than he had for a long time.

Focussed on the BP sign ahead, he weaved in and out of the Dead, and the abandoned, silent cars. The air began to freeze, and fog with violently swirling debris. Which meant that at least one the creatures was close behind him. He was not going to outrun it in a straight line and he was growing tired.

He dodged to the left and stumbled into the stunted front garden of a grey-walled semi. Its door was open and Lewis burst in. He stopped long enough to slam it shut behind him then scampered down the hall toward the kitchen.

The hall was full of objects, paintings, pieces of china, clothes, all piled against the wall. In the few seconds it took to get to the kitchen, Lewis saw that the paintings were originals, still in their ornate frames. They looked as if they might have been stolen from one of the big galleries. The clutter wasn't junk, it was loot, gathered in response to the Deads' desires for what they saw as good living. Perhaps they had some currency in Dead society, or perhaps it was a jackdaw instinct.

Lewis crashed into the kitchen and found it dusty and unused. The Dead didn't eat at home. The Dead feasted on live meat at their fancy restaurants. They had no need for ovens, hobs and refrigerators.

Glass shattered. The sound emanated from what Lewis presumed to be the living room. He scrambled towards the patio doors. They were not locked, thank God. Lewis stumbled through into an overgrown lawn and garden, inhabited by a Dead woman, frozen like all her comrades, facing north and appearing to register nothing.

Lewis had made it to the fence when the scyther appeared, framed and bent almost double in the open patio doorway. Lewis leapt at the rough wood and clung to the top edge. The panel shuddered unnervingly and for a moment Lewis thought it was going to collapse under him. He hauled with his arms and scrabbled at the rough wood with his feet, driven by the proximity of the scyther which must have been close enough to hack off his leg.

He rolled awkwardly over the top, tearing himself and his already filthy and ratted clothes on slivers and nails. When he dropped into the overgrown service road beyond, his legs gave way and he was pitched forward into the dense plant life. The fence shuddered as the scyther's claw ripped through the panel, just above Lewis' back.

Sobbing with exertion and fear, Lewis launched himself down the narrow passage. The air was torn into a rage of icy wind. Shrubs, buddleia, that denizen of the wasteland, overhanging branches and brambles all slapped and tore at his hair, arms and face. But he kept going, driven by a raw terror more intense even than that he had experienced in the battle of St Cyprian's and in his coffin beneath St Paul's. It was the nature of the thing behind him, its sheer destructive energy, its utter, implacable need to destroy him.

Lewis burst out of the passage into a side street. He saw more Dead and, beyond them, a narrow glimpse of the A40. The sky was a merciless blue. The sun beat down and Lewis gagged on the stink it created. No time to think, there was a scyther behind him. And another, bounding up the side street. The first scyther was about to emerge from the service road behind him.

There was the entrance to another service road on the other side of the alley, a continuation of the one he had just run down. Lewis sprinted into it and was, once again, forcing himself through thorns and branches. He could only hope that what made progress difficult for him, would also make it difficult for his pursuers.

Battered, scratched and bleeding, he reached another side street, all but identical to the first. He turned right again and made an attempt at the main road. A loud crash. He looked back to see the first of the scythers emerge from the passage.

Then he collided with a Dead. It was a man, middle

aged, smartly dressed and in reasonable shape. Lewis hit the body hard and over it went. It smashed to the pavement with Lewis on top of it, to lie on its side, in much the same attitude as it had been when standing. Things gave way horribly under him, and a foul smelling fluid gushed from the Dead's mouth.

There was no time for revulsion though, a whirling fury of cold air announced the approach of the scythers. Lewis struggled to his feet and pushed himself on until he reached the A40. For a moment, he was disorientated then he saw the garage and without stopping to catch his breath, ran towards it. He weaved precariously through the Dead, not wanting another collision, unsure of what was going to happen once he reached to the petrol station.

He also wondered how much further he could push himself without collapsing.

A loud moan and a blast of freezing air drove him out into the road. His run becoming a stagger, and when he reached the far side he almost tripped over the pavement. There were cars and Dead scattered over the forecourt. Presumably Dead who had just driven in and helped themselves to fuel. As he stumbled, towards its entrance, Lewis saw that the shop was in disrepair, its door wide open and its windows broken. Inside was little better. Unsurprisingly, most of the food was gone. What was left was spilled and mouldering on the floor among the shards of shattered glass and discarded packaging. Lewis finally gave way to his exhaustion. He leaned forward, hands on knees, sucking in as much air as he could, but never seeming to get enough.

The debris about his feet was whipped up into a gritty, glass-bladed tornado. Lewis stumbled back, glancing up as he did so. Scythers, at least half a dozen of them had swarmed onto the forecourt. They stopped, looked round, reptilian in their movements, alert. One of them rushed at the shop's broken window.

Lewis watched its approach, transfixed, unable to move.

It was coming fast, jaws wide, slavering, tongue writhing as if trying to reach Lewis first. It skipped round a Dead woman in a fur coat, a small deviation, but enough. Lewis remembered Katherine's order. The toilet, he had to hide there. Now.

In the moment before he finally turned to run for his refuge, he saw fluid sprayed across the forecourt. There were rainbows speckled in the droplets. Its smell was dangerous. Some of it splashed the front of the shop and spattered the shelves nearest to the broken window. There were figures, running away from the petrol pumps. There was a flicker of light; a match, a cigarette lighter.

Then hell came to earth.

The scythers disappeared, the paralysed Dead vanished and all was flame and wave after wave of heat that slammed into the shop and drove Lewis onto his belly. He couldn't breathe. It was too hot. There was a horrible, poisonous smoke that gouged at his eyes and ripped at his throat. He remembered that you were supposed to stay near the floor. He crawled, dragging himself over the filthy, litter-strewn surface, knowing he had to get to the toilets, hoping he was headed in the right direction.

He bumped against a blank wall, felt it and realised that it was the frontage of the counter. He had to follow it round and he had to hurry, the smoke was growing denser, a heavy boiling cloud of it just above his head.

A gap. He slithered into it, snake-like now, coughing and gasping for something resembling air. A door. He pushed at it and it gave so he risked getting up into and lurched inside.

It was a toilet, ladies or gents, he didn't care. He lay down on the floor and huddled himself in a foetus curl. The place still smelled, faintly, of disinfectant but thankfully nothing worse. His relief was short-lived. Smoke began to slither into his throat through gaps and cracks under and around the door.

Coughing and gasping, unable to stay on the floor, he scrambled to his feet then up onto the toilet seat. The smoke was thick, dark and almost liquid in its density. It steadily filled the tiny room, rising towards him like water filling a submarine's airlock. Its perfume was terrible, clawing and tearing at Lewis's lungs, burning his eyes. There was a small window above Lewis's head and he began to fight with its latch. The thing was jammed; corroded, perhaps even locked. He slammed the unyielding glass with his fist then began to yell for help.

It was no use. He was trapped in there and finished. In a few moments the fumes would have him and he would join the ranks of the Dead. He would fight it, try hold on the way Caitlin had done.

The door rattled as something slammed into it. Again. There was shouting, coughing. The Dead, scythers...

Another impact and the door crashed inwards. Figures stumbled in. They grabbed him and he struggled. There was shouting and swearing and then a blow which smacked against the side of his head and stunned him. They dragged him out into the heat and smoke, but not into the shop. He was hauled the other way, through a storeroom then out via some back door. Out into air that was breathable, though still smoke-laden.

Somebody kissed him, breath as hot as the flames had been. He tasted terrors and felt Melissa's arms tight about him.

***

It took several minutes of shambolic running and walking to get fully clear of the smoke. A number of houses were also burning and hundreds of Dead, consumed where they stood. The stench of burned, necrotic flesh added to the general stink.

The party slowed and sat down on a low brick wall that divided the front garden of a terrace house from the edge of the A40. Lewis wondered how much harm the smoke had done to his lungs. The air was heavy with the scent of petrol. He closed his eyes and pushed his hand into his shirt to check on Anna. He felt her warmth, movement, the pulse of something that could have been a heart. And fingers, under a thin membrane, flexing, clawing his flesh. The sensation was not pleasant, and yet, at the same time, oddly comforting.

Again he felt the connection, the flare of light, within his own mind. Something else, a whisper, a stir of ill-formed thoughts and sensations. He let himself be drawn into the light. He felt warmth, security, the thud-thud of his own heart, and the echoes of the din and horrors of the last few moments. All had been absorbed into the evolving mind.

Lewis sighed wearily and drew his hand away.

He became aware that there were only three Enforcers remaining with them. He studied the silent, impassive creatures, hidden within their stained, smoke-blackened suits and black, impenetrable visors. Mindless or not, weariness was evident in their stance; heads slightly bowed, shoulders slumped, flamethrowers still in their fists, but seemingly unheeded.

The numbers of Living who had escaped with him from the cage seemed to have dwindled. Some had armed themselves with lengths of wood, iron bars and broken bottles. Most looked tired and shocked. The young brown-haired woman sat close to Hillier. The coughing man had gone. Lewis was dispirited by his own lack of concern or sadness at his disappearance and probable Death. The sucklings maintained their aloof stance, keeping their distance.

The position of the sun denoted afternoon and it was hot. Lewis wanted shade but was reluctant to leave the others. He sensed he was not the only one. There was comfort in numbers and in closeness. Nick produced a handful of bottles of water and some bread from his back pack and they ate and drank. Lewis gagged on the stink of the Dead, but managed to force the food down his throat. He had to eat; he was weak and dehydrated.

It was Li who saw it first. He stood, suddenly. He took a step into the road. The others were instantly alert.

"What is it?" Katherine said.

"They moved," Li said. "The Dead moved."

Lewis felt his strength give way.

Hallucination, trick of the light, the smoke –

Then they moved again and everyone saw it.

CHAPTER SIXTEEN

THE MARCH OF THE DEAD

It was their hands, flexing as if testing their strength, followed by a piano flutter of fingers, then still again.

Lewis stared at the others, who were as frozen as the Dead, with faces as ashen. Everyone seemed stunned, unable to think. Even Nick looked afraid. Lewis's own fear was a giant thing. There were thousands, millions, of Dead all around them. They were stretched to eternity in all directions. There was no escape from them, no sanctuary. He and the rest of the party would be ripped apart so quickly he doubted they even feel their own deaths.

The Dead moved again, in awful unison, a sharp jerk of their necks that lifted their faces skywards. They opened their mouths and the noise started. It was a drone, gurgling from ruined throats, low and unsettling. The volume increased. The sound pressed at Lewis's eardrums. It would be deafening very quickly.

Lewis knew what to do.

He grabbed Melissa's arm and wrenched her into motion. She cried out in shocked protest and struggled to free herself. Lewis ignored her. There was a van, a big Iveco, a few yards ahead of them, white, gleaming and once cared for. Its offside front door was open. As he drew closer, Lewis could see a set of keys dangling from the ignition. The Dead didn't care about security. Who was going to steal their cars? He let go of Melissa's arm and barged through the last of the Dead, desperation ripping away any concern about waking them. Almost there-

The Dead took a teetering awkward step. Some had deteriorated so badly they almost fell. A second step, stiff,

207

more like Hollywood zombies than the raging, hyperactive Dead Lewis had come to know. Then a shout, as loud as an explosion, loud enough to hurt his ears, as every Dead in London who could make a noise, yelled some guttural and incomprehensible word.

And they walked.

All heading in the same direction, together, the biggest army ever created. Silent again but for rustle of their clothes and their various footsteps; the click of heels, slap of trainers, beat of shoes and boots. None seemed to be aware of Lewis and the others, all their attention seemed focussed on their destination, which was north.

The ghettos.

Lewis was at the van. He scrambled into the driver's seat and reached for the keys, fumbling, awkward. The passenger door opened. Someone came in, Melissa...

Not Melissa.

But a stinking necrotic wreck of a woman. Her face was rotted. Bone showed through, her mouth, which was open and drooled juices and rot. Lewis screamed. The Dead grabbed his arm and shouted at him, though the ruin of her throat made her speech unintelligible. Lewis beat at her face and head with his fist. More Dead had turned from their pilgrimage and were hurrying towards the van. A slightly built, frail old man leapt onto the bonnet, face contorted, teeth bared.

A gun rattled and the old man was swept off his perch. The woman was jerked back, her destroyed face showing surprise before it disappeared out of the van and was replaced by Nick. He yelled at Lewis to start the fucking engine and get them out of there. Others were suddenly in the back, dragging the doors shut, out of breath and white-faced. Lewis saw Katherine lead the remainder towards a silver people carrier, abandoned at a forty-five degree angle on the side of the road ahead. Hillier was with her, along with half a dozen of the escapers, including the brown haired girl who had attached herself to him.

The Dead seemed to become aware of them. A few of the creatures broke away from the march to home in on the people carrier. Lewis willed the Living to hurry. Katherine had the driver's door open. Hillier covered her. His rifle flickered, chunks flew from the oncoming Dead. Not enough to stop them. They started to move faster, their old energies returning. Lewis flinched, afraid that a stray bullet would shatter the vans windscreen and possibly his own skull.

The first of the Living reached the people carrier. A moment of struggle, then the rear hatch swung open. Li, stationed himself by the car to help the escapers scramble inside. The sucklings ranged themselves about the vehicle and occasionally darted into the swirl of Dead to tear and slash with fangs and claws.

More Dead turned towards the vehicles and the world became a thunder of fists on metal. Lewis saw faces, pressed against the windows on either side, more of them tried to squirm onto the bonnet. Lewis scrabbled at the keys, twisted them and the van kangarooed; in gear, shit. He crashed it into neutral and tried again. A moment of engine turning then it fired and he revved hard. The fuel tank looked to be half full. Plenty of diesel, thank God. He rammed his foot hard down on the accelerator and the van leapt forward, careering through the Dead, knocking them aside. There were impacts and horrible bumps and crunching as they drove over the fallen.

The Dead turned towards them as they passed by, a moving island of turmoil in the sluggish, necrotic river. Some of them leapt at the van, drove fists and feet against its metalwork, but with no real effect. Lewis drove as fast as he could and quickly abandoned any attempt at avoiding the Dead. Instead he simply battered his way through. Nick was yelling and laughing.

"Fucking stenchers"

He tried to carve a path to the people carrier. The rear hatch was still open. Two, no three Living struggled towards the vehicle. The sucklings grappled with the Dead, but the sheer weight of numbers was overwhelming. The car lurched forwards. A Living tumbled, out of the back. The two others disappeared in a sea of Dead flesh. The people carrier almost broke free. Then it too was buried beneath a wave of Dead. Nick was yelling, Melissa screamed out her horror.

Lewis rammed the van forward again. He caught a glimpse of the car then saw a figure being hauled out, thrashing, then gone. Katherine. He was sure it had been Katherine. Then another figure, beating at the Dead around him. Firing bursts into their rotten bodies. Hillier, his hand about the girl's, dragging her behind him.

Lewis stopped. Nick yelled at him again to move, to go, go, *go!* He couldn't. He could not drive away from Hillier. The Resistance fighter fired again then using his gun as a club clawed his way towards the van.

Then there was fire, Dead flesh melting and disintegrating, and that terrible scream they made when they burned. The surviving enforcers appeared, carving a path through the Dead and giving Hillier and the girl enough time to throw themselves at the van. In the mirror, Lewis saw the door open. Then his own passengers were hauling at the pair, and fighting off Dead who also tried to get inside. Two of the enforcers appeared and clambered in.

Lewis slammed his foot to the floor. Above the howl of the engine he heard shouts and cries for the back of the van, then the hard slam of its door. The van suddenly broke free. But there were more Dead ahead of them, thick clusters blocked their way. Lewis swung right into some side street, where was able to drive round the Dead, relieved because the endless carnage had begun to sicken him. He relaxed a little. He was wet with sweat, from tension and from being shut in a van on such a hot day.

"Left," Melissa shouted. Lewis did so, racing into a street lined with shops. There was a pub, its windows smashed, its woodwork charred and broken.

Wipers on, which was almost funny. The view ahead was smeared. Things slithered and scuttled over the glass. Other fragments came into the car, through the heating grill. Nick swore and crushed them with his fist. It reminded Lewis of Andy Campbell, his theatre technician, dealing with the demon-fired detritus of their operations. He was surprised at how much grief the memory brought with it.

The road slowly cleared and the houses became derelict. Lewis realised that they had entered some sort of no man's land, a band of ruin that stood between the city and the ghettos. What puzzled him was why the Dead had not simply infiltrated this area. Surely there was nothing to stop them. Sheer weight of numbers would guarantee them success.

But they were heading this way now. Perhaps they had needed time to build their strength for the final assault. The Living who existed out here, on the other side of this firebreak, needed to be warned, to move out before the Dead arrived.

He accelerated, the need to get to the Living becoming urgent. Someone in the van shouted in protest. He had almost forgotten that there were others in there with him. He was driving too fast, the place was dangerous. Although the roads were no longer littered with Dead, they were covered in debris, glass, rubble, abandoned cars, all manner of furniture and items. Fierce fighting had taken place here, by the look of it, and looting, though whether by Living or Dead it was impossible to tell,

The wasteland of burned-out and wrecked houses tore a sudden grief out of Lewis. These were ordinary homes, the sanctuaries of countless ordinary people living whatever lives they could manage. The inhabitants of these places had been the living and breathing, fools and saints, the kind-hearted and the vicious. Complicated, struggling, neither good nor bad. None of them deserved the horror that had been inflicted on them by demons and angels and whoever the hell else was carving up the planet between them.

At least this was honest, he supposed. These monsters had been squabbling over their perceived rightful places in the universe since time began. In the past they had used the human race deceitfully. They had deluded them into believing that their causes were just enough to excuse murder, rape and destruction. Now they had come out of hiding and revealed themselves for the vile things they really were.

His anger kept him driving fast in defiance to Melissa's protest. His passengers were silent and he couldn't tell if it was from general shock or fear of his driving skills. He didn't care.

"Home, sweet home," Nick said quietly, opened the van door and climbed out.

There was a wall.

It sliced, at least twenty feet high, across Wembley High Street on the city side of the station. It was a muddle of brick and rubble, corrugated metal work, empty tin cans and iron spikes. All topped with coils of rusty razor and barbed wire. It ran up against fronts of what had once been shops. Lewis could only suppose that it continued on the other side of them.

He had stopped the van about a ten metres short of the barrier and now he waited while Li and Nick walked towards it. They were unarmed, hands above their heads.

Pink Floyd's music rattled incessantly through Lewis's head, an odd yet appropriate accompaniment to the obstacle in front of them. He had been indifferent to that particular band, but Caitlin had loved them. She had an incongruous affinity for all 1960s psychedelic music, despite not having been born when it was at its brief, surreal height. She claimed that the hard fist of protest and subversion hidden behind the soft-voiced surfaces of the music was its appeal. Unlike most of their counterparts, Pink Floyd had survived its journey to the heart of the sun and lived on into the next century. Their soft voice had gone, replaced by a world-weary bitterness that had no place in Lewis's self-contented little universe, not then, before the Uprising. He could never understand why anyone would want to be angered and depressed by music.

Suddenly, he understood what she had meant and how it fitted so perfectly with her character. Caitlin was warmth and love and intelligent kindness, but she was also tough, driven and a rebel against all foolishness and form. But this vivid flashback, this oneness with her, was unnerving, and he understood that it was because of Anna. Some part of Caitlin, some spark of her being, her soul, lived on in the child.

Melissa spoke. Lewis became aware that she was leaning over the passenger seat. "You did well."

"Thanks," Lewis said and realised that he meant it which was an odd juxtaposition; the nurse telling the great consultant surgeon that he had handled things well and the surgeon feeling a genuine gratitude for the praise that had nothing to do with ego.

"There can't be much time before the Dead get here," Melissa said. "God, we've only just made it."

"God? Where is He in all this?" Lewis said.

"Too big," Melissa answered. "I get the feeling that He is something far beyond anything that goes on here."

"So it's a skirmish between insects, is that it? Or are we pawns and bishops on his chess board?"

"Bitter."

"You've got it. Isn't it time He put in an appearance?"

"I think He's holding back to see if Azazel means what he says."

"Oh that's all right then. A world's been lost and a million, million people are Dead or about to die because of a little test God, or whatever it is, has set for one of His wayward minions."

"It's always been like that, Robert. Don't we do that for our own children? Let them make their mistakes so that they learn?"

"Yeah, but parents are always there to pick them up when they fall."

Lewis felt Melissa's hand on his shoulder and it felt like an invasion. He didn't shrug it off though. She did not deserve harsh treatment.

"I don't pretend to understand what is happening," Melissa said. "All I can do is try to make a little sense out of it."

"I know, I know. It's always been like this. There's no such thing as justice or fairness. I should know better. When I was a junior doctor, doing my stint in A&E, there was always the balance between the undeserving bastards who survived terrible injuries and near fatal illnesses, and the innocent little kids who died through no fault of their own. A smaller version of this I suppose. If I'm honest, though, I never thought about it much, just a passing uneasiness now and then. I even remember being proud of my skill in saving a convicted rapist from a near fatal heart attack when he was rushed into A&E from prison. Perhaps I should have let the fucker die."

"You couldn't do that," Melissa's hand was still on Lewis's shoulder. "I saw the care you put in, even with the Dead. You think you're a selfish bastard, but I don't think you are."

"That's nice -"

"Shut up, Robert. Bitterness won't help us right now. So, was offering yourself as a decoy to that scyther selfish? And fighting at St Cyprian's?"

"That was survival, the most selfish act of all."

"And this? You took on the child, you've fed her and nurtured her and it's almost killed you, but you did it because it means the end of the Dead."

Lewis didn't answer.

Then Nick was waving to them to come and hurry up about it. Figures had appeared atop the walls and a ladder was being lowered. Lewis was suddenly too tired to move, but the weight of the approaching Dead was enough to break through his inertia. Even so, the distance between the van and the unsatisfactory-looking ladder, which turned out to be two long, wooden ladders tied together with only an overlap of three rungs, seemed a very long way to travel. The sunlight was a brutal glare and the air suffocatingly hot. His head was aching and he needed both a cigarette and a drink. His hip flask was long empty and abandoned and as he began the precarious climb to the top of the wall, he became aware that he had given up both vices without much in the way of withdrawal symptoms.

There were four people on top of the wall, two women and two men, all in their thirties, thin, grubby-looking and wearing the pseudo-uniform of Resistance fighters. Beneath the grime, their faces were pale, drawn and underfed. They were obviously glad to see Nick. There was much hugging and back thumping.

One of the women, who introduced herself as Aafreen, seemed to be the leader of the group. She shook Lewis's hand and seemed near to tears.

"You're a doctor, yes?"

"I am. Look -"

"There are a lot of sick people here."

"I'll do what I can but there isn't much time."

"I know, the Dead are coming. Nick has told us. We have to fight."

"You can't," Lewis said. "It's all of them, there are too many."

"Someone has to make a stand. If we fall, the next circle will be attacked and the next and the next"

"You don't stand a chance," Melissa had moved in now. "Please listen, there are millions of them. They'll walk straight through your enclave. You have to pull out."

"Where do we go? Tell me that? Who will want us? We can barely feed ourselves. No other enclave will want to help us."

"Then get out of the city altogether," Lewis said.

Aafreen looked at him, and Lewis saw a disconnect in her eyes. Things were breaking inside this woman, the sheer weight of responsibility, the suffering and struggle were slowly pulling her apart.

"We have our orders and our duty," she said. She became matter-of-fact. "Shame we can't get that van in here. At least we'll use the fuel for Molotovs and anything we can prise off it for the barricade. Now, Doctor Lewis, I am aware of the child and how important you are. But we need your skills here."

***

There was little he could do for the sick. They were collected in the ground floor of what had once been a branch of Boots the chemist. The shelves and pharmacy still held some stock, most of it past their effectiveness or safe-to-use dates.

The make-shift hospital was, in fact, a hell of human suffering, flavoured with the stench of human disease and waste. A large number of the shivering, feverish victims were suffering from some bowel or intestinal disease, and it was contagious because he saw more and more cases with identical symptoms. There was a fishy smell pervading the stink, and from what he could see of the diarrhoea was watery and thin. "Rice water" faeces. When he stumbled out into the relatively fresh, but stifling air, he slumped down to the cracked, debris-strewn pavement and searched his memory for a name to the fit the symptoms. He already knew, but he wanted to be sure.

If he was right, the cause was obvious. The enclave, part of the Living ghetto, was a place of filth, poverty and desolation. The Living existed as one squabbling, desperate community, sleeping together in the derelict shops, filthy, unsanitary, but, oddly well-armed and in possession of food, from somewhere.

He told Nick first. The big fighter had seen Lewis and wandered over to hunker down beside him.

"It was always bad, but never like this," Nick said. "There's been an outbreak, and the aid has stopped coming."

"Aid?"

"From the next circle, they keep us armed and supply as much food as they can spare."

"It's cholera, Nick," Lewis said. "I'm sure of it. From the water probably, or an open sewer. It won't be hard to find its source. It doesn't have to be fatal but these people are weak from lack of food and general stress. On top of that they're badly dehydrated, which is the problem, it's the water that is killing them."

"Fuck. Is it contagious?"

"Not from person-to-person contact thank god."

"Something I suppose."

"The survivors have to get out."

"We're trying to make them see it, but Aefreen won't listen. She's so fucking stubborn." Nick sighed. "But then again, I understand what she's saying. The other ghettos and enclaves won't want us, especially if we've got some sort of plague."

"Then get them out into the countryside, out of London, anywhere but here."

"We'll keep trying." Nick indicated the hospital with a jerk of his head. "But what about them?"

Lewis swallowed and felt a stab of nausea he hoped was reaction and not symptom. "They're not going anywhere, we have to leave them. They're Dead already."

"Come on, the others need to hear what you just said to me."

"*We* should go," Melissa said.

"I'm staying," Nick said. "These are my friends."

"You can't. No one is going to survive unless we get the Doc to the next circle," Hillier said. "If it isn't too late already."

"I'm not fucking running anymore," Nick growled. "Aafreen needs me and I'm staying. You go, now, get out of here."

They were gathered in the relative cool of a small shop. Outside, the enclave seemed to have come to life, people were running. Despite their sorry condition, they were well-armed and supplied. Lewis saw drums being rolled towards the wall. Petrol, or some other flammable liquid he presumed.

As he watched and the argument raged around him, he saw someone stagger then collapse. It was a man, stick thin and long-haired. He vomited, his body wracked with violent spasms, then his arms gave way and he dropped into his own mess, shivering. Another fighter hurried over to him and began shouting. A moment later the body was burning. The stink of it snatched away Lewis's strength and he dropped to his knees, holding his belly, gasping for air.

Then all argument was academic because the ground, the building, the world was shaken by an explosion and the rattle of gunfire.

The Dead had arrived.

CHAPTER SEVENTEEN

HELL'S FIRST CIRCLE

Melissa, Hillier and Nick didn't hesitate and ran for the wall with the other fighters. Lewis prevaricated, unsure whether to return to the makeshift hospital or join the defenders. And what exactly could he do for the sick, other than try to defend them?

Resistance fighters were lined up on the top of the barricade like cavalry on the walls of a wild west fort. They were already shooting at what Lewis could only assume was the vanguard of the Dead. Not that bullets were of much use, but they could still do some damage.

In the end, Lewis joined in with the production of the inevitable Molotov cocktails. The work was hot and the petrol fumes brought on another wave of nausea. He could not see what was approaching from down here at ground level and that added to his panic. In his mind's eye he saw wave upon wave of Dead, shattered by bullets but walking inexorably towards the wall.

The smell of burning seeped into Lewis's consciousness. Smoke had begun to taint the air. There were more explosions, caused, presumably, the grenades the fighters were hurling down on the attackers. Then the first of the defenders fell, crashing down from the ramparts, blood spraying from his chest. The Resistance were not the only ones with guns.

Or explosives.

When it came, it hurled Lewis to the ground amid breaking bottles and spilled petrol. A gout of flame, smoke and debris erupted out of the top of the wall. Bodies were thrown outwards like broken toys.

As the smoke cleared, Lewis looked up and saw that the jumbled nature of the barricade meant that enough debris had fallen back into the breach as to make it still all but impassable. Another hit, another avalanche of debris and bodies. Lewis flinched, arm over his face. Dust and fragments of wood and brick pattered onto his head and shoulders. This time the wound was more effective. When he had recovered enough to peer through the swirling dust and smoke, Lewis saw a swarm of Dead clambering into the gap. Some clawed their way up onto the rampart, others slid down the rough inside flank of the wall. The rough surface tore their clothes and their flesh, but what was flesh to a Dead man?

Those that reached the street first were treated to Molotov cocktails and staggered back, screeching and writhing. More burned on the wall, but the sheer weight of numbers drove the defenders back. Lewis watched them come, unable to move or act, transfixed.

Fluid was poured over the Dead from the rampart as they surged through the gap. There was a bright flash and a wave of heat as petrol was lit and hundreds of Dead were engulfed in flame. More smoke boiled from the other side of the wall. Time gained.

As Lewis turned to run, the petrol spilled from the broken Molotovs sparked into life. Almost the entire street was on fire leaving only a small gap for the defenders to struggle through, coughing and gagging, and escape the wall. His own eyes streaming, Lewis tried to locate Melissa, Nick, Hillier or Nathan. He saw Aafreen, rallying her forces and drawing them back into a second defensive line. The fire wouldn't burn forever.

Lewis joined in the effort to drag furniture, boxes, pieces of wood and metal, even wrecked and long-abandoned cars across the road. More petrol drums were rolled into position and the work of filling cocktails began again. This group might lack the basics of life but they were well-armed, which was both a puzzle and unnerving. Why wasn't their supplier bringing them food and medical supplies along with the rifles, bullets and a seemingly inexhaustible supply of petrol, and wine bottles?

As the defenders took up their positions behind their hastily constructed second barricade, the first figures erupted from the smoke. Firing broke out, deafening, and adding cordite to the stink. Bullets tore at the Dead, ripping open wounds that released waterfalls of writhing vitals that carried on the advance and slithered towards the defenders.

Vulnerable to fire they might be, but the Dead carried some heavy weaponry of their own and tore at the barricades with bullets, grenades and then with something that looked like a bazooka.

Then the rest of the Dead appeared, many of them horribly familiar; fighters who had fallen, and now ran, shrieking, at their erstwhile comrades, before being forced back by a hail of Molotovs. Lewis saw many of the Living break down and weep, no doubt over some friend or lover, now Dead and immolated.

Lewis lit a Molotov of his own and hurled it towards the Dead. It was an awkward throw, but it was effective enough. The bottle smashed against the tarmac directly in front of the vanguard and doused them in liquid fire. Living began to rush forward from their positions to shorten the throwing distance. Most made it back but some fell, briefly, only to be burned themselves a moment later.

The smoke cleared for a moment and Lewis saw the nightmare. He wasn't the only one. He heard cries and sobs and screams. He saw Living lurch to their feet and run. The break had revealed the ruined wall and shown Dead pouring over the top, unstoppable and unending. Scrambling and laughing and howling, each wielding some weapon, or picking up lumps of rubble, and lengths of iron pipe and wood.

Aafreen leapt to her feet, weapon raised above her head.

She cried out for fighters to join her in what Lewis knew was to be a last suicidal charge. And despite knowing that it was a hopeless act of defiance, despite his anger at her for not getting her people out while there was still time, he found himself moved by Aafreen's courage and the courage of those who stood with her.

Nick was beside her, his last stand then, his chance to take as many stenchers to Hell with him as he could. Melissa, meanwhile, was also on her feet, helping Hillier and a shocked-looking Nathan to arrange a retreat, and screaming at Aafreen to pull back.

A few latched onto Melissa and followed her as she began to run down the street, away from the battle. Lewis scrambled to his feet but was unable to look away from the final act. He saw the Living break into a charge behind Aafreen and sweep into the oncoming horde. They hurled Molotovs and grenades, tore rents in the attackers, then crashed into the sea of Dead and were swallowed. There was a brief swirl of turbulence, fire and firing and that, Lewis supposed, must be glory.

But it was enough. A moment won.

Lewis grabbed the arm of a child who seemed frozen with fear and stood, lost in the chaos. He cried, tears cleaning the murk from his tiny, ashen face. There was something of the feral about the child, a blank canvas painted with the horrors he had witnessed. Lewis dragged him in his wake as he ran. He saw Melissa ahead, others streaming down the road. He didn't look back. Smoke boiled over and past him, laden with the stench of burning flesh, both Living and Dead. The world rang with gun fire and Lewis felt bullets crack through the air and slam into the road and into the walls around, ahead, and beside him.

He saw the makeshift hospital, and Dead running from its doors, the cholera victims, revitalised, hungry and raging.

They surged out into the fleeing Living. Shots were

fired, a Molotov burst. He saw someone go down, two Dead piled on top of him, struggling and screeching as they tore him apart.

A glimpse of Melissa again, turning, rifle raised and for a moment he thought she was going to lead a second insane charge at the foe. But it was a signal, a rallying call for the frightened and fleeing. She turned again and disappeared into the murk.

Lewis saw a snub-nosed weapon abandoned on the ground and scooped it up as he ran. He swung round and saw the last of the Dead rush out of the hospital. He squeezed the trigger and the weapon bucked and rattled deafeningly in his hands. Bullets sprayed in all directions but some found targets and tore flesh and bone. For a moment he experienced a grim exhilaration. There was something of the shoot-em-up computer game about the work.

But his efforts also drew their attention.

The child he had rescued was gone, then glimpsed, running ahead. The gun was empty. He held onto it, it would work just as well as a club. He ran again, through the thinning smoke down the street towards, what he saw was a second wall. The far boundary of the enclave. People were already scrambling up its flanks. Melissa was there, with a handful of surviving Resistance fighters that included Hillier and Nathan, the new recruit. They helped the children and the unarmed as they made their desperate, ungainly ascents. Lewis was startled to see sucklings there as well. Lewis set to work on yet another collection of oil drums, twisting off their tops and pushing them over to flood the road in a shimmering rainbow-covered film of petrol.

It was already lethal, one spark from the other fires, one hot, discarded bullet case and they would all die.

The Dead appeared, running shrieking and howling. Aafreen was at *their* head now, as fanatical in their cause, as she had been in the cause of the Living. As bullets thudded into the walls around him, Lewis wondered at his calmness. It would only take one hit, one white hot fragment of metal travelling at close to the speed of sound to kill him. And yet he was working the fuel cans without so much as flinching.

Jesus, how he had changed. How the whole universe must have changed.

"That's enough," Melissa screamed. "Go, go, Robert, now, for fuck's sake *go*."

Lewis leapt at the ladder and scrambled over the wall's jagged, brutal face, driven by absolute panic, a primal animal fear that lent him strength.

There were already Dead at the wall behind him.

A brief flare, then Melissa tossed a Molotov cocktail onto the street below.

The inferno was sudden and complete. Heat seared Lewis's back. He cried out convinced he must be burning too, but then he was at the top of the wall, before sliding and flailing down the other side. He hit the street heavily, rolled, and was kicked and tripped over by the panic-stricken rush of Living who had slithered to earth around him. Someone helped him up and he saw it was Melissa. Nathan was with her, smoke-smudged and shocked. His mouth worked but no words came.

There was nothing but smoke, and the shrieks of the agonised Dead. Hundreds must be burning but it was a pin prick in their numbers and no fire lasts forever. God knows how many more had breached the walls on either side of the shops and houses that lined the enclave. Then there were the others who had simply moved on past to the east and west of them, great stinking pincers of necrotic flesh, rampaging through no man's land and into other ghetto enclaves.

And all moving towards the mysterious second circle

that Aafreen had been so desperate to save.

They ran, walked, stumbled, then ran again. The group was loosely centred round Melissa but splintering failing, concerned with nothing but putting distance between themselves and the battlefield. Lewis focussed only on movement. He had to keep going, he mustn't look left or right, and certainly not over his shoulder. What is not seen can't hurt you, wasn't that the lie that had soothed his childhood fears and night-dreads? Close your eyes and you become invisible. He had done some insane things during the battle, had stood in a hailstorm of bullets, millimetres from death. There had been no thought at the time, no consideration or fear even, not then, but now it replayed through his head and shook him like a piece of rag.

So, don't look behind you. Don't *see* them.

He could feel them though, the Dead, moving in parallel with the Living survivors through the streets, clambering out of the fire and over the wall, running, mouths open, hungry and angry.

A young, stocky man stumbled and fell in front of Lewis. He began to vomit and convulse and Lewis wanted to help but he had no means. Even a mercy killing was no mercy.

The man was left behind.

It was evening, the air warm, the light dipping towards dusk. It would be dark soon. The worst time. Lewis was exhausted and needed to rest and knew he wasn't the only one. Rest was dangerous, however, because it would give the Dead time to gain ground, if not catch up completely.

But living flesh was not remorseless. Melissa finally ordered a halt and they dropped, gratefully, onto the overgrown front lawn of a derelict block of flats.

"We can't stop for long. We're not far from the second circle," she said. "We have to keep going tonight or they'll catch us."

Melissa remained standing, weapon in her hands. Strange, Lewis mused as he went over to her, how the pragmatic theatre nurse, wife, and mother of three, had transformed so quickly into a warrior.

"So what is this Second Circle?" Lewis asked her. "You've never mentioned it before."

"There wasn't any reason to."

"Is it just another enclave, is that it? The next stronghold to fall?"

"It's where we'll find safety."

"You know a hell of a lot, Melissa. I thought you were just a recruit who never got a chance to fight."

"I've never been there if that's what you mean. It's a Resistance legend, okay? A well-stocked stronghold the Dead can't overrun." She glanced round, as if checking for eavesdroppers. None of the thirty or so survivors remaining in Melissa's group looked to be in any fit state to eavesdrop on anything. "It's close to a Source, one of the ones under Azazel's control."

"Do you believe that?"

"I believe that it's close to a Source, but I don't believe it's invulnerable. It's probably just a network of big enclaves. But it's all we've got and it's where Hillier told me to go after St Cyprian's."

Lewis regarded her carefully for a moment. "Hillier seems to know a lot." Then he sighed. "We need to get moving."

Melissa nodded, then caught his arm. "Please, Robert, please trust Hillier. He's not your enemy, I want this to be over and you and Anna are our best chance."

Her hand moved to Lewis's face, but he flinched away. Something had broken between them. Their attempt at closeness had driven them apart.

Melissa was right about Anna, though. The reminder brought Lewis face-to-face with the reality of his mission again, forced him to consider what he had been denying since he began this journey.

A familiar gust of cold air slithered over Lewis's skin. Startled, he looked round. Again. A brush, a kiss then stronger. The unkempt shrubs that had once decorated the borders of the lawn stirred, rubbish was picked up and tumbled down the road.

"Scyther," he said. "Melissa -"

"Up, everyone up, *now.*"

Some didn't get up, some couldn't, and would have to be left. Hillier and a handful of other Living, those still armed and in a reasonable condition, moved to the rear as the group shambled back into life.

The winds were strong now; the scythers were close. There was a sound too; yells and shouts, a joyous, hungry cacophony. The Dead, in full voice and at full tilt. Lewis helped stragglers to their feet, urged them to run. Then he set off himself, back onto the straight, wide, tree-lined road. He glanced back and saw Hillier and the rest of the rear-guard trying to run and look back at the same time. The first of the scythers bounded into view and the air was sucked into a raging swirl of debris, and dust that scraped skin and peppered eyes.

Then, in the rapidly greying light, the rest of the horde swung into view.

Scythers first, bounding ahead of a dark, indistinct mass Lewis knew to be the Dead. The Dead were running, tireless, fast, howling with lust.

Hillier swung round and waited, weapon raised. Lewis shouted at him to run. He opened fire and the closest of the scythers went down, its chest and belly torn open. The Dead swarmed past and over the body and Lewis realised that running was useless.

But he kept running, kept hold of a last flickering hope.

He turned again, compelled by the nearness and sheer weight of the horde behind him. It was a wave, a wall of flesh. Rising behind the scythers, who, in turn, were rearing over the Living, slicing at them with their huge claws as they ran. Their kill-rhythm.

Lewis pushed himself on, grasping now for every second of life.

And the first shell tore the air and broke the world into pieces behind him.

The shock-wave threw him face down onto the road, which bucked and heaved under the impact of more missiles. Something was wrong, out of joint, and not just the sheer weight of firepower raining down around him.

Because, deafening as it was, the roar of high explosives could not blot out the clattering rhythms of a helicopter.

CHAPTER EIGHTEEN

THE SECOND CIRCLE

It was a shadowy bulk against the darkening sky, an ugly insect, lit up by the flicker of rocket trails as it unloaded its weapons. Spent, it swung away and swept northwards at rooftop height. As it did so, ground forces burst out of the gloom and through the exhausted, straggling knots of Living survivors, to douse the Dead front ranks with flamethrowers and grenades.

The newcomers wore uniforms and helmets. They looked professional and were efficient and effective. Another helicopter raced in and lit the newly fallen night with a second salvo of rockets. The dark dissolved into hellish orange. The din of the rocket strikes ripped away Lewis' hearing and breath, the world became a darkened chaos of heat, light and formless white roar.

Lewis struggled to his feet and stumbled away from the fight. More soldiers appeared in front of him, boots pounding on the road and pavement. Two of them broke away and came for him. Lewis saw Red Cross armbands as they moved in to support him and guide him to a waiting lorry. He was helped into the back, confused by their care and concern, by the fact that he didn't have to scramble and struggle but that people were lifting him and helping. People were encouraging him.

He found himself among the Living from the enclave. He saw Nathan.

"Where's Melissa?" Lewis asked him.

Nathan didn't know, and neither did anyone else.

The lorry groaned into life and the fire and pulses of war

receded quickly.

There were too many Living. The sheer numbers of breathing, warm-fleshed human beings overwhelmed him. He wasn't sure where they had taken him. The view through the back opening of the lorry had been of endless, abandoned streets, with nothing to orientate by. There was a wall, a huge concrete thing, not a ramshackle barricade this one. It was topped by barbed wire, the gates were steel. There were guards, searchlights. Business, activity, soldiers, weapons. Then something that resembled a village, a steep hill, a cluster of venerable looking buildings.

***

There was a bed in a dormitory of some kind, on which a neatly folded set of clothes had been placed. There was also a shower. Lewis immersed himself under the hot water for a million years. He couldn't leave it, but simply stood, head bowed, as the warmth seeped into his flesh and down towards his soul. Finally, however, he forced himself out.

The Anna had changed. The primal arms and legs were more fully formed, the head, though her face was still buried in his chest, was recognisably human. The child moved constantly with a lizard-like crawling motion. Lewis could see a spine, veins delicately webbing the thin flesh. She was losing her translucence.

The clothes consisted of camouflaged combat trousers and a khaki tee shirt which, he was surprised and childishly pleased to note, was actually filled out in all the right places, when he pulled it on. The fugitive life obviously suited him more than the medic's life he had led before the uprising.

Anna, however, was clearly visible through the tight-stretched cotton.

Despite this, the military cut of the clothes made him self-conscious. He was not a soldier and felt like an imposter. Especially since he now sported long hair and a beard.

Lewis lay down on his bed. The soft mattress and sheer luxury of rest was almost too much to bear, but not so much so that he would contemplate laying on the floor for old time's sake. Nathan and Hillier had also been assigned beds in the room. The young woman, Hillier's devoted companion was also there, and a handful of other assorted survivors of the ill-fated Wembley enclave and the live meat cages.

"Where the fuck are we?" Nathan grunted as everyone settled down for the night, most silent and too disoriented for conversation.

"Somewhere you've never been to in your life," Hillier answered and chuckled gruffly. "Harrow School."

"What's that?"

"It's where Sir Winston Churchill learned to read and write."

"Oh."

So now Lewis knew as well. The Second Circle, as Melissa had called it, seemed to be some sort of ring of steel around the edges of the city. Which meant that there was ample personnel, equipment and supplies. So how could this be? Did it mean that the Dead had not penetrated outside London? Was it the same for all the other cities in the country, in the world even?

The school appeared to be the headquarters of the Second Circle. The regiment or battalion certainly wasn't another desperate Resistance cell. They had chosen a good position for their base. Harrow-on-the-Hill, The "Hill", being one of the highest points in London. Easy to defend, Lewis supposed.

He forced his eyes shut, but he was too worried about Melissa. He had not seen her since the Second Circle's counter-attack on the Dead. His mind was alive with imaginings of her death, her resurrection and fiery destruction.

It couldn't be. It wasn't possible for her to be gone.

The battle was not over. The thud and crackle of the distant fire-fight could be heard through the open window. The dark flickered and flashed in sync with the explosions. The Dead were taking a terrible battering but they would keep on coming and eventually they would break through.

Lewis tried to recall the pre-Uprising population of London; six or seven million if he remembered correctly. An unstoppable number.

He closed his eyes, but knew he wouldn't be able to sleep. The stronghold was seething with activity; soldiers running, some carrying boxes and weapons, setting up positions atop the wall. Radios crackled, orders were barked. The ground shuddered under the hammer-fall of explosions, the stink of burning flesh pungent even here, five or so miles from the battle. No one had time for questions. War was coming.

***

Lewis was awakened by a knock at the door, which opened before he was fully conscious, and before any of the others in the dormitory could actually offer an invitation. The visitor was a young, hard-face soldier, who wore the double stripes of a corporal.

"You're to come with me sir." He was gruffly polite, but his tone brooked no argument.

Lewis dragged himself off the bed. "Where are we going?"

"Can't say sir."

The corporal marched on ahead, taking corridors and stairs at a killing pace. The architecture swung back and forth between ancient wood panel and stained glass window to modern, bright and bland. Lewis's weariness and traumatic adventures were obviously no concern of the corporal. He had an order to obey and that was all that mattered.

The journey ended at a venerable-looking, wooden door. The entrance to "Meeting Area One" according to a hand-written sheet of paper, pinned to the woodwork. Meeting Area One turned out to be a surprisingly small conference room, dominated by an oak table. A large map covered the far, wood-panelled wall, made up of dozens of smaller maps neatly fitted together to form a composite view of London. Segments of the map were shaded in different colours.

There were five people seated around the table, including Reeder. Three of them wore some form of military field uniform. Lewis noted the pips on their shoulders. Reeder wore his threadbare suit, and sat a little apart from the others. There was strong smell of disinfectant, but it wasn't enough to hide the realities of Reeder's condition. His face had been roughly repaired, the stitching grotesquely crude.

The other civilian, though clad in the same style of pseudo-military garb issued to Lewis and the others on their arrival, was obviously no soldier. His salt and pepper hair, was collar-length and neat, his face held the softer edge gained from a life of civilian comfort and privilege. This did not detract from his air of authority, however. He was the boss here and the fact exuded from his pores. He was also familiar. Lewis disliked him immediately.

It was this man who spoke first. "Thank God you're here," he said. His accent was Public School correct and confident. He stood and extended his hand. His grip was firm. "Johnathon Baker."

Christ.

Baker was the former Minister of Defence, or was it the current one? Had the government survived somehow, even though their house of mirth had been turned into a giant Dead brothel?

"And you must be Doctor Robert Lewis"

Lewis did not shake the proffered hand. The Minister stared at him for a moment, then withdrew the hand, his expression more rueful than offended, which was a pity. Lewis wanted to offend the man. "May we see the child?" Baker said. It was not a request. It was an order. Lewis was no longer interested in orders.

"Say please," Lewis answered.

Baker frowned. "I'm sorry?"

"'*Please* can we see the child, Mister Lewis.'"

"We're not here to play games," one of the military types snapped.

"And I'm not a dog," Lewis said. "If you want something of me, ask nicely."

The officer leaned forward. "We don't have to *ask* for anything, Lewis -"

"No need for threats," Reeder purred. "Mister Lewis has been through more than any of you can imagine. He deserves your respect and good manners. Minister?"

Baker sighed, but maintained a mask of good humour. "I apologise for my rudeness, Mister Lewis. *Please* may we see the child?"

Slowly, Lewis stood and lifted his tee-shirt.

The people round the table started, stunned, shocked, outraged almost, at what they were seeing.

"*That* is the child?" the officer muttered.

"It, she, is an empty vessel, Major," Reeder said, his voice level, pleasant-sounding. "A distortion, an abomination in a world of abominations." He looked round

235

the table, obviously aware of the distaste he engendered in his new allies. "As am I," he finished and smiled.

Anna clawed at her father's chest. Then the *presence* returned; Caitlin, so strong and close it caught Lewis's breath for a moment and he almost sobbed her name. He slumped back into the chair.

The Minister was first to recover. "Are you all right, Robert?"

As much as he loathed Baker's familiarity, Lewis was grateful for his concern. Baker pushed a coffee pot and a mug towards Lewis. There were sandwiches too.

Lewis attacked the food and drink with the fury of a starving man. He forced himself to slow down, not for appearances sake, but because his body was probably not in any fit state to cope with such a sudden avalanche of food. The sandwiches contained some sort of meat. God, when was the last time he had eaten meat, other than as unidentifiable lumps in broth or soup?

"Robert, I'm sure you have a lot of questions. You may even be angry," Baker said, adopting the annoyingly soft-spoken concern beloved of politicians. "And we can all understand that anger."

"Can you?"

"Yes, I can. Many of us here lost families during the Uprising."

"I'm sorry to hear that," Lewis said. "But I don't understand how that justifies the abandonment of so many Living in the city. You have helicopters and tanks for Christ's sake. What the hell are you doing?"

"We have to move carefully."

"With all due respect, I think we need to focus on the current situation." The speaker was a craggy-featured, deep-voiced character whose shoulders were heavy with pips and insignia. Like Baker he carried immense authority, although this man's authority was undeniably and overtly military. "The important thing is that we have rescued the entity."

"She's a child. Her name is Anna."

"That isn't helpful, Lewis."

"What isn't helpful?" Lewis managed. Defying this man was not easy for him, because the officer carried enormous personal power.

"Giving the entity a name and a gender. We mustn't personalise it."

"She's not an animal, or a machine."

"Are you suffering from some sort of amnesia, Lewis?" the officer was on his feet, leaning across the table. "What the hell do you think is going on out there?"

"And exactly what the hell *is* going on out there?" Lewis demanded. "People are suffering while you sit on your arses here and do nothing."

"You *know* nothing!"

"Colonel Mitchell." Baker's order was harsh, startlingly authoritative. "Robert has been through a terrible ordeal. *We* have to remember that."

"And we don't have much time," Mitchell growled. "There are seven million Dead heading this way. Lewis is here, the entity, the *child*, is safe, so we need to finish this, now."

"I am aware of that, Colonel," Baker said. "But we need Lewis to be strong enough for the...the action. He also deserves some sort of explanation."

"I just hope we can keep the Dead at bay long enough for Lewis to have his rest and explanation. I've received messages that the same thing is happening in most of the major cities. They're trying for breakout." Mitchell turned his attention back to Lewis. "You can stop it, Lewis, today, the whole thing." He stood and walked out, followed by the other officers.

Lewis poured himself more coffee. He was still hungry but the food was gone now. He also wanted to sleep, to lay in the dark with the child and so, with Caitlin.

"Colonel Mitchell is a good man," Baker said.

"I'm sure he is. What's going on here, John?" Deliberate counter-use of Baker's first name. "You're not some desperate Resistance group, you've got an army here."

"What happened on the day of the Uprising?"

"You know what happened."

"Please, Robert, play along with me."

"The Dead rose up, broke our society, tore down its structures and took over. A few Living enclaves were left to fight back. Some, it seems, bigger than others."

"And what happened to you?"

"I was captured and survived because of my skills."

"You've got it wrong, Robert. It didn't happen that way."

"What are you talking about?"

"We, the Living, managed to contain them in our cities. It was a bloody hard fight but somehow we stopped them spreading out and taking everything. The structure has gone, no more central government, no more railways or television and internet. For us, it's like a return to the old Britain, splintered and tribal, the centres of power regional rather than national. I believe it's like that throughout the world. We receive communications now and then, not much though."

"Barons in their castles," Lewis said. "So you, Baron

Baker, with all this hardware, these trained soldiers and tanks and helicopters, why didn't you do something for the Living trapped in the city? You abandoned us."

Baker looked genuinely pained by the accusation. "What could we do? Bomb London? Even if we had the means, we would have killed as many Living as we would have destroyed Dead. We had to wait, train, and gather strength."

"And leave the Living enclaves to starve. There was an enclave in Wembley for God's sake, a few miles down the road. They were so hungry and desperate they ended up with a cholera outbreak. Why the hell didn't you at least send supplies to them? Why ignore them?"

"I understand your anger, Robert. But the good of the many -"

"How many times have I heard that? Those people were Resistance fighters, risking their lives, trying to do something about what was happening. You should have seen the way they fought at the battle of St Cyprian's. Fucking heroes, all of them. And you let them starve."

Baker's calm was faltering. "You're over simplifying the situation."

"Yes, the way Stalin oversimplified the liberation of Warsaw by letting the Polish uprising dash itself to pieces against the Germans, before he sent his tanks in."

"You cannot seriously compare us to Stalin." A moment. "Robert, an attack would have been fruitless."

"Like the fruitless attack that got Anna and me out of the Harley Street Compound? They were all inner enclave fighters weren't they? No one from here was dying in the middle of London that night, were they?"

"This can all be over."

"Why won't you answer my questions Baker? Too much

of a fucking politician?"

"This can all be over in a matter of hours. You can end this, Robert. You. And are *you* willing to make that sacrifice? You're very happy to accuse me of doing nothing, of playing it safe." Baker shook his head, the act redolent with disdain. Then suddenly he was the passionate leader, leaning across the table, eyes burning. "Azazel *will* unleash his energies. But only if we give him what he needs. Once he has struck, once the Dead are wiped out, he'll be too weak to return to hell. He will need the vessel, the child, in which to gather his strength. She will be a messiah, an angel in the flesh. She will be a rallying point for the rebuilding of this country. Probably even the world. But are you willing to give the child to Azazel?"

"What about when he's finished slaying the Dead and saving the world? Where does the great angel go next?"

"We work with him to rebuild, the world. He is a force for good."

"From Hell?"

"He seeks atonement, redemption."

"And you trust him?"

"What choice do we have?" Baker sat back. "Your arguments about our supposed inaction are purely academic now. The Second Circle is fighting for its existence out there. Seven million Dead are closing in on us. We'll run out of ammunition long before we've even made a dent in their numbers. We can pull back. But then we'll have to pull back again, and again. All the time the Dead will be spreading across the country, they'll break out of the other cities." Baker leaned forward across the table, palms spread flat on the polished wood. "What are *you* going to do about that, Mister Robert Lewis?"

Lewis looked across at Baker and saw the fire in the man's eyes. He saw the energy, the fever, and it was *all* he needed to see.

CHAPTER NINETEEN

THE GHOST HOUSE

Caitlin woke him, sometime in the small hours. She woke him with her scent and her touch, with her voice and with her presence. He rolled over onto his back, opened his eyes and saw her. She leaned over him, hair fallen about her face, and said, "Robert."

Lewis reached up for her. His hands closed on darkness. Bleak, full-awake reality revealed that he was in the dormitory. Outside, the war between Living and Dead thundered and flickered, now louder and brighter than when he had left Meeting Area One and returned here to sleep. Doubtless, its noise and light-show had painted an image of Caitlin in his sub-conscious and given her voice.

No, she *was* here.

Heart pounding, Lewis sat up. He could still smell her and taste her. She was in the shadows and in the jagged dance of yellow-white and dark thrown up by the explosions beyond and around the enclave wall.

"Caitlin?" No answer, but that didn't mean anything.

Lewis crossed to the window. Her presence grew stronger. She was outside. He could see her, glimpsed, running across the playing field, then standing in the shadow looking up at the room, then framed in the window of the building opposite to his.

"Robert." She was behind him, voice sharp, demanding his attention. He spun round and the dormitory was empty of anything but its beds and meagre furnishings and utilitarian, shadow-stained geometries. Lewis rested his forehead against the glass and tried to shock his senses back to the mundane by grinding in the truth that Caitlin was not here. She had allowed herself to be consumed, extinguished. What was left of her body thrashed in maddened rage in a coffin under St Paul's Cathedral. No shred of her remained now.

But it did.

Was he so blind? A shred of her lived on, a splinter of light.

She touched him again, the lightest trail of fingertip over flesh that convulsed Lewis into helpless shivering. He groaned, shook his head in a gesture of denial he knew he would be unable to sustain for much longer.

Leave me alone for Christ's sake, Caitlin...

"Robert," she whispered, urgent now. "Robert, you have to give her up."

He crushed his hands over his ears, he closed his eyes, and he begged her to leave him alone.

"She's ours, but not ours. Don't you understand? She is the saviour."

He saw Caitlin, suddenly, vividly. She stood in the grass quadrangle, naked, but for the long diaphanous cardigan she had worn on *that* day. Shaking, fumbling, sobbing with panic and grief and urgency, Lewis unlatched the sash window and pushed it up. The dormitory was on the first floor but there was grass down there. It was a long drop, but not a fatal one. Not if he was careful. He clambered awkwardly through the gap, gripped the bottom edge of the frame with both hands and for a moment dangled from the window. Then he let go and his stomach surged up and he was falling. The shock of impact was a brutal punch to the soles of his feet. He let his knees buckle and went down.

He rolled across the grass then lay, aching, unable to move because his body was in some sort of physical shock. He waited for a moment then got shakily to his feet and ran for the shadow of the nearest building. He slumped against the wall and, instinctively placed his palms on the swellings and landscapes of Anna's body. He looked up. Caitlin was still there, walking towards him, serene, holding the garment about herself, the way she had done when...when what, when she was alive? Living?

Then she touched him and her touch was electric. He couldn't see her anymore. Caitlin's voice burst into his mind, her voice, her presence, and her fear. So vivid that he trembled and stopped breathing. Despite his shock at Caitlin's nearness, felt through the child, Lewis kept his hands firmly in place.

"Give her up." She was crying, but determined. "Oh Jesus, Robert, we have to give her up, or it was all for nothing."

She filled him, and he lay back onto the cool, dew-damp grass, closed his eyes and tried to hold her inside his flesh. He couldn't. That other light was calling him, a star in the red-blackness. He reached for it, mental arms thrust into the night.

"No!" Caitlin gasped, and he felt her hands on him but he held the light that was Anna, and held her tight.

"Don't...Robert...Give her up..."

"Caitlin," Lewis breathed. "Where are you? I'm sorry, Caitlin...Come back..." There was no answer, only the fierce thud and stutter of weaponry, distant shouts, the revving of vehicles and the clatter of a helicopter.

She flared into him again. He started, and was jerked up into a sitting position by the strength of her presence. It was like an electric shock that emanated from his chest, and from Anna. The child became restless. She rippled and squirmed. Her fibrous roots stung his skin. Lewis pushed himself from the wall. The sensation faded.

Soldiers crossed between the buildings to his left. They carried boxes and other burdens. A sergeant shouted at them to hurry up. Caitlin's presence was replaced by that other light, the ill-formed glow that pulsed in time to his own heart. Brighter than before now. Stronger. But still a tiny seed, a fragile thing, easily crushed and swept aside.

Anna.

Lewis struggled to his feet. The night was alive with light and sound and urgency. His own panic was barely contained.

"I can't," Lewis repeated. To the night now. Caitlin was hidden from him. "I can't because of *him*."

Because of what he had seen in The Right Honourable Jonathon Baker's eyes. He understood what that was. Baker *had* been passed over. He was one of the Mutineers, a gang of five Cabinet Ministers who had risen in open revolt against the Prime Minister in the months leading to the uprising. It had been one of the most dramatic political insurgencies since the deposing of Margaret Thatcher.

The Prime Minister's position had become untenable due to his anti-Dead stance, very unpopular with the general public at the time. No one wanted to be cautious when their loved ones were back from the Other Side. Riding on a populist, pro-Dead wave, Baker and his cronies had seized the moment. He tried for the leadership, confident that his ministerial experience and populist policies would hand him success. But when it came to the vote, the Party had chosen a younger, better looking and highly photogenic man.

Lewis remembered Baker's desolate smile, his bitter magnanimity as he stood before the battery of television microphones to publicly wish the new leader well and pledge his full support. He had not, Lewis remembered, taken his defeat well. He had also paid dearly for his revolt, losing his Ministerial portfolio and sent into backbench exile.

Well, it was purely academic now. Presumably the young

and photogenic Prime Minister ended his short term of office on the day of the Uprising. The exiled traitor was set to make his triumphant return to the sort of power any politician in a democratic society could only dream about. And to add glory to his glory, Baker would have a child messiah, an angel in the flesh, to back up his claim to the throne.

The battle noises seemed suddenly louder, the flashes, brighter. Lewis heard shouting, a scream. Then came an explosion, so close, the ground bucked under his feet. Its shock-wave slammed into his ears and he was down again. The night was ripped into splinters of hot light. When he looked up, Lewis saw that a nearby building was on fire. Someone ran, body ablaze.

Soldiers appeared. "It's him," one of them shouted. "That bloody doctor!" They had him on his feet and running before Lewis fully comprehended that *he* was the bloody doctor.

"The Dead," one of them said breathlessly as they ran. "The Dead have broken through."

Lewis followed the soldiers through the thickening smoke, and into a world of panic. There were plenty of vehicles. Some on fire or smashed to twisted metal. Defensive positions had been set up. A mortar thumped at regular intervals, a machine gun chattered.

"We got him!" one of the soldiers yelled and Lewis saw Baker, who was engaged in what looked like a fractious discussion with the craggy-browed, Colonel Mitchell. Baker seemed glad of the distraction. "Thank God," he called back. "Get him into a vehicle. We need to get to the Source, now. Come on, bloody hurry up!"

The escort bundled Lewis towards a Land Rover. It looked substantial enough, armoured even. A long aerial waved from its roof.

"Doc. Hey Doc!"

Lewis turned to see figures running towards him. The voice belonged to Hillier. His companion was Melissa. They were part of a unit of anonymous, grim, dirty-looking soldiers.

"Jesus, Robert, I thought...God..." Melissa was in his arms, crushed against him. He held her tight, never wanting to let go but prised roughly from her by Hillier.

"We haven't got time for that shite," he snapped. "Get in. Fucking hurry up."

"Robert?" Melissa said quietly.

Lewis sighed. "What choice do I have?"

She kissed him. "The right choice."

Baker was issuing orders. He stood, one foot in the Land Rover, holding the door. The pose was self-consciously heroic. Mitchell was the butt of his proclamations. "Hold them back," Baker said. "Give us time to get to the Connection. Once they break through, they'll be all over us."

"I'll do my best," Mitchell grunted back at him. He sounded as if he wanted to throw Baker to the Dead, but maintained a modicum of professionalism. "But you need to get moving, now, come on, bloody move!"

"Lewis, hurry up, come on!" Baker, impatient.

Lewis held Melissa tightly, partly from need, and partly in defiance of Baker. He nuzzled her hair, kissed her neck and it was good. An explosion, about fifty yards away, finally broke them apart. Fire billowed from the heart of the blast. And then, silhouetted by the glare, Lewis saw scythers. Behind them, a tank. It flanks were covered with passengers, clinging on, shouting and laughing, most in uniform, but all of them Dead. Its machine gun rattled, soldiers fell. Someone grabbed Lewis's arm and he was stumbling towards the Land Rover. He saw a body crumple ahead of him. He heard the whine and patter of bullets, and then the thud of the tank's gun.

The shell tore over his head and erupted beyond the Land Rover; another shock-wave, another searing wash of heat, but no damage. The vehicle door was open, Lewis clambered into the front. A soldier, sergeant's stripes on his sleeve, was already at the wheel. Baker sat between Lewis and the door. The others, Hillier, Nathan, Nina and Melissa and a pair of grim-faced soldiers, clambered into the back.

The vehicle was noisy and heavy but handled well. As the driver reversed round in a tight arc, Lewis saw a Dead soldier with only the top half of a face, his abdomen ripped open. The man's vitals trailed along the ground behind him as he launched himself at the Land Rover, grenade in hand. The driver rammed the accelerator down hard.

***

Harrow-on-the-Hill was burning. There was war here, among its cafes and pubs and high priced school uniform shops. Soldiers moved along the street, towards South Harrow, crouched behind armoured cars and tanks, or settling into defensive positions behind barricades of broken vehicles and other wreckage. Others were manhandling huge drums into the road, breaking them open, spilling fluid onto the tarmac. Nothing but a few moments to be gained from all this weaponry and hardware. Few armies could stop seven million immortals.

The Land Rover turned right and raced away from the oncoming hordes, down towards West Harrow town. Here the night became darker, less fraught, although as they neared the bottom of the hill, a few ragged groups of people, then crowds began to form. These were not in uniform, these were civilians, the citizens of the Second Ring. The inevitable war refugees.

The driver slammed the horn with the heel of his hand. People scattered, some looked back and shouted angrily. The driver shoved the heavy vehicle through, Lewis heard a body bounce from its armour and shouted in protest but the din of the engine and the crowd outside smothered his voice.

Harrow town centre was a ruin. Smashed windows and broken buildings. Not the result of this current conflict but established ruin, a neglected, uncared-for ghetto which seemed to be home of the Second Ring serfs. All the best resources went to Baker's private army it seemed.

There were people everywhere, streaming away from the town, clogging Station Road, the main route out. There were few soldiers here, and little in the way of order. The driver swore and revved and shunted his way through the refugees. Lewis sat, grimly silent, his hand splayed over Anna's back, feeling Caitlin here with him and knowing how much she would have hated what they were doing to these people.

Hundreds, thousands of people. Thousands of Living. The sheer numbers brought a previously unconceived reality to Lewis. The Dead had not conquered the world. There was still a Living population out here, a broken-down, un-unified mess perhaps, but a population nonetheless. Disjointed and oppressed by chancers like ex-Minister for Defence and self-styled Baron of North London, John Baker. Lewis saw the terror of these people and felt the weight of the Dead army at his back.

The far wall of the Second Ring cut across the end of Station Road, where Harrow became Harrow Wealdstone. There seemed to be some sort of gate set into the concrete. The gate was guarded by soldiers, complete with barbed wire hastily strung across the road. There were machine gun posts and an armoured car.

The way to the gate was also blocked by a panic-stricken, desperate mass of Living humanity, all wanting to get out.

"Fuck," Baker snapped. "Can't we drive through them?"

"Of course we can't drive through them," Lewis yelled

back at him. "They're people, they're on our fucking side."

"I don't even think this thing will be able to force its way through that lot," the driver growled. "They're packed in as bloody solid as a brick wall."

They were turning, glaring in through the windscreen, hammering at the bonnet.

Baker swore again then, before Lewis could stop him, rammed open the door and scrambled out. In a moment he was clambering up onto the roof. Well, the man had guts, Lewis told himself, reluctant to give Baker any credit. The two soldiers had climbed out of the back of the vehicle and were trying to push the crowd back. Baker was shouting, Lewis could hear the megaphone quality to his voice, but could not pick out any words.

The effect was that the crowd began to open, awkwardly, slowly. And a moment later Lewis saw why. An armoured car was carving a way through. A soldier sat in its turret, firing the machine gun. Tracer hurtled over the crowd's heads, sending them fleeing in all directions. Other soldiers moved along in its wake, to keep the tide from returning.

When the armoured car was virtually nose-to-nose with the Land Rover, Baker slithered back. As the armoured car began to reverse, the Land Rover followed.

Progress was slow, and involved, to Lewis's disgust, rifle butts and boots, but in a few minutes they were at the gate which was being opened to let them out. The armoured car drove through then swung away. A few people escaped with the Land Rover, stumbling past and into the dark. Then the armoured car moved back into the exit and Lewis heard the rattle of weapons as the gate swung shut.

"Why don't you let them out?" Lewis demanded as the driver accelerated and the Land Rover surged forward into the unlit outskirts of the town. "They need to escape. Your troops won't hold the Dead for much longer. And those people will be slaughtered."

"We need to stay together," Baker said. "When Azazel is here, when we rebuild, it will be easier if everyone is in one place. Don't you understand?"

"What I understand," Lewis yelled back, "is that you need serfs for your fucking empire."

The driver hit him, a forearm across the face. The shock of the impact was brutal and disorientating. Lewis slumped back in the seat. He tasted blood. He was angry, but in too much pain to respond.

All he saw was the helicopter as it roared over the Land Rover, its lights blazing. An airborne escort. Christ, they were determined to get him to the Source. Then it stopped, spun about and hovered in the air straight ahead.

Wrong, Lewis thought, very wrong.

The driver spun the wheel and the Land Rover bounced onto the pavement. A side road opened up, an alley between rows of deserted, semi-detached houses. The world lit up, hissed, roared. Lewis looked to his right and saw something fiery hurtled towards the Land Rover. Then the world disappeared in flame and smoke and noise.

Lewis was picked up and thrown into a hell of white heat and sound and smashed against a wall over and over again. Until it became silent and still and dark again.

He swallowed and the simple reflex reminded him that he was flesh and blood and alive. He was lying down, he was still and there was no pain if he didn't move. He slowed his breathing and let himself drift back towards the dark.

The voices wouldn't let him rest however. They were loud and insistent and accompanied by things that battered and shook him. He forced open his eyes so he could see who it was and tell them to leave him alone.

He saw broken glass first, glinting around him like ice.

And then he became aware that he was lying on his side, on top of something reasonably soft and comfortable even though it was moving and grunting.

"Lewis, Lewis. Wake up, fucking wake up you stupid bastard."

He twisted his head to the right, and saw a figure, leaning in through the skylight and yanking at his arm. Slowly, Lewis came to understand that the skylight was actually the broken window of the driver's door of the Land Rover. The vehicle was on its side. He was still in the vehicle, which had been hit. Because he was in the middle front seat, he was now lying on top of the door-side passenger. He struggled to remember the man's name and why he didn't like him that much.

The driver should, in turn, be lying on top of Lewis, but he was gone, so he must have already clambered out. Lewis was cold, shivering in fact. His teeth clattered and his jaw was stiff and ached. But the vehicle was hot, not summer evening warm, hot.

It was fire. Crackling from under the bonnet.

Fire.

He knew panic then, gripped his rescuer's hand and tried to gain some sort of purchase with his feet. The other passenger, Baker, swore and cried out in pain. Too bad, he couldn't be helped until Lewis was out of the way, so Lewis stood on him and clambered towards Hillier and the broken window. He heard other voices. And remembered someone else.

Melissa.

She had been in the back. This memory became another panic and he battled his way over the steering wheel and out, cutting and bruising himself on the way. He heard Baker's cries for help but left the politician to Hillier and a battered-looking soldier, who turned out to be the driver.

There was pain but none of it so acute Lewis couldn't bear it. Nothing broken, it seemed. He managed to stand, dizzy and weak, but upright. The Land Rover was shrouded in smoke but, as far as he could see in the dark, intact. Lewis took a step towards it and his foot came down on nothing. He stumbled, back, almost fell. A crater, in the road. The rocket had missed by inches and ripped up the tarmac. Its blast had thrown the vehicle over.

More people were clambering out.

"Melissa? Melissa, are you okay?" Lewis's voice was hoarse and weak. He doubled over and began to cough. Then heard his own name.

And the helicopter.

He saw Melissa skirting the crater, hurrying towards him. Loud now, the helicopter swept in. Lewis saw Melissa look up and shouted a warning. Then he threw himself at her and drove both of them into the crater. The torn earth was hot and viciously rough. Lewis pressed himself down onto Melissa, held her tight, fiercely so. Above and around them, cannon shells ripped into the tarmac and flesh. Lewis could hear it, above the drumming thud of the aircraft's engine. He heard the heavy impacts and the softer ones, and the yells of pain and the screams. The thing hovered over them for a million years. Then it was gone again, its clatter dwindling to silence.

The Dead had airpower now.

Hillier shouted orders, obviously unhurt, but his urgency sounded a lot like panic. So it should, Lewis mused as he clung to Melissa and she clung to him, here in the dark warm earth. There were fallen among them who would soon be Dead.

"Robert, we have to get out of here," Melissa sounded close to panic.

Lewis lifted himself away from her then helped her to her feet and together they scrambled out of the crater. The

Land Rover was burning now. The shifting, hot light revealed bodies. Lewis didn't try to count them. One of the soldiers was up, roaring and swearing. No shreds remained here. The Dead soldier was crouched before his two comrades, who trained their rifles on him, but seemed reluctant to shoot. The glow of the flames showed the extent of the soldier's wounds, and his identity. It was the driver. A length of intestine lashed and writhed from his open abdomen.

Baker appeared and scrambled for safety behind Hillier and a large figure, Lewis recognised as Nathan. Hillier saw Lewis and strode across to grab the front of his tee-shirt.

"You fucking well get to the Source and save us Lewis. Do you hear me? Fucking save us." Hillier snarled.

Lewis shook his head, still stunned from the rocket attack.

"Leave him alone, Hillier," Melissa snapped.

"Just because you've had his cock doesn't mean you own him," Hillier answered her.

"Fuck you," Lewis yelled and drove his fist into Hillier's face.

It was an inelegant, inexpert and clumsy punch and it slammed a sudden and brutal pain into Lewis's hand. But the shocked Hillier released his tee-shirt and stumbled back. There was blood, from his nose or his mouth, Lewis couldn't tell. His rage had turned to fear. Hillier was going to come back at him and Lewis knew he would be beaten badly.

Hillier rubbed his face and glared at Lewis then made an odd, choking sound that Lewis realised was laughter.

"Fuck me," Hillier said. His voice was thick. He spat blood. "The doctor is a man after all." He moved in towards Lewis. "Now, we have to -"

The helicopter came back and the world was torn in two. Something unthinkably violent and hot erupted from the heart of the wound and hurled Lewis aside and against the ground. Coughing and gasping for breath he levered himself onto his hands and knees. He could see no one. Heard nothing, but the ringing in his ears. He struggled to his feet and stumbled away, from the flames and smoke. Into the darkness.

***

His house, the ghost house, was exactly as Lewis had last seen it, even down to the darkened windows and lack of electricity. And there, lying on the ground where he had dropped it, the petrol can he had gone to fetch on that last day here. As he crunched wearily across the gravel drive, in the gold edged light of the rising sun, Lewis saw that the front door was still open.

Caitlin had opened it, thinking that it was him, rushing back inside with his can of petrol. Caitlin had opened it and died.

He did not hesitate at the front step. The air inside was dank. He ran his hand over the wall and felt the bubbled, peeling paper. The open door had let in three winters as well as the stifling heat of this summer. As he walked towards the stairs, his feet crunched on what he realised were the remains of the vase, broken during the Living Caitlin's last struggle. There would also be dried blood on the floor.

Breathing hard, he forced himself to mount the stairs.

By the time he reached the landing, Lewis was shaking so badly he could barely walk. He was tired, bruised and he ached. His ears still rang from the destruction of the Land Rover. The journey from the wreck, had been fraught. Edgeware was burning. There had been scythers everywhere, each one at the head of hordes of Dead. The Dead themselves had looked bad. They had become more shambolic. Their injuries were terrible and their deterioration awful. There was no one to repair them anymore.

And for all he knew, Baker, Hillier, Nina, and Melissa had now joined their ranks. He had seen or heard no one after that final attack. He had simply walked away and eventually found himself here. A place of raw pain and wide-open, bleeding wounds. This was where he needed to fight the hardest battle of his life. This was where he would make himself bleed. Where he would slash open his own heart. And save Anna.

Lewis came to a halt at the door to the main bedroom, the master bedroom, as Caitlin had called it, with no trace of irony or self-mockery. The door was open. He had left it like that when he rushed downstairs to warn the crying, brutally hurt Caitlin, that things had gone very wrong in the world.

He should have stayed inside the house. He should have been the one who fought Brian and Kate Thurrow, and the rest of the Newly Dead down there in the hall. The vase should have shattered while *he* defended his home and his lover. He should have bought enough time for Caitlin to escape. He should have burned the house down around them. But he didn't, so the only way was to atone for sins committed. His hand went to the child.

"You and me," he whispered.

He stepped into the bedroom and was surprised by how mundane it felt. There was the bed, its duvet pulled back exactly as he had left it. There was the radio on the bedside drawer unit. The air was stale and damp. He ought to open a window, but he wanted to breathe whatever was in this room, the lingering molecules of Caitlin, her scent and substance.

Her presence strengthened in here, because there really were parts of her scattered over the bed, the floor and in the air itself. Lewis dragged the duvet onto the floor and smelled dust. He lay down on the bed. The sheet felt clammy, but it was *the* sheet. Eyes closed, he pushed his arms out a little way, opened his palms and pressed them onto the sheet.

When they are both at home, Sunday afternoons are sacred. Doors are locked, the world shut out. It is a ritual, and as such, prone to highs and lows, successful and less successful completions.

This Sunday, this dark-skied, bitterly-cold, stay-indoors Sunday, Lewis knows he must service the ritual but does not really feel like it. Forced romance and lovemaking can be flawed, clumsy and unsatisfying. On rare occasions, can even lead to disappointment and argument. Caitlin is intelligent and wise enough to know this, of course, so he's worrying about nothing. Despite this, the ritual is important because it guarantees time and intimacy together.

Lunch eaten, Caitlin had gone upstairs first, to shower and scent herself. Sometimes she dressed up. Lewis is hoping she intends to do that today because it might heat up his lukewarm desire. Perhaps he should have asked. Caitlin always encouraged open-mindedness and never rejected any of his requests, not that they were ever particularly outrageous. "Hey, Caitlin, why don't you wear your fur (faux, of course) coat and high heels and nothing else" hardly constituted out-and-out kinkiness.

There is something else, Lewis knows, as he climbs the stairs en route to his take his own shower. Caitlin has been quieter than usual today, her conversation a little forced. She is worried about something, the Dead perhaps. The Return has oppressed her badly. She will tell him, eventually. Caitlin never keeps a secret from him for long.

Freshly scrubbed and wearing only a dressing gown, Lewis steps into the bedroom. The curtains are open to the promised storm. The room is warm and lit softly, in red. Candles burn and gives off a sweet scent.

Caitlin lies on the bed. The duvet is a crumpled mess on

the floor. Caitlin is naked. Her arms slightly out from her body, her palms against the sheet. Her skin is pale and her red, red hair is splayed over the pillow, strands of it on her face. Her eyes are wide and green.

She smiles. "Robert?" she says quietly, her voice small, and that is what warms him and stirs his tired desires. He doesn't move, but stares at her. She is vulnerable and fragile. delicate and elegant, and achingly, painfully, impossibly beautiful. Surely touching her would sully this moment.

But he does, in the end, because he cannot resist touching her. He goes to the bed and stands over her and lets his dressing gown drop the floor then he reaches out and her hand comes up to meet and clasp his.

His breath is ragged. Lewis climbs onto the bed and lowers himself onto her and she is hot and damp. He slides into her immediately with no foreplay, no touching. She wants union and he needs union and he slides inside her and stays there, hardly daring to move.

He wraps his arms around her and she locks her mouth onto his. Her breath is scalding hot. Her tongue dances over his and he is driven halfway to madness. She begins to move and moans and sighs and he hangs onto her because her movement is driving him towards his climax.

Afterward he holds her and they lie in each other's arms, forever. He has heard the term timeless but has never understood it until now. The sky darkens. The wind batters the house. After a while he touches her and kisses her lightly and she sighs and kisses him and they are moving together again, this time slowly, relaxed, until it's time again and he slides into her and she cries out and laughs and then subsides and they lie quietly again.

He smells her. He gently kisses and tastes her. The air seems cold so he pulls the duvet over them. A gust of wind rattles the window in the frame.

After a moment, Caitlin pulls away.

"I'm...I'm sorry," she says.

"Sorry? What have you got to be sorry about?"

She is lying beside him now. Lewis can see the sky beyond her, through the window, black before its time.

"I've got to tell you something, a confession I suppose you'd call it"

He stares at her, holds her face.

And this time, he says "It's all right, Caitlin. It's okay. You don't have to tell me. I know and it's good. I love you, but now..."

Her expression changes to concern.

"Now you have to go."

She shakes her head. "I have to stay with you. Robert I can't leave you..."

"No, my darling, you have to go. You can't stay. This is Anna's time."

He reaches out to her, knowing that this is what he has to do, and he lays his hand on her abdomen and feels Anna's energies pulse outwards. "I'm sorry. I love you Caitlin. I will see you again, but not now, its Anna's time."

Caitlin opens her mouth to protest, distraught. She tries to come to him, but Lewis pushes her back, gently firmly and she shatters to a million glinting shards.

And is gone.

And only Anna's tiny light remains. Tiny, but bright, and growing ever stronger.

Lewis sat up, fists clenched, gasping for air through his sobs. He felt bereft, utterly alone. She was still there, Caitlin, still in existence somewhere, waiting for him.

His groan became a shout of anguish and he held his face and tried to rip away the image. But he couldn't. He fell back onto the bed, exhausted. Now the bed was an empty, dank thing under his back. He closed his eyes again, this time to sleep. Then he would try to make it out into the countryside in search of Hillier's near-mythical communities.

He felt cold, even though it was a hot summer morning.

A shout. His name, yelled from outside. He scrambled from the bed and crossed to the window. There were figures, indistinct at first, but as they neared the house, they resolved into the broad stocky form of Hillier, the giant bulk of Nathan, Baker, and another, stooped holding a cane. Enforcers brought up the rear and when they stopped under the window, formed an arc about them. Another figure knelt in front of them, hunched oddly, something wrong with its head.

"Tell him who you are," Reeder said to it, voice distinct despite the quietness of his tone. He leaned towards the kneeling figure. Lewis caught a reply, quiet, too quiet to make out any words.

He knew who it was anyway.

"Again. Louder."

"Melissa! I'm Melissa. God, Robert...please..."

Now Lewis could see her clearly, hooded, hands bound behind her back.

"It's time to stop all this running away foolishness and do your duty," Reeder shouted up to him. He held his hand aloft, and although Lewis could not see what he was holding, he knew what it was.

The Stanley knife.

"Do it willingly, or Melissa will die and when she is Dead, I will send her into the house to fetch you out."

CHAPTER TWENTY

CONNECTION

The journey was fast and rough, not least because armoured troop carriers were not known for their soft suspension and concessions to luxury. Lewis was huddled in the back, shaken and thrown by every bump and pothole in the road. Hillier and his new woman, whose name it seemed was Nina, were crammed between Lewis and the rear door, to his right. The taciturn giant Nathan, and thenauseous-looking Baker, sat on his left. There were two soldiers in the front, the driver and a guard, separated from their passengers by a steel bulkhead.

Sitting opposite Lewis was Reeder, one arm about Melissa's shoulders. The knife was in his free hand, its tip pressed against her throat. Melissa's hands were still bound, though the hood had been removed, whipped away by Reeder with a conjuror's flourish. Melissa was deathly pale, and looked exhausted. She avoided eye-contact with Lewis, as if humiliated by her role as hostage. He wanted to reassure her, but decided that it was best to stay silent.

Lewis focussed on Anna instead. He folded his hands over the child, who was becoming increasingly, and uncomfortably, restless.

The vehicle stopped. Nothing happened. Baker looked round wildly. He seemed close to breaking point.

"What the hell is going on?" Hillier muttered. "Fuck this." He slammed open the back door and leapt out. He was gone for a few seconds and when he came back he was ashen. He was accompanied by a burly soldier Lewis had not seen before.

"You'd better come and have a look," Hillier's voice was

ominously quiet.

Lewis and the others climbed out and found that they were on an open, grassy expanse. Reeder dragged Melissa with him. Lewis recognised the place as Elstree aerodrome. What concrete remained was cracked and punctured with grass and weeds. Despite the early morning sunshine and warmth, the place felt bleak and desolate.

There were twelve other armoured carriers strung out in a line across the battered runway, their drivers were gathered in a knot nearby. Facing them, at a distance of about five hundred metres, was a dense, seemingly impenetrable wall of Dead that stretched as far as Lewis could see in either direction.

"They knew we were coming," the burly soldier growled. "We're fucked."

"No, we're not." Reeder said.

"And what do you suggest?" It was obvious that Baker was trying not to shout, but his voice had risen an octave and he was red-faced and shaking.

"We go through them."

"Jesus Christ, are you serious?" Baker did shout this time. "Look at them, there are thousands of them. We can't...Oh shit." He rounded on Lewis. "This is your fucking fault. If you hadn't scuttled off to your bloody house -"

"Fuck you," Lewis said to him and it felt good.

"There's only one way to *get* through them." Reeder's decay-hoarsened voice was startlingly authoritative. "And that's to *go* through them."

"Seems simple enough" Hillier said. "It won't work and we'll die, but it does seem like an elegant sort of plan."

"We can't." Baker again. Lewis wished he would shut up.

"Have any of you a better idea?" Reeder asked. "I'm open to persuasion."

When there was no response, he continued. "Our vehicles are made of steel. Their bodies are deteriorating, and made only of rotten flesh. We will get through. If we decide not to make the attempt they will eventually lose patience and swarm all over us anyway. I really don't feel that we have anything to lose." He turned to shout at the other drivers. "We keep together, form a wedge. Follow our lead." There were answering salutes and nods. The soldiers looked pale, grim and showed little enthusiasm for the plan. But Reeder was right, and they knew it. Even Lewis had to admit that.

Everyone climbed back on board. Lewis got in first and curled himself against the front bulkhead of the carrier. The engine revved hard. There was a lurch and he sensed the vehicle gather speed. He imagined the others racing along beside them in a sort of glorious charge. He felt it accelerate, faster and faster. The roar filled his head and it felt as if they were headed for a cataclysmic collision.

"Brace yourself," Hillier yelled. His face was glowing with some sort of wild joy. It seemed that he had come round to Reeder's way of thinking.

Faster. The carrier shuddered and rattled and sounded as if it was about to fly apart.

Faster.

They hit the Dead and the vehicle slowed with gut-crushing suddenness. Lewis was rammed against the bulkhead hard enough to drive the breath from his lungs. The engine howled, the walls of the carrier reverberated with the pounding of Dead fists. Lewis heard them clambering up the flanks and onto the roof. The carrier stopped. Wheels spun, rubber burned.

Another lurch forward. There were thuds, the crunch of bones, other terrible sounds and sensations. The Dead roared and raged outside. Their massed voices swamped the howl of the engine. It was if they knew that their time was short and were driven into a crazed desperation to stop their end.

The doors flew open and Dead slithered in. Hillier and Nathan were on them immediately, beating at them with their rifles, fists and boots. Lewis scrambled to join in. The images of the last moments of so many Living, flared bright in his mind and unleashed a kind of berserker rage. Hands closed about his ankles, he kicked and felt something soft break under the impact. The Dead were horribly decayed, many of them barely recognisable as human anymore. He beat at them and each blow sank deep into mouldering bones and flesh.

Nina screamed. Lewis saw her slide towards the open rear doors. Hillier grabbed her wrist, Lewis, her hair. It didn't matter, anything was better than letting the Dead take her. Her screams became an inhuman shriek. Nathan fired his rifle, emptying the magazine into the stinking, writhing mass at the open door way. The rifle's noise crashed against Lewis's ears.

Nina was free, crying and shivering in Hillier's arms. The vehicle leapt forward. Nathan leaned out to scrabble for the rear door. Lewis's heart stopped beating. Nathan was precariously balanced. Beyond him the ranks of the Dead closed in again.

A Dead's hand reached in. Nathan found the door and hauled it shut. The door crashed against the wrist and the hand flopped onto the armoured carrier's floor and scuttled blindly about like a fat, fleshy spider. Lewis crushed it under his heel.

He saw Melissa, curled up at the front of the vehicle, struggling to free her wrists. They were bound with a single, black cable tie, and her efforts had made her wrists bleed. Lewis scrambled towards her, but was slammed back against the carrier's side. Ruined as he was, Reeder's strength was inhuman. He yanked Melissa closer to him, the knife back at her jugular.

Lewis bit down on his frustration and curled his arms about his knees. He sat and waited as the vehicle ploughed on, revving and roaring, go-stop-go. Fists pounded the sides, voices growled and shrieked and raged. On and on, never ending. And there was Melissa, head bowed now, helpless and desolate. It was if darkness was pressing in, gathering in every corner of the vehicle.

Then they broke free and the carrier accelerated, its passengers bounced and rattled into submission.

***

The air outside was chill and fresh, despite the tang of the Dead drifting in on the breeze. Lewis breathed deep as he followed Hillier and Nina out through the carrier's back doors. The four surviving armoured vehicles had stopped at a large, electricity substation. Beyond it, Lewis could see trees. The compound was overgrown with grass and weeds. The fence was rusty, the equipment inside, weather worn. The main gate was open, guarded by dusty, tired-looking Living soldiers, the officer in charge looked frighteningly young. A dozen or so Enforcers waited in the compound itself.

Lewis became aware of the gore, splashed over the flanks of the carriers. Streaks of ichor, gobs of tissue, some of which, still writhed and slithered over the metal.

"It's called the London Connection. Appropriate venue," Reeder said, bringing Lewis's attention back to the complex. Reeder kept Melissa close. The blade of the knife glinted in the bright, late-morning sunlight. There was no chance of pulling her free. Lewis had seen Reeder's knife work.

"It cost forty million pounds to build all this," Reeder continued. "Gas insulated switchgear, whatever that means, and a twenty kilometre tunnel carrying electrical power all the way to North West London and the City via St John's

Wood. An ambitious project by any standards. Shame it didn't have much of a life."

Lewis said, "Let her go."

"Not yet, Robert. You know how to free her."

"You miserable little bastard, untie her. I'm going to do what you ask. Let her go, Reeder."

Reeder grabbed Melissa's hair and wrenched her head back, forcing a brief cry of pain from her. Reeder brought the blade up to her throat. "Not until the ceremony is complete. Not until I am sure. Then you can have her again."

"Why should I trust you, Reeder?"

"Do you have a choice?"

Yes, he had few choices.

"Can we hurry up?" Baker was beside Lewis now. "There's an army of Dead behind us, we haven't got much time."

Lewis had forgotten about the wall of Dead. He looked across the airfield. They were not in sight yet, but they were coming.

"You're right, Baker," Reeder said. "To be here for you, I had to deliver myself of my deceptions. The Seven, the Six rather, want me obliterated. Their rage against me, the traitor, is unthinkable, and unthinking. Their new world is already falling apart."

And so are you, Lewis mused. Half Dead. Half stencher.

Entry into the tunnel was by a fixed metal ladder which plunged into near darkness. Enforcers waited at the bottom, carrying a variety of torches and lamps. Even though there was little visible, Lewis avoided looking down. Darkness did not ease his vertigo, if anything, the sensory numbness made it worse. No choice though.

Melissa was already down there, carried over the shoulder of an Enforcer, closely followed by Reeder and his knife. Which he was going to use on her, Lewis was convinced of that. He would ruin her flesh from sheer spite, for the joy of seeing Lewis's agony, which would be far deeper than anything physical the bastard could inflict on him.

But he's Dead.

The thought was an odd one, obvious, seemingly of little consequence. Yet of enormous import.

Once at the bottom of the ladder, clinging to the last of the cold metal rungs until his shaking subsided, Lewis could see that the Connection was a circular tunnel, about ten feet in diameter, and, as such, intensely claustrophobic. The Enforcers' flash lights chopped the place into brightly lit circles separated by bands of deep shadow. The lights penetrated twenty feet or so into the tunnel proper, compressing the blackness beyond into a solid wall of nothing. As with Lewis's previous journeys through the underworld, he was oppressed and terrified by the sheer, immeasurable weight of earth bearing down on them from the other side of the tunnel's concrete shell.

They walked, in pairs or singly, strung out into the gloom; a vanguard of four Enforcers, followed by Reeder and Melissa, then Lewis with Nathan at his shoulder, whether gaoler or protector, Lewis couldn't tell. Behind them were Hillier, Nina and Baker. More Enforcers brought up the rear. The tunnel was endlessly monotonous, lined with huge, black, cables, fixed to the curved walls via heavy metal brackets and occasionally jointed using formless, black junction boxes.

It was difficult to concentrate, because there was a low-level hiss, that sounded like static and grew louder the further they walked. There was also a sense of something building, a tightening of the very air he had felt in St Cyprian's, when the Reverend Jack Martin was opening the Source in his church. But this was bigger, much bigger.

Lewis shook with fear. The tremors were out of his control, his body reacting to signals and energies his mind could not fully discern. The noise, the thrumming of energies, beat at his nerves. His combat trousers crackled with static, drilling tiny shocks into his legs with every movement. He felt his hair rise, his skin itch and tingle. Anna was agitated, squirming and struggling, as if desperate to tear herself free and be gone.

Lewis was sure this was his final trek into hell. Yet he didn't feel the terror of the walk to the scaffold. The bleak realities of the situation and its outcome seemed remote. His mind and body had focussed their machineries on survival.

Then he saw the glow. It flared bright and the white noise in his head became unbearable. Ahead of him Reeder hesitated, Melissa dropped to her knees, her head bowed, her body tense from the pain the noise brought with it. He saw blue-white sparks burst over his skin, heard their hot, electric snaps.

Someone brushed past, Baker, his own carefully coiffed hair awry and waving like Medusa's snakes. His hands were over his ears. Despite his obvious discomfort and fear, he took his place near the front of the column. So that he would be one of the first Azazel saw when he emerged, Lewis supposed, a mark of just how important he was.

"You are clinging to your sanity, I trust," Reeder said without turning round. He yanked Melissa back onto her feet and they continued to walk.

Lewis didn't reply.

Now there were insects, creatures, hard to tell. They infested the walls, a few at first, but as they neared the light, there were more; some many-legged, others slug-like, all with bloated pulsing bodies, and given to sudden, nerve-shredding burst of speed. On either side and overhead, arachnid, cockroach, worm, and centipede, yet not quite, too big, hand-sized, arm-length, heads too human-looking.

Then roots appeared, like the ones that grew down that cramped passageway under the First House, the entrance to the Madam's chamber. These were bigger, increasingly complex, burrowed into the concrete itself. The insect-creatures fed off them, bodies quivering as they sucked the roots' juices through long, fierce looking proboscis

Someone groaned, Nina, muttered "Oh God, Oh God, Oh God" over and over again. Lewis could hear Nathan's hard, tremulous breath, could see Baker's unease. And Melissa, flinching, shaking her head as if trying to clear her hair of crawling, scuttling life.

And there it was, filling the tunnel ahead.

The Source.

Its light was produced by the web of crackling, writhing blue-white energies that poured outwards from the blackness inside, flowing over its rim and crawled onto the walls and snapping at the air. Blackness. Not an adequate description. It was black, yes, but it was deeper than that. It was, an absence, yet pulsing with something indescribably powerful; its heartbeat was a relentless, slow thud that thrummed through the tunnel and underlay the roar of static that ratcheted from its mouth. The closer they came, the more restless became the blackness, more serpentine and sinuous.

"Can you feel it?" Reeder shouted above the noise. "Azazel is coming, like a train, like a fucking rocket." He grinned, euphoric.

But you're Dead, Reeder...

The hiss became a locomotive roar, a jet roar, and light exploded out of the Source. Lewis dived to the tunnel floor as the light gushed into the world to enfold him.

"I need to know," a voice whispered to him, soft and calm in the maelstrom. "I need to know your intention."

"My intentions are good," Lewis answered and giggled.

"Please, Azazel, don't let me be misunderstood."

"I NEED TO KNOW."

"She...She's yours. The child, Anna, you can have her." The words were painful. "Come and see for yourself."

Azazel did so and Lewis discovered that what he had seen in St Cyprian's was only part, a fingertip, a touch. Tentacles boiled from the Source, writhing and groping, translucent things, dripping mucus and covered in tiny but lethal-looking barbs. They tore the back of his tee-shirt, raked his flesh. Snagged him. He clenched his jaw tight shut and let it wrench him in the darkness.

Which was ice. Which had texture and clung to him and smothered him like plastic. He struggled, but each movement drove the barbs deeper into his flesh. So he fought for self-control and stillness. There was sensation, a softness moving over his face, his head, over the child.

He opened his arms, exposed his chest and abdomen, and Anna. The thin material of the tee-shirt was scant protection. She burrowed at him, pitifully small and vulnerable. Lewis fought his own protective instinct and kept his arms apart, fists clenched, nails breaking the skin of his palms. He whispered 'sorry' over and over again, until it became a litany, as the angel slid into his daughter and laid its egg of light.

The barbs tore deeper into his flesh. The pain was unspeakable. Energies, liquids, voices ran into him and every one of them was ice and darkness. Then he was thrust out of the black and slammed sideways against the wall. His body was driven into the cables which smashed the breath from his lungs and cracked ribs. He wanted to slide to the floor and curl about his pain and hide, but the tentacle held him fast.

As the angel came.

The Enforcers were obliterated, turned to ash so quickly their suits remained intact and frozen in place before they crumbled to nothing. Lewis saw Baker bowled over backwards to slam into Nathan and Hillier. Melissa was hurled onto her back on the floor. He saw Reeder, briefly, then obscured as all became light and heat and ice and noise.

The light gushed from the Source and within its depths were glimpses of form and structure and wings and beauty and monstrosity. The angel was vast, miles long and wide and high, a landscape rather than a body, a presence, a structure, a place, an explosion. The tunnel shook and flexed, like a worm, a snake, like the tentacles that held Lewis. The whole earth trembled and twisted and cracked, then healed.

It ended.

A shocked silence. Only an ember remained of the light, floating towards Lewis. Instinctively, he reached out and took it in his fist. There was little sensation, the tickle of a spider perhaps, a thorn prick. Then nothing.

Perhaps Azazel had spent itself, had miscalculated in some way.

No.

Oh no.

The light came back, and exploded inside him with such intensity he was only dimly aware of his body hitting the floor and the convulsions that rippled through his torso and limbs.

The angel had planted its seed and now the flower was blooming. Lewis slammed himself shut. Doors in his mind, closed, locked, barring the way to the room that was Anna.

Azazel hurled itself at him, shattering his mind-image, sending pain and shock-waves through him. He gathered himself and pressed back, strength failing, but Azazel was weakened too.

Lewis opened his eyes. He was on the bed.

"Robert? Robert where are you?"

Caitlin?

Caitlin, yes, touching his face, offering herself to him. Naked and sweet scented. Her hair red, her skin pale and her eyes green. She smiled and wrapped her arms about him and she was real and he could taste her skin and her perfume made him dizzy.

Not Caitlin. Not Caitlin.

Her mouth was on his. Her breath scalded him and her tongue probed and teased at his tight-closed lips. It was snowing outside and she had come back to the bedroom to tell him she was sorry. He rolled over and touched her face.

Of course he would forgive her. How could he not forgive her? He loved her with everything he had. She curled up beside him and he curled about her and she cried and he drew her close. She was warm and fragile and he loved her and -

He flinched back. "No, this isn't right." He tried to understand why. What was happening here? The truth was slippery, something he could not catch. He wanted to stay here. But he couldn't. That was all he knew.

"Robert please don't go," Caitlin said and crushed herself against him. "Robert, they'll take me, if you leave me. Please."

They? He heard them. People were bounding up the stairs, shouting; "Warm flesh bastards!" The Thurrows, the others. He couldn't let it happen again.

She was lying. Caitlin was lying -

The door crashed open and in they came. Thurrow, wearing that black roll neck sweater, his wife, Katie, in her dress, both of them snow-frosted, but not cold. They would never be cold again. Thurrow carried an iron bar, Katie wielded a kitchen knife. Lewis clung to Caitlin as they tried to wrench her away from him.

Let her go...

Her face was distorted with raw, primal terror. She was screaming his name. He held her, taking the blows from the iron bar across his own shoulders, shielding her.

Let her go. Let her go...You've already let her go...

"Robert, God, Robert please..."

There had been others, that day, there had been others in the garden. Where were they now? Why weren't they in the bedroom, helping the Thurrows?

The nursery.

They didn't have a nursery.

The fucking nursery, for God's sake.

Anna.

He let her go, rolled clear and watched as Caitlin was dragged from the bed. He heard her crash to the floor, saw the iron bar and knife rise and fall. He heard her begging him, howling out his name.

Out onto the landing, fighting the urge to go back, sobbing and choking, trying to block out Caitlin's screams and the other, awful sounds. Not right, not real. Wrong. The door, his study - the nursery. The door was open, someone inside.

Lewis rushed into the room. Which was no longer his study. The light was soft red, its source a night light shaped like the face of a teddy bear. Instead of a desk there was a cot, guarded by a mobile of fairies and cute animals. In the cot lay the bundle that was Anna, swaddled in blankets, and silent, barely visible in the shadow.

Leaning over the cot -

- was Caitlin.

She spun round as Lewis slammed into her. He was hurled back, his body on fire. Flames licked at his flesh, agonies tore through him, and yet, the fire and the pain were disconnected. Both consuming and separate.

He crawled back towards the cot.

"Anna, wake up."

Caitlin, weeping and smiling, reached down for the bundle.

"Anna wake up!"

She pulled at the blankets.

Lewis screamed in pain as he surged to his feet and ran at the cot and, with the last of his strength, grabbed it and tipped it over. Caitlin swept her arm into his burning throat and he was thrown across the room to crash onto a drawer unit that splintered under him and erupted into flame at his touch. Smoke filled the room. Darkness slithered in from all sides. Lewis's agonies became a distant thing as he felt himself dissolve into final oblivion.

From somewhere deep, within the heat and smoke, came a soft, puzzled whimper.

Then a full blown baby shriek. A pumping rhythmic caterwaul that filled the room, his head, the whole world. The cry of a new, freshly-minted, whole and complete soul. Caitlin spun round, face contorted with frustration, hate and rage, blistering and peeling. Her body split open, Lewis saw glistening reds and blue-greys, then the illusion, the seed of the angel Azazel, exploded outwards and Lewis choked on dust.

"Robert!"

He rolled onto his back and saw Reeder once again grab Melissa to himself. The Stanley blade glinted in the crazed lights of the dozen torches dropped by the Enforcers in their last moments.

"Cunt!" Reeder screamed. Melissa twisted out of his grip and kicked at him, her foot connected, but she overbalanced and went down heavily. Damaged by the kick, Reeder staggered back. Lewis was on him, but Reeder struggled like a crazed thing and in those eyes Lewis saw something half-mad but familiar.

Azazel.

Now Anna's soul had quickened, there had been only one place left for the angel to go; the rotten hulk of a near-soulless Half-Dead. Azazel's disciple in whom it had been well-pleased, and whom it had spared.

Reeder-Azazel slashed at Anna. Lewis jumped back and found himself slammed against the wall. Lewis watched the knife, swinging in towards his face. He grabbed Reeder-Azazel's wrist, held on. Lewis felt his grip weaken. The knife point touched his throat; a pin prick of pain.

Then Reeder-Azazel flew backwards and onto the floor. A large figure stood over him. Nathan.

"Leave him alone, you fucking stencher. He got us out of your fucking cages," he roared. "You would have killed all of us, you old bastard, but he saved us."

"I'm not Reeder. Listen to me. I'm not Reeder. I am -"

Nathan *wasn't* listening. The steel pipe he held in his huge fist arced down and crushed the fragile, mouldering bone of Reeder's skull, pounding it until there was nothing but dust and the rot that had once been his perverted, malfunctioning brain.

The angel quivered and gathered its broken vessel onto its hand and knees and scuttled in circles, gibbering and sobbing.

Lewis snatched up the knife, crossed to Melissa and sliced through the cable tie. Her skin was grazed and bleeding, two deep wheals had been cut into her flesh. Lewis drew her to him and they watched the wreckage of Reeder-Azazel in its crazed dance.

Hillier stepped into view. Venom dripped from his lips. "You fucking traitor."

Lewis merely shook his head. The words meant nothing. His body ached. He was exhausted. It was finished. Hillier held a flame thrower, dropped by one of the Enforcers. He raised the nozzle until it was level with Lewis's chest.

"No," Melissa pulled away from Lewis and for a moment, he thought she too was turning on him. She put her hand on Hillier's shoulder. "Don't. It's over. It's too late. It's down to us now."

"There's' nothing left," Hillier said. The energy seemed have drained from his anger. "Azazel would have...There's nothing..."

"There is. There's always something left," Melissa said. "The world belongs to us, not to angels and fucking gods."

Hillier frowned then lowered the weapon. "Get out. I'll finish this."

When Lewis, Melissa and Nathan reached the ladder, they heard the roar, felt the heat, and smelled the stink, of Reeder-Azazel's ending. Lewis turned back before he began his ascent, and saw Baker, alone, walking like a somnambulist in their wake. They climbed, but didn't wait for him.

On the surface the sun was bright but there were clouds gathering. The soldiers outside looked questioningly, but made no move against them. The young officer stepped forward. "What happened? Are you...is she..." He nodded towards the child.

Lewis shook his head. "We're leaving the gods out of this one."

"What's going to happen?"

"It's up to you," Lewis said.

***

There was ash, windblown. Presumably, the remains of the Dead army that had been smashed by Azazel's fist. There were people moving across the airfield, civilians and exhausted looking soldiers, all headed out of London. The herd instinct keeping them together, but seemingly without leadership or purpose. They would survive though. The Living always found a way, wasn't that what Melissa had said? She was right, Lewis was convinced of it.

Hillier and Nina emerged from the sub-station, smoke-smudged, quiet.

"We'll need food and shelter." Hillier said. He was subdued, uncharacteristically awkward.

Could it be possible he felt guilty for his treatment of me, Lewis wondered. "We should go back to the second circle," Lewis tried to put the man at his ease. It was over. In-fighting was the last thing they needed. "See what we can find. Set up camp."

"Not questing for those legendary communities, Doc?" A little of Hillier's rough and ready attitude was returning.

"No need," Lewis said, nodding towards the Living. "We've got one of our own." He saw Baker, sitting on the grass, alone and disconsolate. Lewis called to him. The man looked up, the effort seemed to cost him. "You wanted to be Prime Minister? Well, take a look around you. You're a self-serving bastard, but we need a leader of some sort so, here's your chance. Get up and do something Baker, or go to hell."

"Are you serious?" Melissa said. "Him?"

"He's got the experience and the qualifications, we don't have to like him. And who else is there?"

As they walked, heading back towards the city, Lewis felt the child move. Then something tore and he was driven to his knees as wave after wave of pain speared into his chest and abdomen. He clawed at his blood-drenched tee shirt, drummed his fists against the earth, but there was no relief, only more agony.

Anna began to convulse. Lewis could do nothing, exhausted by pain, he slumped onto his back, and stared up at the cloudless blue sky above him. When the pain eased, he reached for the child, but she was gone, replaced by raw, torn flesh. It would heal, but it would hurt. And it didn't matter, not at this moment. He lifted his head and saw that Melissa held the child now, tight in her arms, laughing and crying at the same time.

Then Anna too, began to cry.

THE END

Terry Grimwood

THANK YOU FOR READING

Thank you for taking the time to read this book. We sincerely hope that you enjoyed the story and appreciate your letting us try to entertain you. We realise that your time is valuable, and without the continuing support of people such as yourself, we would not be able to do what we do.

As a thank you, we would like to offer you a free ebook from our range, in return for you signing up to our mailing list. We will never share your details with anyone and will only contact you to let you know about new releases.

You can sign up on our website

Http://www.horrifictales.co.uk

If you enjoyed this book, then please consider leaving a short review on Amazon, Goodreads or anywhere else that you, as a reader, visit to learn about new books. One of the most important parts about how well a book sells is how many positive reviews it has, so if you can spare a little more of your valuable time to share the experience with others, even if its just a line or two, then we would really appreciate it.

Thanks, and see you next time!

THE HORRIFIC TALES PUBLISHING TEAM

ABOUT THE AUTHOR

Suffolk-born Terry Grimwood started his working life as an electrician and is now a college lecturer, having travelled full-circle from doing the job to teaching it (which he prefers).

Along the way he has been a quality assurance manager, project manager and technical author. He is the author of numerous short stories and reviews which have appeared in Midnight Street, Bare Bone, Murky Depths, All Hallows, FutureFire and Eibonvale Press's Blind Swimmer anthology, among others. He has written and directed three plays and runs the Exaggerated Press which started when he published his first collection, The Exaggerated Man.

Terry Grimwood

ALSO FROM HORRIFIC TALES PUBLISHING

High Moor by Graeme Reynolds

High Moor 2: Moonstruck by Graeme Reynolds

High Moor 3: Blood Moon by Graeme Reynolds

Of A Feather by Ken Goldman

Whisper by Michael Bray

Echoes by Michael Bray

Voices by Michael Bray

Angel Manor by Chantal Noordeloos

Bottled Abyss by Benjamin Kane Ethridge

Lucky's Girl by William Holloway

The Immortal Body by William Holloway

Wasteland Gods by Jonathan Woodrow

Dead Shift by John Llewellyn Probert

The Grieving Stones by Gary McMahon

The Rot by Paul Kane

COMING SOON

Song of the Death God by William Holloway

High Cross by Paul Melhuish

The Veil (Testaments I and II) by Joseph D'Lacey

http://www.horrifictales.co.uk

www.ingramcontent.com/pod-product-compliance
Lightning Source LLC
Chambersburg PA
CBHW030238200626
46816CB00002BA/420